T0355974

No Life for a Lady

NO LIFE FOR A LADY

Hannah Dolby

An Aria Book

First published in 2023 by Head of Zeus, part of
Bloomsbury Publishing Plc

9 7 5 3 1 2 4 6 8

A CIP catalogue record for this book is available from the British Library.

ISBN (HB): 9781804544365
ISBN (XTPB): 9781804544372
ISBN (E): 9781804544341

Cover design: Nina Elstad

Printed and bound in Great Britain by
CPI Group (UK) Ltd, Croydon CR0 4YY

Head of Zeus
First Floor East
5–8 Hardwick Street
London EC1R 4RG

WWW.HEADOFZEUS.COM

To my mother, Ann Grace – my rock and my inspiration for joy, creativity and laughter

Prologue

It was hot, the night my mother disappeared.

It was a Saturday, and she had been going out. I had wanted to go out with her, because I was eighteen, and bored, and because the world and my exciting future beckoned.

'You can't come this time, Vi,' she said, stroking my hair. 'When you've had your debut, perhaps. Then I can take you to a few parties, we can have fun. Girls together.' She was wearing a dress in dark green silk, her hair tangled up with sprigs of flowers and a scattering of ruby pins, and she smelt like gardenias or some other exotic bloom.

'Where are you going?' I asked, because she had as ever been vague.

'Just to see a few friends. Nothing dramatic. I will probably be bored.' She yawned, and stretched out her feet, examining her silk evening slippers. 'No dancing, I hope.'

'You look beautiful,' I said, because it was expected and also true.

'It's not all it's cracked up to be, this beauty lark,' she said. 'A lot of the time it's more trouble than it's worth. Just be glad that you don't have to put up with it.

'I don't mean it like that,' she rushed to say, seeing my face. 'You are just as beautiful as me, when you sparkle, and make funny jokes. We all love, love, love your jokes. Your personality makes you gorgeous. I just mean that it can be a trap, too. People want too much from me. It's not all good. But you are my beautiful, funny, sweet little daughter and I love you.' She grabbed me in her arms and squashed me tight, while I resolved to give up my role as comedy daughter.

These scenes of lamentation were not new, but I did wish she would stop using me as a comparison.

'I should like to do something useful in life,' I said, when she had released me. 'Something that could perhaps earn money. Do you think there might be a way?'

'There are always ways, but it's not easy,' she said. 'There is a gazette, I think though, that has ideas for employment for women. Interesting ideas, like book binding, or botany. Let me have a think. But don't you want to get married?'

'Not quite yet,' I said.

'Well then, I must be away!' she said. 'They are expecting me half an hour ago. Enjoy your evening, my Vi.'

She wafted out of the door, and that was the last time I saw her. There had been no sign from her that she might leave, no real difference in her behaviour to make me suspect she planned to go away.

That was why it would be easier to think her dead. But even now, ten years on, I could not let her go.

Chapter One

I first suspected I had hired the wrong detective when he gently stroked the photograph of my mother with his thumb.

'Attractive lady,' he said. 'Hastings pier, you say? When was it?' He laid the picture down beside the pile of pound notes I had given him and stared at it. 'You don't look like her.'

'It was ten years ago, the summer of 1886. No, I don't,' I said.

He was dressed in a puce and yellow striped blazer and a straw boater, as if he should be strolling along the beach instead of sitting behind a desk. It was no reason to dismiss a successful man of business, but my instinct was a live creature, squealing at me to leap off my chair and scurry out.

I stayed because I had dreamt of hiring a detective for a long time. His advertisement in the *Hastings Observer* promised, in splendidly large capital letters, to deal with investigations with discretion and valour. His office was in a smart glass-fronted shop on the St Leonards' Colonnade, on the very finest stretch of the Marine Parade, and he had a shining brass pen and inkstand on his well-varnished desk. These things should inspire confidence.

'Lily, Lily Hamilton.' He scrawled it on a sheet of paper and circled it twice. 'And the disappearance was in the newspapers? What did the police say?'

I realised I was clutching the edge of my chair, so I loosened my hands and smoothed them flat across my skirts. 'Yes, it was in the local newspapers. I don't think it went further. The police did not investigate for long. They thought she had left us, and my father agreed.'

'Where is your father today?'

'He does not need to be involved,' I said, firmly. The man looked at me with a small smile and his moustache, sleek and rat-brown coloured, smiled along with him.

'To be frank,' he said, and that was silly, because he was Frank – 'Frank Knight', the sweep of gold lettering said on the window behind me, 'Detective'. A name full of hope, of chivalrous adventure and pioneering spirit; now of slowly deflating dreams. 'There are ladies who don't like what they are made for, the cleaning and the domestic business, the caring and the mothering. We might think badly of them for it, but it does happen.'

A philosopher, then. 'I don't think she would have wanted to leave,' I said. I could not talk about love to this man. 'I think she would have let me know. She—'

'And it's such a long time,' he said. 'Ten years? She will have a whole new life by now, started again somewhere else. A lady who looks like that, could.' He looked past me out of the window, at the bustle of carriages and the gaggles of people thronging the promenade. Outside I could hear chatter and laughter as well as the cries of seagulls and, distantly, the squabbles of a Punch and Judy show. 'If she's alive, that is. If she drowned, well, of course, that's tragic. It is surprising she didn't wash up somewhere along the coast, though.

'What age are you, twenty?' he said to the window behind me. 'You should be thinking about your own life, not raking up the past. Creating your own brood.'

It had been a mistake to come without a chaperone. 'I am twenty-eight, and not inclined to marry,' I said. It sounded grown-up, until I said it aloud. 'Will you take my case?'

He whipped his eyes back to me and smiled again, his teeth as pearly white and small as a child's. He was in his mid-forties, perhaps, genial, avuncular. I could not fathom my sense of unease.

'Of course, Miss Hamilton. Happy to help a lady in trouble. I'm in the middle of another case, so I can't be doing anything else for a week or two, but it's waited this long, hasn't it? She's a lady – not that you're not one,' he added. 'Only that she is a real lady. Of means, I mean. And there are a lot of men – she needs a lot of men – there isn't the resource immediately. But Frank Knight is not one to leave a wilting flower without water.

'Tell me about your mother.' He leant forward in his chair with a creak of leather. 'Was she happy at home? Any arguments, domestics? Was she the faithful kind? How was she dressed when she disappeared? Did she have enemies?' He spread his fingers out flat on the desk, starlike, and waited.

It was not how I had imagined a detective's office should be. The room was cavernous, his desk and our two chairs the only furniture in it. The walls were lined with shelves from floor to ceiling, all empty, and the surface of his desk held only a single sheet of paper, an unused blotting pad and the pen and inkstand. It was as if he had wandered in and set up office that morning, on a whim.

But I had been dreaming of finding my mother for ten years and searching for a detective for two. The advertisement, and then a leaflet posted through our front door only last week, signalled fate might finally be on my side. It was no time to take fright.

'Can you tell me how you will conduct the investigation?' I asked. He looked taken aback.

'You needn't concern yourself,' he said. 'You can leave it all safely with me. I will follow a well-trodden path. I have years of experience. Just tell me what I need to know and then you can get back to being a young lady again. This must have been a distressing time for you, but now you can leave everything in my hands, and relax.'

He stroked the picture again with the tips of his fingers, smoothing it.

'It would be useful to know your plans,' I said. I was not normally argumentative, but I did not want to hand over the baggage of my life without knowing what he would do with it.

He sighed. 'A lady who knows her own mind. Well then, here's a new idea. A sign on the side of a building. We could use the brightest of the new paints, vermilion, pink, gold.' He flashed his fingers as he mentioned each colour, like a magician, and then stretched his arms out full width, embracing the room. 'I can see giant letters saying "missing person". Something everyone sees and no one can pass by. Eight feet tall. The signwriter might even be able to catch a likeness of your mother. "Lily Hamilton, Missing". Publicity is everything these days. That'll stir things up, bring out the rats.'

'No,' I said. 'No. This has to be discreet. You said in your advertisement, in both your advertisements, all cases of a private nature would be discreetly investigated. It's very important to me. I don't want any signs, or publicity. No publicity.'

He frowned and scratched the back of his head. 'When I said leave it in my hands,' he said, 'I meant leave me to it. Seems you've been fretting too long, and you've forgotten that this is a man's business. Tell me about her.'

'I must ask you to be discreet. I would prefer that society generally does not know about this investigation. And I do not want my father to know,' I said. A smile slipped onto his face again.

'Indeed? Well, then, I suppose I can keep it quiet, for a lady's sake. I'll have to ask questions, of course. Of the police, etcetera. But I'm good at keeping secrets. Very well, no sign, although it would have moved things along more speedily. Now, to your mother.'

'She was happy,' I said. 'She was happy, and all was well with her and with our lives. There was no reason for her to go. She was wearing a green silk dress. There was nothing on the day it happened to suggest she would leave. Everyone who knew her, loved her. Can I have the photograph back? It is the only one I have.'

It was not true but, for a reason I could not explain, I did not want him to have it. I reached across the desk and took it, but he lunged over and snatched it back. He was not a tall man, so it was a dramatic lunge.

'No, I need it,' he said, and as he sat back down again his

arm knocked over his inkstand and black ink flooded over the desk, dripping off the edge onto his lap. 'Christ,' he said, leaping up again. He shoved the photo in his breast pocket, grabbed sheets of paper from his blotting pad and tried to stem the spill.

'I am sorry,' I said. 'For, for…' I looked away because he was blotting the front of his trousers. 'Perhaps I should leave you to…? Is that enough for today? Shall I come back?'

'Christ,' he said again. He was wearing white flannels, so it would stain. 'Yes. Leave it, I'll sort the preliminaries, look out the newspaper cuttings, and then we can speak again in a week. I'll need a full and frank account, though. A proper warts-and-all discussion. You can't go missish on me, if you want me to find your mother.'

'I shall endeavour not to be missish,' I said, and I rose and left him there, dabbing at his trousers.

So it was done. I had taken a step, a terrifying step, to find out what happened the night my mother disappeared. I felt sick and exhilarated. It had not gone as I had pictured, and he was not the Mr Frank Knight I hoped for, but at least life was moving forward, as it should. For too long I had felt pinned to the past, a butterfly on a board.

To my right was the beach, dotted with bathing carriages and day-trippers, and beyond it lay the blue sea, glinting silver in the sunshine. To my left was the grand row of apartments that ran the length of the promenade, as far as the eye could see, and behind them, rising up on the hills, the fine houses of Hastings and St Leonards and, higher, the castle ruins.

It was early April, and although the wind was sharp the Marine Parade was already packed. As I spun round to walk home a seagull flew past my hat, almost dislodging it, and a small boy dressed in a sailor suit dropped his ice-cream cornet at my feet and wailed. His mother sent me a glare and hustled him on.

The woman on the seashell stand shouted, 'Queen Conch! Sea urchin! Giant cowrie! Mother-of-pearl!' at passersby, briefly drowned out by a one-man band, who marched along crashing his assorted musical instruments in painful discord. A goat bleated past, pulling a smartly dressed little girl in a goat-chaise, but it was not a biddable animal, and it lunged to the left, aiming for the fish and chip stand, and the girl shrieked as if her life would end.

People were lured here by the promise of free fresh air, but smells of fish, seaweed, burning wood and popcorn drifted on the breeze. There were many fine ladies out promenading, as well as several gaudy-blazered gentlemen. It was definitely the start of the new season.

Just past the rows of pleasure boats, I saw the Misses Spencer coming towards me. Of even height, as if nature had decided on perfect symmetry; dressed prettily in pale green from head to toe. I saw the second they spotted me, the panic in their eyes as they decided what to do. It was too narrow and crowded a path to leave a wide berth, so they turned sharply right, tilting their parasols in front of their faces, just before I reached them.

It was not new. They had been doing it for the last ten years, as if I had an infection that would make their mother disappear too. It did not sting so much as it had. I carried on, comforting myself with the knowledge their turn led them directly towards the gentlemen's entrance of the public convenience.

The Misses Spencer and I had attended the same school from the ages of eleven to sixteen; a small school run by over-frilled ladies who prepared us most passionately for a destiny of flower-arranging and découpage. The Misses Spencer – Janice? Mavis? – two years or so younger than me, close to each other in age, were not unfriendly but were prematurely prissy, perfectly moulded for the world they were to enter. I had not encouraged friendship much, to be fair. I had been too excited by life and its possibilities, which then had seemed to stretch as far as the horizon and as high as the clouds. Once I had used the school's entire supply of green and red thread to embroider a dragon, fire pouring from its nostrils, a small heap of mutilated people at its feet. The sewing instructor had warned my mother about my bloodthirsty sensibilities, but my mother had only laughed. 'Let her embroider dragons while she can,' she had said.

I walked to the edge of the promenade and rested my arms on the railing to look out across the beach to the sea. There was a frenzied desperation about the holidaymakers below, as if a day out meant every second must brim with joy and contentment. It was a tough ask for any portion of humanity, let alone those set loose on a shingle beach on a windy day. The ladies and gentlemen struggled to maintain propriety and order amidst a chaos of deck chairs and picnic blankets while their children, faced with the novelties of ice-cream, swimming, rock pools, ham sandwiches and the impossibility of building sandcastles with stones, veered from happy to hysterical.

There was a small red boat bobbing about far out and I envied whoever was in it, surrounded by the peace of sea and sky. It was hard, in the sunshine, to remember why I had felt a creeping sense of disquiet in Mr Knight's detective parlour. Perhaps all detectives were mildly unsettling. Perhaps they needed to be, to get the job done.

Chapter Two

We lived in a detached red-brick house in St Matthew's Gardens, one of the many new houses that had sprung up in the town over the last half-century. The bricks were bright red-orange, untrammelled by the blackness of city smog, and it had a dark green front door with stained-glass panels on each side. We had moved here when I was ten, and I had loved it, in the early years. My mother had liked to cover any available surface with ornaments, vases, coloured lamps, family photographs, candlesticks; she had draped our furniture and our mantlepiece with bright fabrics that brought cheer to the rooms. A year or so after she disappeared, my father had arranged for many of these reminders to be packed away in the attic. He had replaced some of them with keepsakes from relatives I had never known: footstools and faded antimacassars woven by long-dead great-aunts; his grandmother's Staffordshire pottery dogs; photographs of his grandfather, who by all accounts had been a terror. But some of the shelves and surfaces stayed bare, and the atmosphere of cluttered cosiness was gone.

***

At breakfast the next day I faced a wall of newspaper, as I had for approximately the past ten years. Today it felt more than usually annoying.

I was a lady. I would be ladylike and rise above it. I straightened in my chair, taking a deep breath. I was an elderly spinster, patient with my lot and with the foibles of others. I was a woman, nurturing, caring. Accepting. My only goal was to foster a happy, contented home.

I hit the edge of the teaspoon I was toying with too hard with the edge of my thumb, and it flew across the table and collided with the back of my father's newspaper with a sharp thwack.

He jumped and lowered the paper.

'Stop it, Violet,' he said.

'I thought perhaps we could have a conversation,' I said. 'It has become a habit, your reading, but perhaps it might be pleasant to talk today?'

He raised the paper again. 'I need to know what is happening in the world. Am I not to be allowed a moment of peace? You will get your chance when I am done.'

The *Hastings Observer* would give him a narrow view. 'You did not read when Mother was here,' I said. She had not let him, but it did not seem wise to raise that. He must have found it joyous and freeing to take up reading the paper after my mother had disappeared. But now we were chained deep within the dullness of his habit, and I hated habits. If I had a choice, people would be forced to do new and different things every single day.

He lowered the paper briefly and looked at me with a

weary patience, as if I was a sack of rocks he was dragging around.

'I have told you, I do not want that woman mentioned in this house,' he said. He folded up the paper so that he could hold it one-handed, and then forked his breakfast into his mouth. My mother would have said it was very rude and American.

Breakfast was eggs and kippers. I also disliked kippers, at every time of day, but especially at breakfast. It was a miserable end for a herring. I thought they should all live out a long and happy life at sea, unsmoked.

Eventually he finished eating, folded up his paper and dropped it beside his plate.

'What will you do today?' he asked, rising. 'My kippers were a little dry, by the way. Best raise it with…' He made a slight vague circular gesture with his hand. 'I have a busy day, and I may be back late. But in time for dinner.' And he was gone, out of the door, off to his manly, worldly business at the bank.

'Today, I will mostly be…' I said to the air. 'Today, I will mostly be…' I stopped and rested the heels of my hands against my eyes for a second. I was not crying. I just needed to rest my eyes.

Cross Edith came into the room to clear the breakfast things, and I straightened up fast. She dropped some letters next to my plate.

'The kippers were a little dry today,' I said, and she harrumphed.

'You haven't eaten yours. And it will be because you are late paying the fishmonger,' she said, clearing the dishes with a clatter.

I sighed and reached across the table for the newspaper. Why could my father not just have handed it to me, knowing I wanted it? It was a small hurt, a stupid hurt. I was oversensitive today, because I had taken the immense step of hiring a detective, while he was content to let our mother fade from our lives as if she had never been.

There was nothing useful in the paper. There hardly ever was, beyond that one glorious advertisement for a detective. Petty crime, jobs I was not qualified for, minutes of endless town hall meetings. There was an advice column for women, mostly preaching cold baths and the ruination of body and soul that might come from painting our faces.

The first letter next to my plate was from that very paper. I had written to them, asking if I could offer my services as a writer. I knew it was possible because the Society for Women Journalists, with members from all over the world, had met here in Hastings only last month.

The Editor returned my small contributions, a recipe for jellied ham and tips on keeping rabbits, mostly conjured from my imagination. His rejection was kindly and perfectly justified. I didn't have enough real-life experience of the womanly arts. My writing lacked real insight. However, as it was the tenth anniversary of my mother's sad disappearance this year, might I be prepared to contribute a few lines in one of the June editions?

It was an offer that would hardly please my father, even if he wished me to have a profession. I crumpled up the letter and threw it in the fire.

The second letter was from the Hastings and St Leonards Society for the Rescue of Itinerant Travellers, to whom I had also offered my charitable services.

'We thank you for your kind offer to volunteer, but as an unmarried person, you may be less qualified to deal with the distressed persons who come through our doors than some of our long-standing married members.' Mrs Withers from our local church was behind it, I was sure. She had stern morals where I was concerned, apparently aimed at ruining any chance I had of living a life.

My life had been only half-lived anyway, since the day my mother vanished as easily as mist on a summer morning. Any gold-tinged dreams had evaporated as speedily as the social invitations. My mother's friends had moved on as soon as sympathy and speculation ran dry, and, perhaps understandably, my few female friends did not want to harm their own prospects by associating with a girl who was careless enough to lose a relative. It was possible I had offended two or three of the notable ladies in society in the succeeding years too, through my unfortunate habit of rejecting their sons.

The disappointments of the decade had been compounded by the realisation it was almost impossible for a lady to take up a respectable profession. I had been set on the idea, but now my attic was filled with the skeletons of half-finished hats, faded botanical specimens and, most tragic of all, dusty portraits of a few worthy occupants of the town. This last career had ended abruptly when I persuaded the wife of the town mayor to pose for a portrait. I had faithfully included all three of her chins, upon which she told me she had only sat for me out of sympathy, forbade me to continue as an artist and left, chins wobbling in fury.

It was but one example of the difficulties I had faced, but it was memorable. I was almost entirely convinced there was no respectable profession for an unmarried lady without a mother.

'Nobody wants me to work for them,' I said to Edith, who had come back in to wipe the crumbs off the tablecloth. We had only two servants, Edith and weary Millie, although Mrs Fitzsimmons came to wrangle with our laundry every second Thursday.

'Did you have to empty the chamber pot for the gentleman of the house this morning, miss?' she asked. 'Or clean the soot from the grates?'

'No,' I said.

'Well, then,' she said, and left the room. She was right, as always, but it didn't make me feel any better.

Edith had been in our employ for fifteen years or so. She had adored my mother and by comparison I was poor leavings. Daughter of a stolid, practical farmer, Edith had dreams of a better life, and my mother's disappearance meant the end of glamour. My mother had loved all the things Edith believed proper ladies should: beautiful clothes, accessories, fashion journals, perfume. Edith had helped her dress for the theatre, style her hair, choose which jewellery to wear; they had giggled together about other ladies' hats.

I liked these frivolities too, but my father was not as inclined to indulge me. A Puritan ancestry or perhaps a banker's caution led him to believe it was his duty to guide me to be more restrained, more parsimonious, and my mother had been far more skilled at the art of persuasion. So Edith was denied her sparkle and her resentment had grown each day, as slowly and implacably as limescale on a dripping tap. I could not blame her for it.

She had tried, at first. One evening a few months after my mother's disappearance I was invited to an evening soiree at some lady's house, and Edith had struggled to style my hair, so brown, so wildly curly, so uncontainable, so unlike the sleek red-blonde submissive waves of my mother's. I had gone to find myself the centre of attention, everyone speculating feverishly about my mother, and half my hair had exploded out of its pins to a frizzy abandonment – I looked as if I had just risen from bed. I went home early and never let her near it again. I would control my own hair.

It was around that time I began to realise my mother might not come back.

Chapter Three

I could not blame Mr Knight for admiring my mother's looks or keeping her photograph, over and above the fact he might need it for his investigation. She was beautiful, with her Titian hair and a smile warm enough to melt snowmen in winter; everyone had wanted bits of her. The postmen fumbled with their letters and the Vicar called at our house far too often. If she dropped a glove in the street, men were reluctant to give it back.

When she disappeared, I had been eighteen and due to have my debut. My mother had even talked about going to London. 'She can't stay here, unless you want her to marry a sailor or a dockyard navvy!' she had cried. My father had acquiesced, as he had always done to keep the peace. But shortly before she vanished I had already decided I did not want to marry, and in her absence it became pointless.

It was unfortunate then that my father wanted me to marry, as his primary execution of parental duty. It had taken all my ingenuity in my early twenties to avoid it. The respectable ladies of St Leonards might point their cold little noses seaward, but for a while at least it appeared my mother's disappearance gave me a certain racy appeal to gentlemen. I could not think of any other reason why so many tried to take liberties. Did they think my mother's disappearance might lead me to abandon my morals? I did not know, but the fact that I was a little brown wren to her peacock did not seem to matter.

The first time was when I was nineteen and Ernest Webb, son of the manager of St Leonards Bank, whom I had passed only rarely in the street and never formally met, brought my father a gold watch and asked for permission to court me. My father graciously agreed, informing Mr Webb of all my best qualities (as well as a few I didn't have). Our courtship came to an abrupt halt on our first outing, when Mr Webb attempted to kiss me under a weeping willow in Alexandra Park in full view of our chaperone, an elderly lady from our church. I had pushed him into the boating lake, and my chaperone had taken to her bed in shock, refusing ever to accompany me again.

Thankfully, in recent years, my appeal to the local male population had declined. I hoped it was because of my advanced age and because I had built a reputation as someone who was not marriageable. It was annoying therefore to return from a walk that afternoon to discover my father was not late but early home, and with a gentleman. I entered the parlour to face them both, squarely.

'Ah, Violet,' my father said. He was in genial mode, a personality he adopted whenever we had guests, dropping it abruptly as soon as they had left. 'You look fresh and lively. Let me introduce you to Jeremy Parchment, who runs the shopping emporium in Bexhill. We have been talking business, and it seems I can assist him with his bank accounts.'

'Delighted to meet you,' Mr Parchment said. He emphasised the last word, as if he would not have been glad to meet anyone else. He took my hand, shook it limply, then dropped it. I sat down on a chair and waited for the rigmarole to commence.

Mr Parchment was perfectly acceptable, as gentlemen went. He was not too old or too young, in his mid-thirties perhaps, and he was smiling. His chin took a gentle slope towards his neck, but this should not be a consideration when a man's interior qualities were what was most important.

The conversation was as hopeful as one could expect between two people who had nothing in common.

'I sell a lot of ladies' things,' he said, bobbing his head generously towards me as if giving me a gift. 'We have counters full of the best fabrics from London, as well as parasols, purses, other gewgaws and giff-gaffs, all the things that young ladies like. Have you been? You must come and visit. We have all sorts of trinkets. Perfume, and suchlike.'

'That sounds delightful,' I said. My father was smiling expansively, but underneath I could sense the strength of his will, as strong as a wave in a gale-force wind, urging me to behave, to be pleasant. He did not need to. These days, I did not push men into bodies of water.

'We are much larger and more popular than Butler's Emporium,' Mr Parchment said. 'People sometimes travel all the way from Brighton. We have a new selection of millinery just in, dainty little bonnets and straw hats with flower sprigs.'

'Incredible,' I said.

'We also sell necessary items,' he said, giving me a half wink and a smile, and abruptly ruining any credit he had gained. I stared back at him, blankly. I did not know what he meant. Underthings? Items that women needed at certain times of the month? Embroidery scissors? Bloomer elastic? The term obviously had some salacious meaning that other women might understand.

My father was, as always, oblivious when suitors overstepped.

'Important not to let your shop become all frivolity,' he said jovially, slapping Mr Parchment on the shoulder. 'Even though women are the ones who love to shop. We gentlemen need clothes as well, and books, collar studs and tobacco pipes, yes, pipes and cigars.' He trailed to a halt as he ran out of ideas, staring into space. It was not something he often had to discuss.

'It is an emporium, much more than simply a shop,' Mr Parchment said, a little sniffily, but he was still looking at me, trying to submit secret messages that I could not understand and did not want to understand, his eyebrows twitching. I kept my face as blank and immovable as possible, as if there was nothing but dandelion fluff in my head.

'Miss Hamilton, perhaps we could take a stroll to the beach?' he said at last, abruptly giving up.

'Of course, yes,' my father said too eagerly, rising from his chair and slapping his thighs. 'That is a splendid proposition. Violet would be delighted.'

I looked at him, silently, but he had long ago given up treating me as a person of any agency, and was already heading towards his study, duty done, although I should not be left alone in the parlour with a gentleman.

'I would be delighted,' I said to Mr Parchment. I had not yet had the chance to remove my coat, so without ado we headed out of the house and onto the street. It was a straight, steep walk downwards to the beachfront from our house. A silver haze lay across the sky, and at the bottom of the road, between the shops and the houses, I could see a slice of grey-blue sea.

He was offering me his arm. I could see him, from the corner of my eye, winging it at me like a flapping bird, and, in the end, I could not pretend to ignore it. When I took it, he held it too close to his body, so that my arm was squashed against his chest. His longer legs meant I was tugged downhill at a speed that was almost a run. A calamity of the falling-over kind beckoned.

'You are very sweet,' he was saying, a little out of breath, 'to accompany me. I am looking forward to getting to know you better. Your father has been most illuminating about you. I can see for myself though, your pleasantness. You seem like a very gentle, a very accommodating young lady. Forgive me for saying so, but you also have the most remarkable blue eyes. I confess I am in danger of drowning in them. I can see—'

I stopped, pulled him to a halt and removed my arm, the action pulling him round to face me. On the steep slope of the street we were almost the same height.

'Mr Parchment,' I said. 'You are too generous. And I fear my father is too generous also. He only has my very best interests at heart. However' – the word hung in the air for a second, a seagull about to swoop on a hunk of bread – 'I do not want to mislead you. I fear I must not, I cannot, I will not ever marry.'

He blinked at me for a second. 'I have not proposed,' he said at last. 'We are only going for a walk.'

'I know this. But I feel it is only fair to tell you, as a man of honour and good breeding, a gentleman, that this can never go any further. It would not be fair of me to lead you on, to create any kind of hope, of expectation in you. It is best that you know now, so that you can judge whether you wish to spend any more time in my company.'

'You are nervous of marriage?' he said.

'I am flighty,' I said. 'I fear I have inherited it from my mother. I cannot promise myself to any man, because I cannot be sure I will not leave. It is in me, a bad quality, a taint if you might call it that, and one day we could be happy, terribly happy, and then the next day pfff! I would be gone. I cannot do that to anyone, to create a family and then destroy it, just because I am like a feather on the wind.'

Something about him had deflated, but at this he perked up again like a rooster.

'It seems to me that you just need the right man,' he said. 'A man who would keep you right and not let you stray. A man who would give you all that you need, keep you... happy. I do not mind a little wilfulness in a woman, a little waywardness. It would settle down with a little domesticity, the right home. I am sure you do not take after your mother.'

I touched his elbow with a trembling hand. 'You mean... you mean you would be willing to take on someone like me? Almost an orphan, friendless in the world? I am all agog. You mean you would marry me, knowing my wildness, my passion for freedom? You would ask me to marry you, knowing all that?'

'Well, yes,' he said, and then his eyes widened, and he looked around a little frantically, realising what he had agreed to and checking if there were any witnesses. 'I am sure I would, once I got to know you a little better. But we have only just met, and I have just remembered that I have an appointment in town, so perhaps we could talk again some other time. These are serious matters, you know. We should take it slowly, ruminate.'

'I am looking forward to it,' I said. 'But please do not drown in my eyes. I should not know how to rescue you.' I stroked his arm again, as if in affection, and he jumped. It was remarkable how men reacted when ladies broke the rules. He gave his farewells in a great hurry and set off down the hill, his coat-tails flapping.

And there it was. I had secured a proposal in under a minute, and sent him running the next, when all he had likely intended was a fumble of my bosom under a beach awning. If he had also intended to propose, some distant time in the future, I had done him a great favour by expediting matters and scaring him away.

Once, I would have congratulated myself on the speed of my execution. Others had taken longer to dispatch. But I had lost my zest for spurning suitors in recent weeks. What lay behind it, after all, but fear? It had seemed fun, at first, to confound expectations. But I could not claim I wanted to live life when I was fleeing one part of it at great speed. All I was doing was condemning myself to an eternity of silent breakfasts.

I took a long route home, to give my father the impression I had given Mr Parchment the time of day. It was not hard, as the town was anchored on a billowing wave of coastal hills, the steep streets a maze leading in all directions. Even after many years I was not confident I always knew my way, especially in the older parts of Hastings. It had been a smugglers' haven for centuries, and its past lingered in warrens of narrow, precipitous flights of stairs called twittens and in dark alleyways that might lead only to a dead-end.

Our house was in St Leonards, the fashionable seaside resort that had sprung up next to Hastings only a few decades ago. Although St Leonards was new and grand, and Hastings old and rough-edged, the two resorts had so thoroughly sprawled into each other that no one could now deny they were one town. Last year the council men had finally demolished the archway that had marked the divide between them, although they had done it in the dead of night, because people were fond of it.

When I got home, there was a letter waiting for me, in a very spiky, agitated scrawl. Someone had apparently been busy.

'I have <u>already discovered</u> some Interesting Matters,' it said. 'Please call on me at your <u>Earliest Convenience</u>. Yours, Mr F. Knight, Esq.'

It was short and slightly disturbing, not unlike the man himself. But at least he was making discoveries, as a good detective should. I resolved to visit him the next day.

There were several reasons I was determined not to marry. One was that I did not trust my understanding of gentlemen, or myself. I had not yet gained a clear sense of my own attractiveness, because I had only been to a very few social gatherings with my mother before she disappeared, and, wherever we went, she had shone the brightest.

There were a few exceptions. 'Whoever is this little pixie?' an elderly gentleman had once asked her, cornering us in the foyer during a matinee at the Gaiety Theatre. 'She looks sprung fresh from a woodland dell, all wondering eyes and fragile innocence. Good evening to you, little fawn.' His eyes flicked lower than they should as he said it, even though I was only seventeen and wearing a dress with a high neck, and he made a low humming sound in his throat, reaching out a smoke-browned finger to stroke my cheek.

'She is a very fierce pixie,' my mother had said, 'so I would watch your hand if I were you.' She had whisked me away, back to our box, and lectured me as we sat down.

'Do not ever think that politeness means you have to put up with gentlemen like that,' she said. 'People may call them roués or rakes, but I call them toads, because no sensible woman would ever let their warty fingers near her. You look very young for your age. Perhaps we should not let you have your debut at eighteen. It is so soon. Too many men like that might feel you would fall for their flummery. And you are not little.'

I had argued with her about my debut then, because I wanted one furiously. It meant parties, laughter, dancing, an entrance into a world far wider and more alluring than the one I had seen. Marriage had not really come into my consideration at seventeen, as we had not talked about it, mother to daughter. It was something to be thought about in the distant future, once I had danced my shoes to smithereens.

Eventually she agreed I should have my place in the sun, but 'You must stick close to me,' she said. 'I will tell you who is who, which men are to be avoided, which ones must be handled with charm, which ones you may insult. Goodness knows, I had to run the gauntlet myself. I think I chose your father because he was the first not to salivate on me when we met.'

She was prone to exaggeration, but I understood what she meant. I was glad she was at my side. She seemed wiser than other mothers, in these matters if not others, because she had already navigated a world in which she had been a significant prize to be caught. She had spurned her fair share of suitors before she had met my father, and I could see why his dignity, his serious approach to courting, had charmed her, especially if she had previously faced a plethora of amphibians.

In her absence, I was not ready for the spotlight and unsure why I had it. Was it because I was the daughter of a mysterious, beautiful, missing woman? Or had I unexpectedly blossomed from a startled woodland animal into a more palatable creature? I was small when she was tall, round where she was not; I was altogether a different proposition to her red-gold, green-eyed, willowy elegance.

My father approached my marital prospects practically, as if a meeting of minds was as simple as a bank draft. I did not trust him to protect me from the wolves and I suspected the gap left by my mother had given me the wrong kind of allure. The suitor I was forced to push in the lake was not the only one who behaved inappropriately. A greasy mutton-chopped gentleman had once dipped his finger in his wine and run it down the back of my neck between my shoulder blades, ruining any joy I felt about wearing my first evening dress. Another, short on teeth and politeness, had tried to embrace me in an orangery, his arms wide as I dodged away from him among the small potted trees. A fourth had seen fit to touch my bosom in my own drawing room, putting his hand on it quite matter-of-factly, as if testing the upholstery on a Chesterfield, and I had had to insert a hot teapot between us.

I felt most foolish of all because I did not know if this was how men always behaved, or if there was a deeper reason.

Without her protection, her wisdom, men and courtship were like navigating stormy seas in a boat full of holes. It was safer to reject them all.

Chapter Four

There had been few balls, no glittering events, in the last ten years, because it did not seem right to enjoy them once she had gone, and because, although he did not say it aloud, I think my father felt that my mother's gaiety was the quality most likely to have led to her disappearance. Any hope of adventure and excitement went with her, so the last decade had been very dreary indeed.

I had found some small solace in reading about other people's adventures. My father granted me a small book allowance and our Vicar, the Reverend Bartle, had a remarkably extensive library for a religious man and lent them to me freely. He had been fond of my mother and kept a close pastoral eye on me now she was gone.

I lit on the idea of a detective when I was reading through his collection of adventure books. There was a series about a detective called Sherlock Holmes, an odd but freakishly clever man, and a collection of short stories by a Catherine Louisa Pirkis about a Lady Detective called Loveday Brooke. Among her cases was the bewilderingly complicated mystery of a missing lady, which she had solved with great expediency.

It was ridiculous, of course, to think a lady could ever be a detective in real life, but Loveday Brooke was a beautiful name. I rolled it around my tongue to comfort myself when my nights were at their most desperate.

The police had given up searching for my mother too quickly, waylaid by other cases more pressing: battles between fishermen and the council over who owned the beach; thefts of building materials from the scores of new edifices decorating the town. The detectives in books overflowed with honour and dedication, going to great and dangerous lengths to solve their cases. After a while, the idea took shape, growing clear and sparkling in my mind until I could think of nothing else. I needed a real, living detective to find my mother.

Two years ago I had pawned a necklace and earrings that had belonged to her, in readiness for salvation to arrive. It turned out, however, that Hastings was not thronging with men of an investigatory nature. I had started to consider going as far away as London to track one down, so when Mr Knight's advertisement appeared, it felt as if my prayers were answered.

It was a grave disappointment, therefore, that Mr Knight did not seem to be living up to his name, in spirit or attire. When I went back to his office he was dressed in another blazer, this one striped camel brown and pink, and he was frowning. The room was as empty as it had been before, and this time there was not even a pen and inkstand on the desk.

'I went to Farnham & Sons,' he said, without preamble. 'The photographer on the back of the photograph. He's based here, so I went in to make general enquiries, to see if he had any other photographs. And he did. He does. She used to pose for him. For cigarette cards, and the like. I've got a couple here. She must have made a bit of extra income from it. Not much, but they were popular. You can see why. A beauty, your mother.'

I picked up the pictures he pushed across the desk. I did not recognise her clothes. A velvet dress in some dark colour, cut deep at the neck. A hat with a curving plume of pale feathers in the first photograph, a white fur stole in the second. She wore a necklace of dark stones and pearls and her hair was piled on top of her head, thick, luxuriant. She was smiling, a genuine excited smile, that had not stiffened into awkwardness in the time it took to take the shot. She looked younger than I remembered. I felt a wrench in my chest.

'When were they taken? Who did she sell them to?' I asked.

'Not long before she disappeared, apparently. Farnham sold them. Sent most of them to London for sale in the big shops. She has a name, a false name, there, printed at the bottom.'

'Miss Evelina Joyce', it read, in white curly print, 'Performer'. Had she wanted to be a performer? A performer of what? It was not a respectable life, but she had always been fond of drama. She would have suited the stage.

'Pictures like this sell better if people think the model's well known,' he said. He was still frowning, and his lips were pursed. They were already protuberant, so pursed they looked like two overripe grapes. 'What do you think of that, then? Five minutes on the job and I have found something out already.' He didn't look happy about it, though, and his hands were clenched tight in fists on top of his desk.

'Thank you, I am grateful to you. So, they weren't sold here?'

He unclenched his hands and drummed the desk with his fingers.

'No, not these ones. So, tell me about her,' he said. 'Why would she have posed for these? It seems... reckless.'

'Perhaps,' I said. 'But I am sure we will find there was a good, sensible reason.' It was unwise of her, to have put her image out in the world so freely, to be bought by anyone who liked her looks. It was the kind of thing less respectable women would do. But I would not say that to Mr Knight.

Something else was going on with him. He folded his arms and then unfolded them again, staring at the empty shelves on the far wall.

'Can I have them?' I said.

'No,' he said. 'I bought them. They are mine. You can get copies from Farnham & Sons, if you want them. I'm sure he'll sell you the... best ones.'

'There are more?'

'A few.' He shifted in his chair. 'But I think these are the ones you'll want. Now. About your mother.'

What did I have against him? Small teeth, a smile that slid off his face too quickly? He was not smiling today. But he had been more than willing to be discreet, once I asked. There was nothing tangible. I could not explain why I wanted to protect my mother from him instead of helping him find her. He was offering, after all, to solve a mystery that had been my most fervent preoccupation for years.

'Can I see the other ones?' I asked.

'I didn't want to say it. I really didn't want to say it,' he said. He stood up and walked around the room. He let himself smile, but it was tight at the corners.

'I know Farnham, he trusts me. He would usually keep

such a thing confidential, but he told me – this is going to be hard, for a young lady – it might shock you. But he told me – I am not sure I should.'

He was going to tell me anyway. I could see the news rising in him, angry bubbles of air, ready to pop.

I helped him. 'Please tell me.'

'Some of the photos are not what a respectable lady – they are on the edge of – they might be called risqué.' He threw himself back in his seat. 'Sadly, it seems your mother was... imprudent.'

'Imprudent?'

'Indecorous. I have copies – purely for the investigation.' He took two more photographs out of his desk drawer. 'I don't know if... perhaps you should not see these. But perhaps it is best, that you know.' He slid them across the desk towards me, face down, one on top of the other. Then he pulled them back towards himself, shaking his head. 'No, no. That is not appropriate. No, perhaps it is better if I describe them.'

'I should like to see them,' I said, and he pushed them towards me again, and then pulled them back, but this time I grabbed the nearest edge and there was a brief battle before he let go.

'Well, if you must,' he said, and shrugged.

I turned them over. She had a great deal less clothing on, in these. In one, she was standing in just her chemise and corset, with one leg propped on the seat of a chair, rolling down a woollen stocking. She was bent over so that anyone could see the top of her chest, and the strap of her chemise had fallen off over her shoulder.

In the second, she was in just her chemise and muslin drawers, sitting on a bicycle, her arms wide, legs spread and toes pointing out as someone might do if they were freewheeling down a hill. There was a painted backdrop behind her, of a road and a country landscape. In both of them she was laughing as if she hadn't a care in the world.

'I didn't know she could ride a bicycle,' I said. I had always wanted to ride one, even though there was so much in the papers deriding modern women and their safety bicycles. I would even be tempted to wear those divided skirts that some women wore, if I could test it somewhere in the countryside, far from town. There was such freedom of movement in them. It would be draughty in drawers, though.

Just then a little girl threw her whole body against the window outside, screaming, flattening her wet face and palms against the glass. She looked like an evil elf, her face all distorted. A woman grabbed her under one arm and lifted her away, but she left a smear, and I was conscious of the world outside again.

'Were these photographs taken for my father?'

He didn't answer, just looked at me, and I knew that was a forlorn hope. My father was unlikely to have approved of those photographs, even if they were private.

'I think I have the right to keep these,' I said, but he lunged across the desk again and before I could blink, he had shut them in his desk drawer again.

'No, I need them for the investigation,' he said. 'They are too shocking for a young lady. Too distressing. I must keep them, for your own good.'

'It would be better if we didn't investigate further,' I said. 'It looks as if there are things it would be better for us not to find out. For her sake I think we should stop this, immediately.'

He looked furious. 'No, indeed no. We need to find out

what happened here, as a matter of urgency. These pictures could have ignited unsavoury passions. No, we must not stop. We cannot stop now.'

'They are not salacious,' I said. 'She was a very good, a very moral person. There must have been private reasons that she posed for these photographs.' The thought that anyone I knew could have seen my mother wearing so little was terrifying. I realised I was one of the scarce few people alive who would not judge her for them. But how could I defend her, when she looked so happy to be wanton?

'Some of these photographs were sold here in town,' he said, pacing again. 'He didn't sell the other ones, the respectable ones, but he did sell a few of these here. What was she thinking, to expose her family in such a way? I have asked Farnham for a list of everyone he sold these photographs to, and I will investigate every single one of them. Every single one. There is a link here, a real link.'

'A list.' I was feeling a little dizzy and faint. 'They were sold here, to a list of people? In town? No, you must stop. I do not want this investigated any further. Please stop.' I stood up. 'I do not want her reputation to be ruined because of a mistake. This may have nothing to do with her disappearance.'

'You must feel betrayed,' he said. 'But don't you see that these could have led to murder?' He took them out of the drawer and held them up high, as if wielding a tablet of stone. 'Men may have become inflamed. Angry.'

I went to the door, needing fresh air. I did not feel betrayed, just confused and upset.

'I have to go,' I said. 'But I would ask you to please remember that my mother is – was – a lady. These photographs are not so very terrible. She is still covered in most of the right places. She looks happy. I do not think they would offend anyone.'

'Your innocence is charming.' He was becoming calmer. 'I will be discreet, as we discussed. Your father will not find out. But it is important we find out urgently what happened here. And we need to sit down properly and discuss what happened the night your mother disappeared.'

'Next time,' I said. 'I need to think. I need time to recover. Next time.'

I did not want there to be a next time. I wanted to stop the investigation, and never see Mr Knight again. But how could I possibly ask him to stop now? What rational reason could I give, beyond that it felt wrong to allow a seaside detective to rummage so freely through my mother's secrets?

Chapter Five

Why had she agreed to such indecency, such lewdness? I did not know. It went against everything we had talked about that night, around three months before she left.

She had decided that as I was eighteen and of marriageable age, it was time to tell me about what occurred in the bedroom between a husband and wife. She had begun pleasantly, but I knew her well enough to know when she was not telling me the truth.

'So, it felt holy?' I said. 'And you were filled powerfully with the joyful song of angels? I am glad it was so magical, but what actually happens?'

She had taken my face between both of her hands, put her forehead against mine and started to cry.

'I am sorry, Violet,' she said. 'I am sorry. But it is best that I prepare you, so that you steel yourself. Perhaps this will help you get through it. Perhaps it will not be so bad for you, perhaps there is something wrong with me. But I could not stand it. I still cannot stand it.'

She told me in great, graphic horror, although she left me unclear on the actual mechanics. My father had been too heavy. There was awkwardness, difficulty breathing, invasion, blood, a great deal of pain. She had shrunk away from him afterwards, and he had tried to comfort her, but their wedding night had been spent in separate bedrooms while she sobbed herself to sleep.

'He was not unkind. But I did not want it, Violet. My body and soul were revulsed. I wanted to peel off my skin afterwards. We tried again, a few times, but once I vomited in the chamber pot he stopped. He told me I was as cold and unwelcoming as a marble statue. I hope it will be better for you. I hope – but it is such an awkward, undignified thing to have to do. Limit it, limit it as much as possible. Men want it, they are beasts for it, but it is the most terrible, terrible thing for a woman.'

She said she was crying for me, for what I must go through. 'But marriage is not so bad, if you leave the... animal part aside. Your father and I, we love each other, and we have built a marriage of strong companionship, an intimacy of spirit and mind. Do not let my experience tar yours. And there is you. I had you, and all that pain was worth it.

'I must tell you,' she said, after we had hugged and cried together at the awfulness of life for a while, 'what it looks like.'

'What *what* looks like?'

'A man's parts,' she said. 'So that you can steel yourself. I have thought about it, and the best way I can think would be for you to go and look at a turkey.'

'A turkey?'

'Yes. The top of a turkey's beak has a loose, wrinkly bit of skin flapping over it, hanging to the side, that looks very much like a man's... parts. It is called a snood. I looked it up in a book. It has no purpose except to attract the female. Yes, when a man is not ready for… for the act, it looks very much like that.'

'Thank you,' I said. I had not looked closely at a turkey before.

'And when he is… desirous, it looks very like a particular type of mushroom, a Matterhorn mushroom,' she said. 'We can go and look for one, come autumn. It smells like rotting flesh, to attract the flies. The mushroom,' she added hastily, as I squeaked in horror. 'The mushroom does. Not… the other. Not a man's parts.'

She sat back against the head of the bed, with a sigh of relief. 'There, I have told you it all. Let that be an end to it. I am exhausted.'

Quite quickly after that, I made a vow never to marry, so I would never, ever have to put myself through it. It sounded like a perfectly nasty way to spend time.

Even now, I sometimes looked at my own father with a flinch, trying not to imagine what mad lust had made him create such carnage behind closed doors. He seemed so cold, so morally upright, it was hard to think of him acting like a marauding beast. But it was best, as a rule, not to think too much about it.

I did go and find some turkeys soon after, of course. There were a few farms on the hills. Turkeys were very odd-looking creatures. They had a wrinkly cowl of skin over their heads, like a judge's wig, and another long flop of red-pink wrinkly skin falling across their beak that looked as if it irritated them, getting in the way whenever they turned their heads. It was not appealing in the slightest, and I left quite quickly, before the farmer could ask why I was staring at his birds.

My mother and I did not get around to searching for mushrooms before she disappeared, so I did not know which one she meant. I could not find it in books. Mushrooms seemed a peculiar shape for procreation. I hoped it was not red with white spots, like a fairy toadstool.

So, what was she doing, posing in those titillating photographs, that presumably encouraged – no welcomed, that sort of behaviour? I walked far along the beach away from Knight's office, until I reached an empty, rocky inlet, sat down on a rock and tried to work it all out.

I could not be angry with her for the photographs. She appeared so happy in them. So free, when she should have looked ashamed. Her expression couldn't have been so carefree if she had been blackmailed or forced into them. I didn't understand it, and it made me wonder how well I had known her. When had they been taken? I had forgotten to ask.

She had not been happy, for several years before she left. She and my father had argued, spat spiteful words at each other. At times they had not spoken to each other at all, using me as a reluctant messenger. She had spent more and more time with her friends, at soirees, at musicales, at the Pier Pavilion, the Gaiety Theatre, the Warrior Square Opera House.

There was no peace for me on the rock. There was a woman in a hooded black cloak, wandering back and forth across the beach in front of where I was sitting. She was almost bent double at the waist, staring at the ground. Every now and then she would pick up something and then fling it aside, with a flourish and a crack of stone against stone. She brought to mind the three witches in *Macbeth*, and I wondered if she was searching for some kind of stone that would help her brew up a curse. She glanced up the beach towards me and I saw her cheeks cleaved inwards to her jaw, the strange sunken, skeletal look of a toothless person. She looked like someone who had lost their wits. I could not sit and think about my mother while a spectre patrolled the beach, no matter how innocent her mission.

As I rose to leave, the thought occurred to me how completely unrecognisable people were without their teeth, how much they shaped a jawline, made a face. Toothlessness made people old, even if they were still young. A flush of horror went through me. I turned and crossed the shingle towards the woman.

'What are you looking for?' I asked her.

She scarcely looked up at me. 'Shtones,' she said. Her voice was muffled.

'Is that so?' I said, desperate to see her face again. 'Any particular kind of stones?' The beach was covered with thousands of them, so it was possible she had lost her wits.

She straightened up to look at me and I stared frantically at her face. Dark eyebrows, brown eyes, a straight nose, those dreadful cheeks curving inwards. Light brown hair, with streaks of white. She looked down again. 'Foshils,' she said, briefly, and then bent over again and carried on walking, dismissing me.

I wanted to sit down on the rocks again to catch my breath, but I made myself clamber up the steps to the promenade and head for home. It was not her. Of course, it was not her. My mother's hair had been gold, tinged with red, and she had had green eyes. As straight a nose, perhaps, but there was no reason she would have lost her teeth like that, no reason at all. And the woman was shorter, more rounded, surely. The curator of Hastings Museum had once told my mother she had the angular gracefulness of a heron. She had not liked the compliment.

The flash of fear stayed with me all day, as if a ghost had walked through me. I wondered how low I had sunk – to think strangers might be my mother.

Chapter Six

It was the third Sunday of the month, the day that the Reverend Bartle came to visit us. I was fond of him. He was one of several men who had regularly called when my mother was around. The others had faded away, but he had carried on, ostensibly to give solace to me and my father but also perhaps to catch some fleeting essence, some memory of her warmth, her joy and laughter. When she was happy, she had spread it around as freely as air.

My father had not seemed to mind the other men who admired her, sure, perhaps, that she would not stray. He had seemed to bask in it, when I was little, watching with pride as she held court. I had sat at her feet, gazing on in wonder as she and her admirers conversed about the world. She had sung beautifully too, and they had joined in, the Vicar with his deep baritone, the others higher, everyone harmonising in a way that made everything feel right with the world.

The Reverend Bartle was a small, kind man who always chose the least fiery, the least judgemental passages from the Bible to read in his sermons. He had adored my mother in a wholly selfless way that asked for no return beyond the chance to spend time in her company.

'How are you, Violet?' he asked today, unwrapping his very long scarf from around his neck. It was a gift from a member of his congregation, who he had told me liked to knit, but not cast off.

'I am in good health, Reverend,' I said, leading the way into the parlour.

'And you, Lucas?' he asked my father, who was reading a book of psalms, to match the genial but pious personality he adopted in the Vicar's company.

'Well, I am well,' my father said. He closed the book with a bang. Millie had set out the tea and biscuits already, and so we set to our usual routine, passing round plates and arranging ourselves comfortably without much need for words.

'What news?' the Reverend asked, and even after all this time, I wondered if he hoped that some miracle might occur, and that my mother might have returned.

'I've taken on some new business,' my father said, and they chatted about that for a while, as the Reverend was a good listener, who responded in all the right places with murmurs of agreement and helpful nods. I worried about those listening skills, sometimes, as I watched him trapped in church pews with members of his congregation who liked to talk. But he didn't seem to mind.

'Violet is doing her usual,' my father said, when I least expected it.

'Her usual?' the Reverend raised his eyebrows.

'I invited round Jeremy Parchment, the man who runs the Bexhill Emporium, and he might have been interested in getting to know her. But heaven knows what happened, because when I saw him yesterday, he stammered like a fool and hid behind the haberdashery counter.' He turned towards me. 'What did you do, Violet? What did you say to him, to make him behave like that? I set up these opportunities for you, and you ruin them every time.'

'I… nothing,' I said. He had never brought up these matters in front of the Vicar before. I did not know what to say.

'It is not that hard. It really is not that hard, to get a husband. Lord knows, it did not take your mother long to hook me. Flutter your eyelashes, look coquettish. Girls have all the power in these situations. I don't understand why you are not married by now. What do you think, Reverend? How is she scaring these men away?'

'Perhaps he did not suit her,' the Reverend said, putting his teacup down. He looked like a worried rabbit. 'It is important in marriage to find a partner with whom there is a mutual affection and understanding. You would not wish her to settle for a husband she does not like just to suit you, I am sure. She is young yet, there is time.'

It was the wrong thing to say. I could see my father's ears turning red. 'What do you want out of life, Violet? Do you expect me to pay your way through it without lifting a finger?'

I wanted to find my mother. I wanted to fill my life with something useful, and not be afraid of living. I wanted to know about life, and not be wrapped and smothered in cotton wool because I was a woman. I could share none of this with my father.

'I do not expect you to support me forever,' I said. 'I apologise. Mr Parchment and I did not suit, but I should have let you know before you saw him again. He is a shop owner, Father. Do you really want me to be married to someone who sells common and everyday goods? I have heard he sells cheap spades and buckets for the seaside.' It was a long shot, but I was desperate to restore calm.

'At this stage, I would see you married to the coal man,' my father said, but his ears were pinker, and he picked up another biscuit.

'I will get wed someday soon, Father,' I said, and hid my crossed fingers in the folds of my skirt.

Chapter Seven

Overnight, I found that my mother had turned into a skeletal spectre in my brain. It seemed almost more horrific if I were to find her alive, a shell of the woman she had been, than if she had passed away. What if she had fallen on hard times, taken up loose ways? What if she had lost her mind? The thought had not occurred to me so strongly before, that the mother I found might not be the one I had lost. She might be gibbering or a drinker of gin; suffering with some terrible pox or working in a music hall.

I would welcome her back anyway, with open arms. I imagined myself hugging an elderly woman covered in sores, wiping her tears while bits of her skin fell onto the floor. I was not so sure about my father, but I, surely, could steel myself to face her, to love her, no matter what?

I was becoming ever more convinced, though, that Mr Knight should not be the man to find her. He was obviously investigating the Wrong Things. What did it matter if my mother had posed for some naughty pictures? He should be concentrating on what happened the night she disappeared. Everything else was distracting.

* * *

My father seemed unusually happy the next evening. It was most disconcerting. He whistled as he came in the front door and asked me how I was. It was such a surprising question I found I did not know the answer and muttered something about mutton for dinner.

'Mutton again,' he said. 'Well, we mutton complain.' I was not used to jokes either, of any calibre, so my laughter came out as a squeak.

'Did you have a good day?' he asked over dinner, still jovial, and I almost looked under the table to see if we had hidden guests. Maybe he had stowed a suitor behind the curtains. But then he ruined that theory by asking, 'Have you scared any more men away?'

'How diverting,' I said. 'No, I have not been fortunate enough to meet any gentlemen recently.'

'Well, so be it,' he said, and then changed the subject. Something was up, definitely. He continued on, in mellow form, and I remembered that sometimes, maybe often, he had been like this when my mother was around, mostly when I was younger. Contented, affable. I began to think how hard the past years must have been for him, too, and then I stamped down on the thought, because it was not wise to let my defences down and think of him as soft-hearted.

'Would you like a sherry?' he asked at the cessation of an endless dinner. I was exhausted, from wheeling out pleasantries after years of rust. He had discussed the weather, the new harbour works, a lugger rusting offshore, the crowds that heralded the start of the day-tripper season. Usually, he read the newspaper, and on special occasions complained about the food.

'No, thank you. I must retire and catch up on my sewing. You seem in jovial form this evening,' I dared to say. 'Is there a reason?'

'No, nothing specific,' he said. 'Just feeling the joys of spring. I feel as if there is a freshness in the air, a clearing away of cobwebs. Perhaps it is time at last for us to have a new beginning.' Was that a small flush of colour, high up on his cheekbones? Impossible. My father was not the blushing kind. I bid him good evening and went to hide in my bedroom.

He would not be so happy if he discovered what I had done, hiring a detective to find my mother. I had meddled beyond my station as a daughter and set in train a calamity heading towards God knew where. My mother might be discovered singing on the London stage, or acting as a lady friend to a dissolute gentleman. If I could not trust the confidence of Mr Knight, the ambience in our house would be worse than the seventh pit of hell for around the next forty years.

The next day was Clean the House Like a Banshee day. This happened around every two months, when I realised that we could not put it off for any longer. Balls of dust could be found in every room and up the sides of the hall stairway. It was important to do it a day or two before my father noticed the mess, a technique I had refined effectively over the years.

It had not always been this way. For the first couple of years after my mother vanished, I had tried to keep house beautifully. But there was something so wearying about it, so all-encompassing; the relentless return of dirt and chaos, and I could never match up to the effortless way my mother had managed the servants. I was the interloper, the poor relation in housekeeping terms; I took over the running of the house before I had built up any authority with those who served us, and my father never quite trusted me to have made a proper transition from dependent daughter to lady of the house. Besides, once I realised that he did not really notice the difference between spotless and spit and polish, I decided the latter would do.

Edith, weary Millie and I gathered in the parlour, and set a plan of action.

'It would be easier,' Edith said, 'if we had more help and then we could do it as we went along, rather than all last minute and topsy-turvy like this.' She despised me, most of the time, but I couldn't blame her, because I couldn't pay her that well and her job was not at all joyful or rewarding. She was often scrambling to keep up with all that needed to be done. My mother had somehow inspired the same devotion in our servants as she had in everyone else and they had forever been doing more than they needed to, purely to please her. I was not my mother.

'I can't afford to hire anyone else, Edith,' I said. 'Right, so shall we divide it by floor? I can do the bedrooms. Edith, can you do this floor, and perhaps Millie, as it is your domain anyway, the kitchens and suchlike? And then we can meet back here at midday and see how far we have got.' It was not their ideal solution, I could see, but I had to look as if I was at least nominally in charge.

We went at it. The key, for me at least, was to actually behave like a banshee. My father had left for work, so I tore into his room and ripped the sheets and blankets off his bed as if fighting a death battle with a ghost. Then I ran into my bedroom and did the same there. I picked up all the bedlinen and shot downstairs as fast as I could run and put them in the laundry basket. After that I ran back up, remade everything with clean sheets and blankets, and wiped all the surfaces, then brushed the floors as if they were a fire I had to douse.

It was past time, I realised, to change the tattered newspapers that had lined our chests of drawers and trunks for the past five years or so. I debated for a while using that day's newspaper before my father had read it but relented. I found older papers, and a new folding technique I called Bundle and Squash helped me put the clothes back in the drawers at record speed.

By lunchtime, I was puggled. If I could have wailed like a banshee, I would have. By the end of the day, I was exhausted. The three of us sat at the kitchen table, sweat and dust in every pore, and agreed to never again let it get so bad. It was the same discussion we had roughly every two months.

'Violet,' my father said later that day, 'all my shirts are crumpled up in my drawers like birds' nests. Can you sort it out, please? I can't have creased shirts.'

He seemed grumpy again, and I welcomed back his old self. But by the time I had ironed a shirt for him for the following day, I was ready for bed. By the grand hour of eight and thirty, I was tucked up, ready for sleep.

I couldn't, of course. I dozed and dreamt of hag-like witches, claiming to be my mother, and oily detectives, their hands outstretched, luring me to a lurid doom. But in between I lay awake and stared at the ceiling, wondering how I could stop Mr Knight from bringing my family into disrepute.

At midnight I gave up on sleep and lit my oil lamp. I had

stupidly taken all the books in my bedroom back downstairs so instead I read the pages from the *Hastings Observer* of five years before. The old news was not interesting, the typeset fading, and it was not long before I found my eyelids drooping.

Seconds before I threw them aside, I spotted another advertisement. It was very small, uncoloured, with no illustrations, no great boasts, barely even twenty words long.

It was for another detective.

Chapter Eight

I had to go. I had to go and find this Mr Blackthorn, Mr Bernard Blackthorn, and see what he was like. If he was like Mr Knight, erring on unpleasant, then I would know that all detectives were like that, and I would put up with it. But what if there were other detectives, who were more as I had imagined them to be? The detectives I had read about, who were principled, upstanding, understanding, heroic. A little like a knight, stuffed full of chivalry and a desire to ride to the rescue of forlorn spinsters.

The thoughts raced around my head all night until eventually I dropped off into the sleep of a mummified person around five in the morning, to be woken two hours later by a seagull cawing outside.

Mr Blackthorn's office was in Hastings, on the edge of the old town. I would lose my way in the maze of streets uphill, so I walked down to the seafront and then along the flat, wide promenade. There was a sharp wind coming off the sea and my skirts whipped around my ankles, but I put my head down and continued, fighting to remain respectable and not be blown out to sea. This was a more familiar battle to me than the much-heralded 1066 event, which had been fought a good seven miles away at a place appropriately called Battle.

Just before the black fishing huts, I turned left up a narrow, cobbled street lined on either side with rows of small houses. In this area the rooftops were all odd heights, walls and windows bulging, later additions jutting out; they were homes built and adapted for living in, across centuries. Many sat on a high pavement that ran above street level, hiding deep cellars and connecting tunnels built for smugglers of years past. The old town was where the real people lived and traded: the fishermen, shopkeepers, seamstresses, publicans; those who did not have the luxury of choosing the town for its fresh air.

It was also rougher here, and I was glad I never adopted the latest fashions. Giant leg o'mutton sleeves or hats adorned with flamingo feathers would only serve to advertise me as prime fodder for pickpockets in this part of town.

Mr Blackthorn's premises were up a side street that led into a small square, surrounded by high walls on three sides. The door might once have been bright red but was weathered to a dull, peeling brown. There was no sign, no gold lettering, only a rusty number three, which had lost a screw and hung upside down. I pulled the bell, and it clanged deep within.

There was no answer. I turned the handle and pushed the door and it opened, sagging inwards, so I clambered over the step and went in.

It was a junk shop. There was furniture everywhere, wardrobes, chests of drawers, bookcases, ornaments piled high enough to cover all but the tops of the windows, so light squeezed in only reluctantly. There was no obvious pathway through it all, and if I headed in any particular direction, I might embrace a roll of carpet.

'Hello,' I cried, and from the depths of the maze I heard footsteps. Or not quite footsteps, but a dragging sound and a thud. I conjured up Quasimodo, Frankenstein's monster and Cyclops, before a man appeared through the gloom.

He had a long beard and he was very tall. He looked at me, making a sound halfway between a harrumph and a cough.

'You want a chair?' he asked. I could not see one that was not covered in piles of books and papers. 'Or a wardrobe?' He ran his hand over his face. 'A bookcase?'

'No, I want a detective,' I said. 'Mr Bernard Blackthorn.'

'Ah… ah.' He stood awkwardly. 'That was my father. He died around a year ago. I am Benjamin, Benjamin Blackthorn. I sell furniture now,' he said. 'I did carry it on for a bit, but then… this.' He gestured at his left leg, which was sandwiched between two wooden splints. 'I'm tall… men like to try. I'm not much of a fighter. My father was shorter. It was better for the business.'

We stood and looked at each other silently for a second. Although he was so injured and unkempt, I did not get the sense from him that I wanted to flee and never look back. The relief outweighed my disappointment that he was no longer a detective.

'I am Violet Hamilton. I am here about my mother. She was very beautiful,' I said. It was always best to get that out at the beginning. 'She disappeared about ten years ago, from Hastings. You might have read about it. The police didn't search for very long.'

'I only moved here in the last year or so,' he said. 'Here, have yourself a seat.' He cleared away the rubbish from the armchair one-armed, dumping it on top of a cabinet and then propping himself against a sideboard.

'Missing persons can be fiendishly difficult to solve,' he said. 'People disappear for all kinds of reasons, and it is harder than you think to find them. There are cities you can disappear in, make a new identity, and no one will question it. It might take a lot of time and a lot of money. And how much are you prepared for the other option?'

'The other option?'

'That she isn't alive any more,' he said. 'Are you willing to face that? Face whatever might have happened to her to prevent her coming home, however horrible that might be? Or perhaps that if she was found alive, she might not be the person you remember? Life is not always kind.'

My eyes were getting used to the gloom, and I could see he looked tired, as if life had not been kind to him either.

'I have already employed the other detective, the one by the seaside, Mr Frank Knight,' I said. 'But I think – he is not – I think I may have made a mistake. Do you take on occasional cases?'

He sighed and ran his hand along the wood of the sideboard, reflectively. It was a strong hand, used to doing practical things.

'I've come across him. He's only been in town a few weeks. He seems a straightforward chap. What's your difficulty with him?'

Mr Blackthorn was the one who was straightforward. He was so different from Mr Knight, so solidly reassuring, without any of the hubris.

There was a strange squawking from a wardrobe, as if a bird was being strangled.

'I beg your pardon,' Mr Blackthorn said, and he opened the door of the wardrobe and took out an angry seagull from the hat shelf. It was furious and tried to peck him. He restrained it easily, holding its wings to its body under his arm and its neck with his other hand. He limped to the door and placed it on a stone mounting block outside. I was sure it cursed at him in seagull language before it flew away.

'It met my window and knocked itself out,' he said. 'I found it unconscious outside the shop this morning. I thought it only needed a bit of a rest in the dark and some water, and look, it's fine now.'

I had risen from my chair but now I sat down again, heavily. This. This was what a detective should be like. The relief of it, that such a detective existed, that kindness existed, was immense. There were hundreds, possibly thousands of pestilent seagulls on the seafront, and he had chosen to rescue one of them. Mr Knight might have killed it and dressed it for dinner.

If I had been a weaker woman, I might have swooned.

'Why are you looking at me like that?' Mr Blackthorn said.

'Won't you... won't you take on my case?' I said.

'I'm not one to get in the way of another man's business,' he said. 'What's your reason for disliking Knight?'

I sighed inwardly, and then took a picture, a clothed picture, of course, of my mother from my reticule and showed it to him. I did not want to let go of it, so we had a brief, awkward tussle and then I realised that he could not easily bend down to look at it more closely and I released it. He raised his eyebrows at me and then examined it.

'A beauty, then, your mother,' he said, and handed it back to me. 'That doesn't answer my question.'

'He seems very quick to judge her,' I said. 'He has uncovered some things about her and he is not treating them impartially, factually, as a good detective should.'

'What sort of things?'

'I would prefer not to discuss them, until you agree to take on my case. They are private.' I knew I sounded like a prim great-aunt, but I was not ready to trust him fully, even though his demeanour, his consideration for birds, his straightforwardness and perhaps even his beard were very reassuring.

'What about your family, your husband, your father? Can they not help?'

'I am a spinster. My father is infirm,' I said. 'Nearly blind and possessed of an uneven temperament. I cannot trouble him with this. I had hoped to reunite my mother and father in marital bliss before he dies, but for his sake I need to put an end to this fiendishness.'

I had gone overblown. Although I could barely see his face under the weight of all that hair and bushy eyebrows, I felt he was suppressing a laugh. He frowned abruptly and ran his hand through the curls on his head.

'If you're paying him, he should work to the brief you give him,' he said. 'Judgement doesn't come into it. Just tell him how you want it done, be firm. Sometimes ladies can be too polite.'

'If I can get my money back from him, I can pay you,' I said. 'It's not much, but I'll pay you whatever I have. I don't trust him, because… because…' Why didn't I trust him? Instincts and feelings would not convince a man.

'Because?'

'He wears a holiday blazer and his teeth are too small,' I said. It sounded pathetic and slightly unhinged.

'Miss Hamilton, I can't help you,' he said. 'I've given it up. Detective work is mostly a filthy business, and I want no part of it. My leg is taking a while to heal and I prefer my limbs intact. My father was the best one. I'm sorry he's not here.'

'Won't you consider it? It seems as if you have some experience in… handling difficulties.'

He shook his head. 'If you have furniture you want to sell, I can buy it off you. But taking business off other detectives on a whim is not something I do.'

I tried to argue but he clumped his way to the door, opened it awkwardly, and then stood upright like a soldier, waiting for me to leave.

'What is that?' I said, on my way out. I was clutching at reasons to stay, I knew. There was a machine on top of a cabinet that looked very pleasing to the eye, black and modern, with fancy curled lettering on it.

'It's a typewriter,' he said. 'They are the modern way, apparently.'

I was about to ask more but he raised his eyebrows at me, patiently.

'Very well, I am going,' I said. 'I just… I really thought you might help.'

He shrugged his shoulders. 'I'm sorry,' he said, and barely waited for my skirt to clear the step before he closed the door. I stood and blinked my eyes at the glare from the pavement and the sky. The sun had come out, the seagulls were wheeling and shrieking and in the distance was the blue, blue sea. It was hard to hold onto how you really felt when the weather decided to be cheerful. I wanted the rain back to match my mood.

I cried a little in bed that night. My future felt very bleak.

I had not minded spinsterhood so much when I had had a mission. But now it was a mission that was likely to end in despair and ruination. At the very best I faced a life of paternal hatred, public shame, dwindling income and knitting bonnets for other women's babies. And the hairy giant that was Mr Blackthorn had chosen to rescue a seagull over me.

Chapter Nine

Lying was utterly wicked, of course, but sometimes being a female required it.

I called on Mr Knight the very next day and told him another detective was taking over my case.

I had tried to write a letter, because I really did not want to see Mr Knight again, but it did not have the firmness, the decisive, final quality I needed. I realised I had to go and see him, even though all of me quailed at the thought.

He was not expecting me, and when I went into his office he had his feet up on the desk, and he was looking at the pictures of my mother again. At least I thought he was, but when I came in, he threw whatever he was perusing in his desk drawer and slammed it shut, swinging his feet to the floor.

'Miss Hamilton,' he said. 'An unexpected surprise. Take a seat, take a seat. You have come to tell me about your mother. Wait, let me get my pen and ink.' He bent down and started rooting around in a lower drawer.

'No,' I said. 'No, there is no need.' My voice was a little raspy, so I cleared my throat.

He sat up clutching the pen and the inkstand, placing them

on his desk, and then dived back down and brought out some sheets of paper.

'No,' I said again. 'I have decided I am going to hire another detective.'

He stopped dipping his pen in his ink and stared at me. 'Two detectives?'

'No, I am going to dispense with you. I mean, your services. I am cancelling your services.' Why was I so weak, so woolly?

He gave a short laugh and threw down his pen.

'Miss Hamilton, you cannot do that. You cannot hire a detective, and then fire him.'

'I can,' I said, but I could hear the uncertainty in my voice, the lamentable similarity to a mouse squeaking.

'No, you can't. I have already invested hours in setting up this investigation for you. It is not done.'

'I am doing it,' I said. 'I should like my money back. I am happy for you to keep whatever you have spent on... outgoings, but I should like the rest back.'

His nostrils flared, and even his moustache looked as if it was perking up and getting angry. He took a deep breath.

'I don't think you understand,' he said. 'You cannot cancel an investigation on a whim. This is not a tea party. I have put considerable effort and money into this case already. I have uncovered significant leads. This may severely hamper finding out what happened to your mother. I do not think you are being rational.'

'I feel very rational,' I said. 'I have found a better detective.' Oh God, why had I said that? He half rose from his desk, and then he crossed his arms and sat back down again, breathing through his nose.

'Who is this other detective? Miss Hamilton, I would not

counsel you pay him. I have no intention of giving up this case. I don't think you comprehend how business is done. I will not give you your money back, and I will see this to its conclusion.'

'He is a very large detective,' I said.

'If it's Blackthorn, he's given it up,' Mr Knight said. 'He runs some kind of furniture parlour now. Did I scare you, with the pictures? I know young ladies are easily shocked. It must have upset you, to know your mother was not – who you thought she was.' He was calmer, as if he had worked out where the trouble lay.

'I was not shocked,' I said. 'I merely wish to move my business elsewhere.' If only my voice was as firm as my words.

'I think that you are just frightening at the gates. Startling, when there is no need to. We'll carry on, and I'll bear in mind that you have sensitivities, that we need to take things gently.'

'I am not a horse,' I said, but he was relaxed, in control now.

'Goodness!' he said. 'You girls sometimes don't know your brains from your elbows. I have got so far, let's not have a fit and run away.'

'Mr Knight, I am ending our arrangement,' I said, but he just smiled, and shook his head.

'Give it a few days, and you'll see things differently,' he said. 'Is it a full moon today? Are you in a fragile frame of mind? Come back in a few days' time, and we'll have another cosy chat, and you'll see all is well. Meanwhile, I'll follow up a few leads. It's all under control.'

He was avuncular again, condescending. I could not hold firm to my opinion of myself and descended to his vision of a wishy-washy female.

'I wish you would listen to me,' I said.

'But of course I am listening,' he said. 'I am just acting in your best interests, as you are not approaching things in a sensible manner.' He smiled. 'I am currently dedicating a great deal of time to you, in the face of some paucity of information, it must be said. You have not yet given me any real insight into what happened. But Frank Knight understands ladies. I will wait until you are ready.'

I did not know if I would ever be ready to trust him with more. 'Very well,' I said. 'But please understand, my mother is – was – very important to me. I should like to be assured that you will treat this case with respect and delicacy.'

He merely smiled again, small white teeth glinting in the light from the window.

Chapter Ten

It took a while for us to realise that my mother was not coming back. We had assumed, Edith and I, that she was sleeping late, as she did sometimes when she had been out the night before. My father and she had always kept their own bedrooms, so he was up and away to work as usual.

So when she did not stagger downstairs mid-morning, yawning, with stories to tell, we wondered if she had had a later night than usual, and it was not until lunchtime, after Edith had gone to check her bedroom, that we began to worry. We had sent messages to those of her acquaintance we could trust not to spread the gossip and then, as panic spread more widely, to those acquaintances we could not trust. Was she staying the night with them, perhaps? Had she stayed somewhere to comfort a friend in need? One by one, the answers came back negative, and we knew the embers of scandal were being stoked. It felt as if we were betraying her in her absence.

I sent a message to my father at around two o'clock and he came home, angry I had disturbed him, convinced that my mother was gadding about and would come home contrite. It was not until four o'clock in the afternoon that he finally contacted the police, and it took them time to realise the seriousness of the matter too, that she had actually disappeared. Those lost hours stayed with me like a fresh wound.

In the days that followed, I hoped too much. I hoped that she would return, gaily, with a ridiculous excuse and a smile, and that we would all forgive her and things would return to normal. I hoped that she had been captured by pirates or other bad men, who would fall in love with her, realise the error of their ways and return her safe and cherished, with a diamond necklace for her trouble. I hoped that she had lost her memory or been offered money to go to Paris to perform at the Folies Bergère and would arrive back with a magnificent story and a feather boa six metres long. I hoped too much, with a blithe optimism drawn mostly from the plots of novels, and it was only when endless day followed endless day, and no clues were uncovered at all, that dread and despair hit like a steam train.

Chapter Eleven

It was the day when Mrs Fitzsimmons came with her fists and beat our laundry to a pulp, so it was a good day to be out of the house.

'I don't need a footstool,' Mr Blackthorn said, bleary-eyed, when he eventually opened the door. It was eight in the morning, but his hair was standing on end and he looked as if he might have been partaking of spirits the night before. 'Please go away, Miss Hamilton. We are not open.'

Even like this, he was so much more fitted to the name of Frank Knight than the man I had hired. He was big and solid, and he looked like someone that a person might lean on for support, in a physical and a metaphorical sense. He wasn't patronising and he didn't want to stare at portraits of my mother.

I had been castigating myself. Why had I not noticed that small advertisement before? If I had seen the advertisement, and hired Mr Blackthorn, or even his father, two years ago, maybe my mother would be back by now, sitting prettily across from us at the dinner table, insisting on proper conversation. Instead, I had been lured in by colour and flash.

But I was sure, on reflection, that Mr Blackthorn had found it hard to turn me down. A man of principle, who rescued wounded birds in his free time and stood like a soldier, must be persuaded to change his mind. Even with a broken leg, all he would have to do was pop his head into the diminutive Mr Knight's empty cavern and tell him he was taking over my case, and Mr Knight would capitulate. If only because it was obvious to anyone with two eyes and a brain that Mr Blackthorn was the better detective.

'I don't think you understand. The seat was woven by my great-aunt,' I said, advancing forwards, so that he was forced to take a hobbling step back into the shop. 'It must be very old. They are birds,' I said helpfully, as he stared at it.

'It looks old. Birds? Not brown snakes? I don't think it is valuable enough to sell in my shop, Miss Hamilton. I usually go through dealers, who know what is valuable, what is worth selling.'

'The thing is, Mr Blackthorn,' I said, a little breathless after zig-zagging up and down the hills, 'it is payment. I thought we could come to a mutual arrangement.'

'An arrangement?' He was laughing at me again. It was very irritating. I put the stool firmly on top of a cabinet and beamed at him. There was no desperation in my eyes, whatsoever.

'I have more footstools at home and also larger pieces of furniture, like chairs. My great-aunt Maud made tapestry covers for many items of furniture in a classical theme. She was known in the family for it. She particularly loved the Greek myths. I think a great many people would like them. Yes, I have run out of money, but I thought an arrangement where I give you furniture and you stop Mr Knight from investigating my mother—'

'No,' he said with great force. 'Please sit down, Miss Hamilton, and let me think for a second. You are a very... whirlwind young woman.' He was quite remarkably dishevelled, the hair on his head sticking out at interesting angles like a bird that had been fighting. He was like a pirate who had only recently given up marauding, or the giant from 'Jack and the Beanstalk', without the propensity to eat people.

I sat. 'I am twenty-eight,' I said. 'Not young. I promise this will not take up too much of your time. I thought, even if you do not want to take on my case, you could have a manly conversation with Mr Knight, where you explain to him that he should stop investigating. You could pretend, perhaps, only to him, that you are investigating this case for me. I am coming to believe, now, that it would be better if my mother was not investigated at all.'

'Let me at least... I am going to make coffee, Miss Hamilton,' he said, with great emphasis. 'Perhaps you will be so good as to sit there while I make one. Just sit there. Would you like a cup of coffee?'

'Yes, please. I do not see many footstools here...' but he had disappeared to the back surprisingly quickly for a hobbling man. In his absence I allowed myself to feel a small sense of shame at trying to exchange footstools for favours, especially from a stranger, but I consoled myself with the knowledge I was doing it for the sake of my mother.

The coffee when it came was good, dark and strong. When I tried to start talking again, he held up his hand and shook his head. 'Wait.' He had brought out a tall coffee pot as well as cups, ornately carved in silver, and it was not until he had started on his second cup and refilled mine that he began talking.

'Now, Miss Hamilton,' he said. 'Let me be clear. It is entirely impossible for me to help you. I have a broken leg, I sell furniture, I don't do investigations any more, and I definitely don't aim to stop other men who are in the same line of business. No' – he held up his hand as I started to interrupt – 'there is nothing you can do to persuade me. You have to stop looking at me like a wounded lamb. I am sorry for your situation, but I think you should seriously ask yourself why you are looking to stop a detective whom you employed in the first place.'

'He does not seem entirely proper,' I said miserably.

'He has been improper towards you?' Mr Blackthorn sat up straight and frowned, with all the ferocity I could have desired. I was tempted to lie, just to keep him on my side.

'No, not exactly. It is more that he…' Oh God, we were back to instinct again. 'I can sense that he does not care for my mother's reputation as I do. And he does not listen to me.'

Mr Blackthorn was listening as I thought he likely listened to everyone, patiently, his gaze steady on my face, giving me his full, focused attention. He was not planning to interrupt, to override. That was how a true detective should behave. If only I had known about him, years ago. If only I had known that there were two kinds of detective, one who made the hairs on my arms stand on end, the other firm and honourable.

'I am truly sorry,' he said now. 'I stood at my father's grave, only a year ago, and I swore that I would not follow in his footsteps. I cannot go back on my word. I hate to lie, either. That's one reason I gave up this business. It's a bad habit, and it only leads to more trouble.'

I clutched my coffee cup in both hands, looking at the delicate willow pattern around its edge.

'Did your father want you to give it up?'

He frowned again, and ran his hand over his beard, and I knew I had intruded badly, and blown my chances again.

'If you will excuse me, my day beckons,' he said, rising abruptly. 'I cannot help you, Miss Hamilton. You must cease asking me. I feel sure that Mr Knight will handle matters as they should be handled. I have heard nothing to suggest otherwise, and he is a professional, after all. I understand that an investigation like this can be unsettling, uncomfortable. I'm sorry that you have to suffer it. But I hope he finds answers, and I hope it leads to some kind of resolution for you.'

He was back at the open door again, the wounded soldier awaiting court martial. I noticed the typewriter was still there. It looked like a fine machine.

'Please, take your footstool. The feet of Hastings' finest can stay unsupported,' he said, handing it back. I took it off him, silently.

'Take care of yourself, Miss Hamilton,' he said, and he looked at me as if he meant it, but then he closed the door on me with exactly the competent firmness I admired.

I left the footstool outside the shop, because I could never like it again.

There was a seagull standing in the middle of the yard, staring at me. I was sure it was the one he had saved. It had probably developed some ridiculous fondness for him, simply because he had been kind.

It cocked its head and looked at me, expectantly.

'Please, put your feet up,' I said, and headed for home.

Chapter Twelve

As I was going into breakfast the next day, my father came out of his study. 'Will you be here this afternoon?' he asked. 'There is someone I want you to meet.'

'Yes, I will be back, but—'

'Good,' he said, and went back into his study, shutting the door. Could I, would I, ever muster up the courage to ask him to cease introducing me to these gentlemen? It could not be long before he had rolled out the entire eligible male population of Sussex, and then he would be forced to move on to the coal man, who despite the black dust that permanently coated his person, was not as off-putting as men with soft hands like Mr Parchment. At least in hefting coal sacks, his job involved good hard labour and created solid hard muscle.

Now where did that odd thought come from? I squashed it down firmly, to a place somewhere under my ribs on the left-hand side, where I put all inappropriate musings. Gentlemen's bodies were not polite topics of thought, especially when I was doing everything in my power to avoid connecting with them.

***

I could not get Mr Blackthorn's typewriter out of my mind. It had looked like such an exciting machine, gleaming silver and shiny black metal, with what looked like a black rolling pin on top, lots of complicated mechanical levers and 'Remington Standard Typewriter No. 2' printed along the bottom.

I had read that many modern offices were taking on lady typists. Some ladies even owned a typewriter themselves and could perform their typing for different people. What glorious possibilities might lie ahead if I could learn to use such a machine? I might even be able to earn an income. Mr Blackthorn's apparatus was sitting lonely and forgotten, and he might be willing to let me experiment on it, if I carried out some typing for him in exchange. It was a terrible shame for such a shiny device to sit there gathering dust and rust.

I should be thinking about what to tell Mr Knight about my mother, what secrets I could entrust him with. But since my foolish attempt to dismiss him, I felt trapped in his perception of me, a weak, vacillating spinster. Keeping information felt like the only power I had, even though I was defeating my own ends.

Instead, because it was the most pleasant avenue, I dreamt about the possibilities of typewriters, lady typists, earning an income and whether I could ever build up my courage to go back to Mr Blackthorn's shop.

In the end, I decided just to get out of bed and go, before my doubts had properly woken up. Accordingly, I crept out of my house at seven the next morning, disturbing a very surprised squirrel at the back gate.

The streets of St Leonards were quiet, and the sea was calm

and silver blue in the gaps between the buildings. There were a few delivery boys pushing barrows, and a man lying snoring under a bush by the side of the road, a brown bottle by his side. He looked like one of the many builders or navvies in the town, his clothes covered in cement and dust. It was not usual this side of town, and I wondered if eventually someone would wake him up and send him back to the old part, where he likely lodged. I hoped they would let him sleep a bit longer first.

As I got closer to Hastings, the streets were busier. The people here could not afford to be laggards. They were sweeping the night's detritus off the pavements, unloading goods from carts and barrows, shouting greetings at each other, wiping sleep from their eyes. The butcher was standing in the window, hanging carcasses on hooks, and a fishmonger was waving a handful of sprats in the air, arguing with a fisherman. I dodged horse dung and a bucketful of soapy water flung at my feet and felt glad to be part of the world.

When I got to Mr Blackthorn's shop, someone was already waiting outside the door.

He was a small man, sitting on a wooden crate, and he had an enormous amount of fierceness. He picked up the crate, as if I might steal it.

'Ah'm here for Mr Blackthorn,' he said, in a strong Scottish accent, and he squared his shoulders, looking like he was ready to start a boxing match.

'So am I,' I said, and this seemed to throw him a little.

'Well, ah'm at the front of the queue,' he said. 'Perhaps go away and come back later on.'

'I think I'll wait,' I said, pleasantly, and after a moment, he put his crate back down again and sat on it.

The silence stretched out, and I could almost see the sirens of politeness winding around his conscience.

'Ah'm here for my milady,' he said eventually. 'She wants a detective, and she doesnae need that fool Frank Knight. Bernard Blackthorn was a good man, and his son's the same, far as I've heard.'

'I agree,' I said. The stranger was still fierce, but I was beginning to see that it was directed at the world and all the frustrations he faced in it, rather than anyone specific. The silence continued, and then with a heartfelt sigh he moved along on the crate.

'It'll be proper if you sit with your back to me,' he said. 'It's early enough, in any event, that no one will see. Whit are ye here for anyway, young sprite of a woman like you?'

I perched gingerly on the edge of the crate, arranged my skirts primly, and took my time.

'I wondered if Mr Blackthorn might let me use his typewriter,' I said. 'But I can see, in the clear light of day, it might not be appropriate.'

He gave a harrumph, which somehow served to reassure me.

'Sounds practical to me. All she needs,' he said, as if he was continuing a conversation already started, 'is someone to go and talk to her. She willnae come here, she's stubborn as a goat, but she needs to talk to someone, and the idea will keep buzzing around her head until she does. Blackthorn claims he's given up, but who would sell lampshades when you can be a detective?'

'I agree,' I said again. 'It's a silly choice. When you could be a detective, choosing to sell lampshades.'

We lapsed into a comfortable silence. The chill of the dawn

air was dissipating under the warmth of the sun, and some blue tits were chattering and flitting from branch to branch in a small tree nearby. I could not see any windows overlooking the square, beyond those belonging to the shop. I was ready to stand up and look respectable at a second's notice, but no one came, and my vantage point in the square would give me good warning if they did.

'Drouth,' he said, at one point.

'Hamilton,' I said, proudly.

'No, I've got a drouth,' he said. 'A thirst. My name's Mr Mackenzie. Do you want a swig of cider, Miss Hamilton? Or Mrs? It's the weak kind, shouldn't be too strong for a lady.'

'Miss,' I said. 'I couldn't possibly.' I was already sharing a crate with a stranger. But after a while, I made sure there was no one around and sidled out my hand, and he gave me a big stoneware bottle. It was not so very different from apple juice, and it felt refreshing and quite suitable as a breakfast beverage.

'Thank you,' I said. 'So, your mistress just needs someone to talk to, to tell them about her case?'

'Aye,' he said. 'She's been on about it for years. Frank Knight came roond but she saw through him quicker than a ghost. The man is all flannel, and I'd be surprised if he's investigated a missing handkerchief. It's Mr Blackthorn or nae yin.'

I thought about that and drank some more breakfast cider. It was strange, how some of the best moments in life came unexpectedly.

Eventually we heard some movement inside the shop and we both stood up abruptly. Mr Mackenzie rang the bell and banged with his fist on the door, and eventually we heard muttered swearing and Mr Blackthorn opened it.

'Mr Mackenzie, Miss Hamilton, it's eight a.m.,' he said. 'I don't open until ten. What can be the possible urgency of this call, at this hour? Has the pier burnt down?'

'You dinnae have opening hours on your door,' Mr Mackenzie said, 'so you cannae expect me to know when to turn up. I've got other business to attend to. Same goes for the lady here.' I liked him, immensely. He was blunt, and he didn't put up with nonsense.

Mr Blackthorn's sigh came from his boots, but he left the door open and went back into the shop. We followed him in.

'The sprite can go first,' Mr Mackenzie said, but some instinct told me to wait, so I shook my head and let him take the lead.

'Mrs Monk needs you to go and listen to her,' he said. 'I know you said you werenae doing it any more, but what kind of fool hocks furniture? Your father was a great man. Seems only right you should follow in his footsteps. This town needs a decent detective, and Mr Knight isn't it.'

'As I said the last time you came, I have given it up,' Mr Blackthorn said. 'In the last year I have been hit over the head with a bottle of whisky and thrown off the side of a boat. I'm fed up of it, and I need a steady job. People don't get violent around furniture.'

'All she needs' – Mackenzie was looking fierce again – 'is someone to talk to her. If you tell her it's hopeless, fair enough. But I dinnae think you can be frightened of talking to a lady, can you? She's in her sixties, and she's not the attacking sort. Are you a man or a piece of mutton?'

'She lives up the West Hill, doesn't she? I have a broken leg, and I can't ride or walk up any hills just now, or in fact very far at all.'

'If it's just a case of visiting the lady and asking questions, then I could do that,' I said. 'And write down the answers for you.'

Both men looked at me as if I had danced a can-can in frothy petticoats.

'No,' said Mr Blackthorn, and at the very same time, 'Sounds braw,' Mackenzie said.

'No,' the detective repeated. 'You are a young unmarried lady. That wouldn't be right. You are gently bred—'

'It would make sense, twa ladies talking. Milady might feel more comfortable with that. I like it,' Mackenzie said. 'Let's do that.'

'It is a wonderful solution,' I said, and I swept my arms out wide as if I was an opera singer. The world was joyous all of a sudden, and I felt tremendously cheerful.

'Are you – tipsy?' Mr Blackthorn asked, and yes, I was, so I straightened up and folded my hands primly together.

'Absolutely not. So are we agreed, then? I will go and ask the lady some questions for you?'

'Aye,' Mackenzie said. 'Ten o'clock tomorrow morning. Blackthorn has the address. See you then.' He disappeared with his crate, so quickly he might have been a leprechaun.

Mr Blackthorn looked at me, frowning.

'This is not your business,' he said. 'Detective work is no life for a lady. Are you sure you want to do this?'

'I am sure,' I said. 'I am very happy to help you.' I gave him my biggest smile, full of simple joy. 'You can tell me how it is done. I am very good at listing…' I actually was listing, about ten degrees to the left, so I straightened abruptly. 'Listening.'

'Very well,' he said. 'But I'm not convinced you haven't been drinking, and it's hardly nine o'clock in the morning. If you can stay off the alcohol tomorrow and it's not a habit, I'll let you go.'

'I have only had a little cider. It is a very refreshing breakfast beverage. I am not accustomed to drinking at all, in the normal way of things, but I was waiting a long time for you to get up. I also wanted to ask you if I might practise typing on your typewriter?'

'I have a feeling,' Mr Blackthorn said, 'you are going to bring me a great deal of trouble.'

I had forgotten about my father. I went for a long walk to clear my head and it was later than I had promised by the time I got home.

'Is that you, Violet?' he asked when I came in the front door, and I realised with horror that he had probably been making stilted conversation with another hopeful gentleman for at least half an hour. But as I approached the parlour, I heard what was, unmistakeably, a female voice.

'Oh Lucas,' it said. 'Beehave,' and there was a high, trilling laugh and then a squeak that hinted at something untoward going on.

It was obvious, even before I entered the room, that my life was about to change.

Chapter Thirteen

The lady was very loud. It was as disturbing to my senses as if someone had marched in and started ripping the paper off the walls.

'You are Violet,' she bellowed as soon as I came in the room. 'How pretty you are. It is a delight to make your acquaintance.'

'This is Mrs Beeton,' my father said. He was as unlike himself as I had ever seen him, his eyes dazed, his hair ruffled. He looked happy.

'I am very pleased to meet you,' I said. I perched on the edge of a chair and watched them both warily.

'We are courting,' my father added. An unfamiliar smirk spread across his face, a schoolboy caught stealing plums from his neighbour's orchard.

'We met a few weeks ago at the regatta,' she boomed. Hastings regatta? I could not imagine my father wandering around there. 'He bet on a boat that lost.' She gave a great guffaw of a laugh, which set her impressive bosom quivering. Her hand went out to touch my father's knee, hovered above it and then returned to her lap.

'I have daughters,' she said. 'A couple are your age, or thereabouts. Married, of course, but the younger ones are not. It would be lovely for you to meet them. I am sure you will get on. They are a bundle of laughs, like me. "Tilda," my dear husband used to say, "there is no room for sadness in this house. When I am gone, I want you to laugh the rooftops off until you die and make sure the girls laugh too," and so it has been, ever since. All the worst bits of life can be got through with a laugh.'

'How true,' I said. My mother had believed in laughter too, but of a more delicate kind. It was like comparing sprinkling fountains with waterfalls. You could never have called my mother jolly, but this lady oozed jollity like warm jam in summer.

'Violet is like her mother,' my father said. 'Funny when it suits her.' He cast a look sideways and I had the feeling they had been discussing my mother, pulling her apart; perhaps discussing me and my failings too.

'I am sure she is a great joy to you,' the lady said. 'What lovely things have you been doing today? Meeting up with friends?'

No one had asked me in so long, I nearly answered honestly. 'I have been volunteering with the Hastings Society for Unfortunate Peasants,' I said. There were numerous such charitable societies, and if questioned I could change it easily to the Society for Discombobulated Voyagers, or some such. 'I was helping to sort clothing for the poor today.'

My father looked at me frowning, before realising that he had no knowledge of my activities in order to disagree with me. 'Admirable,' he said. 'It is good for a woman to be useful in whatever way they can be, when they are not married.'

The word sat between us all, heavily, and I wondered what his intentions were towards this new arrival or, in light of my mother, what they could be.

'I have certainly kept busy,' she said. 'My husband was a farmer, Violet, and I have continued to manage the business on the dairy side. We have a great many cows, all fine milkers. You must come and see the farm, someday soon. We own fifty acres, on the far slope of St Leonards. It's a hard life, and there are plenty of early starts, but my brothers-in-law manage a lot of the daily graft and it's a good business.'

What would my mother have made of this bovine force of nature? She had none of my mother's delicacy or beauty, but her bosom was four times the size, and I caught my father staring at it before he looked back at his teacup, guiltily.

Perhaps for such a woman, the act of marital joining would not be so unpleasant? Perhaps she would approach it practically, like a farmer might approach the mating of a bull, with the knowledge that suffering must be borne and endured for the sake of male pleasure. Perhaps her body was made more robustly and, after all those daughters and with extra padding, could accommodate male desires and cope with excessive pain.

'It sounds as if you have an admirable operation,' I said, trying to shut down the visions in my head. 'I am fond of milk and cream.'

'I shall arrange for some to be delivered to you both,' she said, looking delighted. 'Fresh from one of our finest, with the top of the cream.' She laughed again for no reason, and my father looked at her fondly, and I realised I had never seen him with that expression before.

'I must go,' I said, jumping up. 'And check on a few

household matters. It was lovely to meet you, Mrs Beetling. I look forward to seeing you again.'

'Beeton,' my father was saying as I left the room. 'Beeton.'

I escaped, but I could hear the cadence of her excited voice and the boom of her laughter through the walls even in my bedroom. Her cheer was almost an assault.

It also struck me forcefully that in the circumstances, my father was unlikely to welcome any insight into his errant wife that didn't involve her passing away.

CHAPTER FOURTEEN

The lady I was visiting on behalf of Mr Blackthorn was called Maria Monk, which was fascinating in itself, as the only Maria Monk I had heard of had written a scandalous account of the hidden life of nuns in a convent, which I had never managed to get hold of. Could it be the same lady? It had been a long time ago, but that might fit in with her advanced age now. I would need to assess her for nun-like qualities.

'Don't make assumptions,' Mr Blackthorn had said. 'Don't talk much, simply ask questions. Find out what she wants me to investigate, don't promise anything, take notes, bring them back to me. Don't try to sell her footstools or turn up intoxicated. I'm still not sure this is a good idea.'

What kind of fool did he think I was? I had no intention of doing those things. I was fully aware of the importance of the task, the need to behave well and impress her and Mr Blackthorn. It was my chance to prove I was not a frivolous female, but a woman of serious intent. It bordered on employment. I was terrified.

She lived high up on Upper Maze Hill, in a gleaming white house with a glass conservatory overlooking the sea, and a garden full of tall exotic plants and elegant statues.

Mackenzie answered the door, cheerfully spry, and showed me to the drawing room.

My imagination was a fine thing, but occasionally it ran away with itself, for reason of knowing no better. I shut the lid on it, took a deep breath and focused on the task in hand.

'Miss Hamilton,' Mackenzie said. He left the room, closing the door behind him, and a graceful lady rose from her chair. She had one of those faces that would always look beautiful, fine-boned and austere. She had kind eyes, a warm smile. I knew instantly we would get on.

'Miss Hamilton,' she said. 'Welcome and thank you for coming. But we have met before, I think. On the beach, a few days ago.'

It took me a while to work out when I had last met anyone on the beach, but eventually I did, and I rushed to disabuse her.

'Oh no, that wasn't you,' I said. 'She was toothless, and hag-ridden.'

If the floor had been covered in rugs perhaps my words would have not echoed so loudly, but it was a wooden floor, and I heard them land, one by one, heavily.

'I mean…' I said, but what else could I mean? Nothing but that. 'I mean I met someone else, who was not you, who was those things. Not you.' Now that I looked, there were similarities, but this woman had white teeth, which had lit up her face when she smiled, and she looked serene and neat, not wind-blown and miserable.

Her face had changed, all warmth dropping from it, and now she looked very much like a nun, who had very sensibly chosen a life of prayer above the evilness of mankind.

'Who are you,' she said, 'to come here and insult me? I told Mackenzie that I only wanted to speak to Mr Blackthorn. Detective work is not for a woman, especially one who has staggered from the nursery yesterday. Go away.'

'I am sorry,' I said. 'I did not mean to be rude. I was wrong to say that. You are very fine-looking. I really do want to help you. I just need to ask a few questions—'

She rang a bell, and Mackenzie appeared.

'Miss Hamilton is leaving,' she said. And although he didn't lay a hand on me, his renewed fierceness and her disdain meant that in under thirty seconds I was back outside the gate of her house, still trying to apologise as it clanged shut behind me. The worst part was that Mackenzie looked so disappointed.

It had all taken place so fast that I stood staring at the gate for around a minute before I understood what had happened, and how thoroughly I had thrown disaster at opportunity.

I could not tell Mr Blackthorn that I had botched things just yet.

I went to the public library instead, and asked for a book on dentistry, so that I could fully understand how someone could have no teeth one minute and perfect ones the next. I was also desperate for a copy of the *Awful Disclosures of Maria Monk*, but unfortunately it was Mr Gallop, the head librarian, on duty, who had strict morals and deep grudges lurking beneath his terrifying handlebar moustache.

'Dentistry?' he said. 'That's hardly a suitable subject for females.'

'It is for my father,' I said.

'If you are looking to take books out for your father, you must bring his library card. You can't get books out for him on your library card.'

He liked rules. It was perhaps in part because I had rebuffed his addresses several years ago, when his moustache was smaller and less fearsome. I had tried to soften the blow by telling him I wanted seventeen children and would likely leave him alone to bring them up, but it had been achingly hard to get books out ever since.

'It is for me, then. But dentistry is a perfectly suitable subject for a lady to read. I am not planning to become a practitioner of it.'

'If I were to consult my good lady wife on the subject' – he liked to bring up my replacement at every opportunity – 'I am sure she would agree that teeth and oral matters are not a delicate or appropriate subject for women of any age, however advanced, especially when they are Unmarried. I have a duty of care to my Readers.'

'Oh, for crying…' I said, but I stopped myself. He liked to think my single status had turned me into a hysterical harpy. 'Fine. Fine. Thank you. Good day.'

I left the library, but it was not the end of matters. I was going to get books on dentistry and any other subject I liked, if it killed me and him. I just needed to work out how.

I was a little torn as to what level of truth to share with Mr Blackthorn. It might not reflect well on me if I admitted that I had insulted his client within the first half-minute of meeting her. But while a little exaggeration in life was acceptable, I did not want to lie outright, particularly as he seemed the kind of man who might see straight through it.

'She has changed her mind about needing our assistance,' I said. 'We had a difference of opinion about – about aesthetic matters, and she has decided not to pursue our— your services.'

'I'm fond of people saying what they mean,' Mr Blackthorn said, 'not tangling their sentences with fancy words. Call it blunt, if you like. What do you mean?'

He was half-sitting on the edge of his desk, his broken leg stretched out alongside, which gave him a casual, lounging appearance. The top button of his shirt was open. It seemed rather informal for a business meeting with a lady. I decided not to mention it.

'I mistook her…' No, that wasn't right. 'I may have inadvertently…' He shot me a look and I stopped and took a deep breath. 'I might have insulted her appearance. By accident. It was an accident. I have seen her before, and she looked very different. It took me by surprise. She threw me out.'

To my disappointment, he wasn't angry, but amused.

'I won't ask you what grievous insult you flung her way, although I quail to think. I didn't want the work, so you've done me a favour. Thank you, for going, and for trying. I should not have asked it of a gently bred lady.'

I was enormously tired of the phrase 'gently bred'. According to my mother, my father had not been particularly gentle in the act of breeding at all. It seemed to be a catch-all phrase for ignorant and foolish.

'It is not the end of it,' I said. 'I am going to go back and see her again and make it better. She just needs a bit of time to calm down, and then I'll do what you asked of me. It is not the end.'

'Miss Hamilton,' he stood up, and now things were too formal. 'It has been fascinating to meet you. You are a woman of great… determination. But I shouldn't have asked you to help me with my work. It wasn't appropriate. We must bring our dealings to a close.'

I could feel tears gathering behind my eyes, another weakness on top of everything else, and I straightened my back.

'There is another matter I wondered if we might mutually assist each other with,' I said. 'As I have said, I would like to learn how to use a typewriter, and it appears you have one that you do not use. Do you think there is a possibility I might learn to operate yours? I would like to become a lady typist, and perhaps I could type some letters for you.'

I summoned the full force of the determination he had assigned me, and let it shine out of my eyes along with a smidgen of hope. Eventually he sighed and propped his hip on his desk again.

'I don't see any harm in it,' he said. 'I'll get Agnes to pop round a bit more often, so we are not alone too much. I can set it up on a desk in the corner, and you're welcome to teach yourself. I think there's a thousand-page manual that came with it. Try not to arrive here with too much of a fanfare each day. Most people mind their own business round here, but we don't want rumours to start.'

I beamed at him. He had a wife, then, so he was doubly safe. There would be no inappropriateness or leering at any point. It was perfect. I felt no disappointment at the revelation whatsoever, not even a twinge. Henceforth, Mr Blackthorn would be as attractive to me as a lump of rock.

'When can I start?' I said.

Chapter Fifteen

A note arrived in a familiar scratchy hand the next morning. 'Discovered something Important,' Mr Knight said. 'Suggest meet St Leonards Public Gardens, by the lake, two o'clock.'

Was I not even worthy of being consulted? Was my diary so unlikely to contain other appointments? Why could we not meet at his office? I could only hope that it was a sunny day and there would be other people around, as I did not want it to look as if I was seeking to be alone with him. Although on reflection, I did not want to be seen with him under any circumstances, as anyone who knew him would suspect I had taken on his services. He was immensely inconsiderate.

There was only one solution. I spent the morning taking up the hem of a mourning dress of my mother's. It was a little snug in the chest area, but it would have to do. I wore a hat with a half-veil in black net and carried a black parasol, and I walked all the way to the park as if I was attending a funeral.

It was lucky that the grey weather had frightened most people away, so hopefully I could go without worrying unduly we would be seen. As I reached the gate a gentleman was leaving, and I think he felt the full force of my grief, for he held open the gate for me with the deepest of bows.

The garden was surrounded by some of the finest villas in town and had been designed by the London architect who had masterminded the creation of St Leonards. It was open to everyone, but until a few years ago it had been closed to everyone but wealthy subscribers, and it still felt like a place where the town's finest peacocks came to parade.

I was early, so I waited by the lake, admiring the water lilies and watching the moorhens. There was a sudden squawk and a group of ducks shot across the lake's surface. As they moved closer, I realised it was a female of the species beneath three drakes, her algae-covered head barely above the water, one of the drakes holding the back of her neck with his beak, the others hemming her in. After a few seconds she fought free and flew away, landing on the far shore and fluffing her feathers in disgust. I could guess what had happened, although I was hazy on how. It was simply further proof of the horror of mating.

'I hope you are enjoying the birds, madam,' a voice said at my shoulder, and there was Mr Knight. He was straw-hatted as usual, in a blue and white striped blazer. 'Ah,' he said, peering at me as I turned, 'Miss Hamilton. I thought it was you. But I could not be sure, because it appears you have suffered a tragic loss.'

'Yes,' I said, without explaining, because he was bound to regard my disguise as another female whim. I moved away from the scene of brutality towards a giant redwood tree that looked as if it would provide suitable cover for a discussion.

'That bench over there might suit,' he said.

'I would prefer the redwood tree,' I said, but as we

approached it, I noticed that Mrs Withers and her little henpecked husband were loitering in the vicinity, smelling the roses. After my mother's disappearance Mrs Withers had complained to the Vicar that I was not wearing black, even though my mother was not, as far as anyone knew, dead. I swivelled abruptly, nearly careening into my companion.

'What you propose is preferable, on reflection,' I said, and I took off back down the path to the bench. It was off the main path and shaded by an ornate iron-wrought roof, far enough away from other people to give some privacy but public enough to avoid accusations of a romantic assignation.

'Anything to please a lady,' he said, frowning as he sat down. 'Might I offer my condolences?'

'Yes,' I said. 'Thank you. Why did you want to meet here, and not at your office?'

'I understand your mother was seen walking through this park on her last evening,' he said. 'I thought it would make sense to visit the scene of the... disappearance.'

'She walked through here to get to the seafront, but she was seen afterwards, on the pier, by several people,' I said. 'So it is unlikely there will be any clues here.' He looked immensely displeased at that, as if I was trampling on the toes of his shoes, so I changed the subject. 'What did you want to see me about?'

'I searched for the name on the photograph,' he said. 'I have been reading the *Hastings Observer* at around the time of her disappearance, and I spotted the name Evelina Joyce in the advertisements for the entertainments at the Pier Pavilion.' He paused, as if he wanted me to clap.

'Is that so,' I said. There was a puffed-up male pigeon in front of us, strutting and cooing after a female pigeon while she performed a series of dodges in an effort to escape. What made one half of a species so rapacious and the other so disinterested? Could there not be a more... equitable way to go about things?

'She is listed as giving a performance there on the fifteenth of February, four months before she disappeared,' he said, and I turned around on the bench and looked at him properly for the first time that day. There was faint stubble on his chin and his eyes looked red-rimmed, as if he had not been sleeping properly.

'What kind of performance?' The Pier Pavilion was a grand building, overlooking the sea at the far end of the pier, built in oriental style with onion-shaped domes.

'I will find out. "The mesmerising Evelina Joyce," the advertisement said. There were plenty of other performances the same night, lantern shows, comedy songs, Black and White Minstrels. Her name is in very small letters. Did she have talent as a mesmerist?'

'A mesmerist? No.' A retired military man had once written a terrible poem about her eyes, melting. Or perhaps the other way around. But if she had possessed the skill to put people in a trance, my father would have been top of her list. 'How could she have performed when she was so well known here? Could there be another Evelina Joyce?'

'Do you think you might lift your veil?' he asked. 'I find it hard to talk to a lady whose face I cannot see.'

'I am afraid not,' I said. Mr Blackthorn had said I was a woman of great determination, and the compliment had warmed my mettle. I was not prepared to do everything Mr Knight asked, wholesale. 'It would ruin the line of my hat.'

He stared hard at me through the veil. 'Very well,' he said.

'Now, can you tell me about what happened the night your mother disappeared?'

I weighed things up in my mind.

'There is nothing really to tell,' I said. 'She said she was going to her friend's house for a choral recital, but when the constable interviewed them, they said she had not arranged to meet them. They had gone to the Isle of Wight for the weekend and were not even in town.'

'So she had planned something else?'

'Well, yes, but not necessarily to... disappear. She would often bend the truth a little, not in a serious way, but because she thought we did not need to know. Usually she was doing something else equally harmless, like flower-arranging or visiting our Vicar, but she liked to muddle her appointments a bit. She once said it was the biggest freedom she had.'

Mr Knight breathed through his nose loudly and sharply and I had the strangest sense he was disappointed. Why should he care how she behaved? I did not like sitting as close as I was to him. His lips glistened wetly in the sunshine like a peeled grape. I moved a little further away from him on the bench.

'And how does the pier come into it?'

'She paid the entry fee, and she was seen there, several times throughout the evening. It was crowded there, as it always is. The police told us the last time she was seen was nine o'clock. No one saw her leave the pier. No one has found any trace of her since. It was a complete mystery. She just never came home.'

'Just', of course, was a weak word for an event which had crashed through my world and, for a while, rent me in two. But Mr Knight was not a man whose shoulder I wanted to lean on. He was smoothing his moustache and staring into the middle distance. I noticed a rat was making its way across the neatly clipped grass, in no great hurry, and I wondered whether Mr Knight had seen it and what St Leonards' high society would make of it.

'So what was the reason for her to leave?' he asked.

'There was no reason,' I said. 'All was well, and she was happy. There was no reason for her to go. That is why I wonder if she was... harmed.' He was not a safe person to trust with too many secrets. I was hoping he would uncover the truth without them.

The rat was heading towards my left, and I swivelled around on the bench to follow its path.

'There will be some clue,' he said. 'There will be a clue to where she went – if she went voluntarily. I must ask you to think more deeply about this, devote your mind to the details. Might she have had an affection for someone else? Might she have wanted to leave your father? I must ask you to try to concentrate.'

I had thought of nothing else, in the aftermath. I had searched my mind as thoroughly as the rat might scour a kitchen for crumbs. I had gone over the events of the previous day, the previous year, until my brain knotted in my skull. I had searched her possessions, read her letters. I could not find any answers, and their absence had stopped me sleeping for too many years.

'I will attempt to bring my brain to order,' I said. Did Mr Knight realise when I was being sarcastic? I doubted it. In his eyes, women were likely not capable of it.

'Do that,' he said. 'We'll speak again soon. I shall leave you now and get to it.'

'When will I hear from you?' I asked, but he had given me a stiff bow and was already walking away down the path. He had a clipped strut of great importance, as if an audience was watching him stride onstage to speak. He fitted in nicely with the other human peacocks, but he was more like a parrot.

Mrs Withers passed by with her husband and I moved my parasol so that she could not see my face, even though I was finally wearing black, as she had wished. I hoped I was not tempting fate by wearing it.

At least Mr Knight was finding things out. Although it was ridiculous to think that my mother would perform on stage in the town where she lived. She had handled her reputation as adroitly as she handled everything else, and she would surely not take the risk of working on the stage.

I sorely wished she had passed on her ability to handle life to me, and not left me at the age of eighteen, floundering like a trout on dry land.

I was finding my way, though. I could finally see my way towards earning an income and independence. I could see, on the edge of the horizon, beckoning me, the glorious possibilities of a typewriter.

Chapter Sixteen

I went back to Mr Blackthorn on Friday, to commence the typing. I knew my way now. I walked downhill past the huge houses, built big enough for Greek gods, and then it was a straight walk along the flat, glistening promenade. I walked past the little weather station with the day's forecast, past St Leonards pier and the huge Russian gun, a trophy of the Crimean War; past the bathing huts and pleasure boats and Hastings pier; and then finally, before the gaggle of black-tarred fishing huts, I took a sharp left up the hill.

The nearer I came to the huts, the more I saw real life, instead of the promenading, bathing-carriage kind. The Bourne Street wash houses dried their washing on the beach, often from the finest houses, and I wondered if anyone ever walked past and spotted their own fine dress, fluttering in the breeze. The fishermen hauled up their fish, and dried it in the sun, and made their ropes and nets. I did not visit this side of town very often and I found myself looking at it all with fresh eyes. I liked to see everyday life in action, with no apology, and I wished I had not left it so long to discover it.

Something had changed. Mr Blackthorn had fitted a bell to

the door, so that it rang when I came in. His hair was neatly brushed, his beard combed, shirt buttoned to the neck. He looked relaxed, in control. The splints had been taken off his leg, although he was still walking with a crutch.

He swivelled at the waist awkwardly, bent down and picked up a heavy-looking box that was resting on the uncomfortable armchair, hefting it with ease on top of the sideboard so I could sit down. An unfamiliar sensation ran through my veins at the sight, but I ignored it. I had no time for sensation.

His shop looked emptier, I realised, less piled high, more like somewhere you could look around and, perhaps, shop. 'Where is all your extra furniture?'

'Sold some of it, rearranged the rest. I'm feeling better. It's lighter to get around now the splint is off. Do you want a coffee, before you get to grips with the Remington?'

'Yes, thank you,' I said. It was edging towards a ritual, this coffee, and it pleased me. I was like all the professional gentlemen who had met in coffee houses across the centuries to discuss important business. Tea was frivolous by comparison. He made it well too, bitter and smooth. It would be fuel for the typewriter battle ahead.

The bell rang sharply, and we were interrupted by a great stream of children of all ages who fell and filed into the shop, seemingly intent on securing half-pennies from Mr Blackthorn for sweets. Their cries of 'Father' and 'Papa' clarified matters. He grimaced at me and then emptied his pockets of change, and they disappeared as quickly as they had arrived.

'Stay away from the slot machines!' he cried after them, and then turned to me, raising his hands helplessly. 'Agnes's brood. What else can I do?'

Did he have other broods by other women? He must be very… busy. There had been at least seven children in the crowd, the youngest barely two, hitched on her sister's hip. He must be one of those men who are very persistent in the bedroom, who could perhaps overcome women's natural distaste, or convince them that the pain of submission was worthwhile.

'How is it going with Mr Knight?' he asked, and I nearly blurted out my suspicions again, my sense that Mr Knight was disappointed in some way in my mother. But it would all sound so inconsequential and imaginary, again, as unimportant as my aversion to his tiny white teeth. I felt too embarrassed to tell Mr Blackthorn my mother had posed in scanty clothing, even though he would likely handle the revelation with much more impartiality than Mr Knight. He was still a man, and I felt an odd trepidation that he might judge me differently for the sins of my mother.

I told him instead that Mr Knight was certainly investigating things.

'He is certainly investigating things,' I said. 'Although I am not convinced you would not do it better. There is something about him that is a little like a self-satisfied parrot.'

'Well, as long as it doesn't affect his detective skills,' Mr Blackthorn said. 'Has he contacted the police?'

'I don't think so,' I said, and he frowned, and then shook himself.

'Well, not my investigation,' he said, and I wished, again, fervently, that it was. Mr Blackthorn was so efficient, so imbued with the best qualities of a man instead of unsavoury ones. The kernel of an idea formed that I should encourage his further interest, but I decided not to push matters, and changed the subject to what items of furniture in his shop were selling the best. It was bookcases, apparently.

'Have at it,' he said eventually, once we had finished our coffee. 'I need to go to an auction down the way, so I'll leave you to it. I'll be back in an hour or so. The manual's beside it, and there's a ribbon in a box that needs to be set up, I think.'

He trusted me so easily to do the task, I nearly embraced him. A strange flush went through me at the thought, but it must be due to the sheer inappropriateness of such an action.

A big woman with a massive bun of curly blonde hair burst into the shop, walked up to him and slapped his shoulder with the flat of her hand.

'You've been giving the children money again,' she said. 'They went straight on a boat on the lake, all seven of them, and all of them fell in, and it was only because Ernie and Ethel have been swimming since they were as small as a pea that they managed to get everyone out. All covered in green slime and duck feathers, they are. I've told you about giving them money!'

'They called me Father,' he said, looking helpless again.

'Yes, because they know you're a big soft pile of mush. They don't need money. They can entertain themselves just fine without it. They spent last Friday afternoon searching rock pools and skimming pebbles in the sea. It's a bad habit to get them in. I'm not telling you again.' She suddenly launched herself around him and gave him a giant smacking kiss on the cheek. 'Great lummox,' she said, and then she was gone from the shop as quickly as she had arrived.

'She has rules,' he said. 'But it's hard when they are all looking at you like that. There are so many of them.'

Fatherhood was not my area of expertise.

The bell dinged again, and this time it was a tall, mutton-chopped gentleman who was looking to buy furniture. A tallboy, specifically, which seemed appropriate. Mr Blackthorn dealt with him and sold him a particularly tall tallboy, relatively quickly, and then he was off.

'Best lock the door when I go,' he said as he was leaving. 'So you don't get bothered by customers.'

Chapter Seventeen

I locked the door, and then because I was alone, I took off my hat, coat and gloves and got to work. It was indeed a manual of many words, but it was possible to skip a great deal. The hardest part was inserting the ribbon, a task more suited to a professional engineer of several years' standing, I decided, after nearly half an hour of fiddling. But eventually the ribbon was in, and I managed to insert the paper in the right place.

I pulled over a stool and began to type.

It was not easy. The keys struck upwards, hitting the paper underneath, so I could not see what I was typing without lifting the carriage. The keys got stuck together every now and then, and I had to untangle them. But other than that, it felt like a miracle. I loved the sound of the metal hitting paper, the ding as I returned the carriage home at the end of each line. I could see myself, sitting at a desk, surrounded by piles of paper, straight backed and nimble fingered. It seemed feasible that I might succeed as a professional lady typist, especially compared with any of the other professions I had tried.

Halfway through, there was some considerable knocking

on the door, so I opened it. A bewhiskered gentleman fell over the step, and when he had picked himself up, he looked about and through me as if I was invisible.

'Where is the gentleman who runs it?' he said, and when I said Mr Blackthorn would be back in an hour, he harrumphed with distress. Then he walked about the shop for several minutes, staring blankly at the furniture. After a while, he drifted back towards me.

'I am looking for a particular piece of furniture,' he said. I waited, patiently, and eventually he harrumphed again, and stared in desperation at the ceiling. 'I am looking, ahem, for a commode. The chair. Not the cabinet. For my father.'

I had not properly examined the furniture in the shop, but I did so now, and after about five minutes, I struck gold. We did indeed have a rosewood commode chair, a white ceramic basin hidden within its seat.

'I'll take it,' he said, but I did not have any idea of price, so I demurred for a bit while I worked out whether I should sell it or wait for Mr Blackthorn.

'Very well, you drive a hard bargain,' he said. 'Here's five pounds.' He gave me the money and left the shop, carrying the chair, even though it was very heavy.

Had I done the right thing? I had no idea. But I hadn't finished typing, so I got back to it.

When Mr Blackthorn returned, I was sitting on the uncomfortable armchair, smiling.

'I have done it,' I said. I handed him a piece of paper, covered in words. There were a few mistakes, and the ribbon had smudged the ink a little in places, but it was a whole page of typed words, and it looked businesslike, important.

'You have typed my name,' he said. I had indeed. I had not

been able to think of many other appropriate words to type. 'It looks – impressive.'

He smiled at me, and it was a warm smile, that made him look younger, more mischievous.

'So, you have become a lady typist,' he said, and I felt my chest puff up with pride, like a pigeon. Then he frowned, and I quickly deflated.

'You have…' He took out a gigantic handkerchief from his breast pocket. 'Excuse me. You have… a slight moustache.' He handed me the handkerchief and I wiped my upper lip, and handed it back, but he wouldn't take it.

'No,' he said, 'higher up,' and he put out a finger and touched me just under my nose, gently. It was only a second's touch, so I had no reason to feel anything, but all the same, I felt something.

I scrubbed the handkerchief hard on my upper lip, but 'It's not coming off,' he said, so I shot across the shop to look in a wardrobe mirror and, indeed, I had a beautifully crooked smudge of typewriter ink below my nose. There was another blotch on my cheek and my hands were blue-black all over.

I used Mr Blackthorn's tap, in the courtyard at the back of the shop, as well as a cake of soap and a rough towel he gave me. The stain did not come off completely, but I looked slightly better by the time I left. The smudges were grey, instead of black.

'Remember to grease your rods every day,' I said, as I was leaving, and he looked confused until I pointed to the lettering painted on a panel at the very top of the typewriter: '*Keep the machine free from dust. Clean all of the top rods – especially the Shifting rod – with a greasy cloth every day.*' It was a precious machine, and it needed excellent care.

I confessed I had sold his commode on the doorstep, in case he got angry.

'Five pounds?!' he said, and my heart contracted, but then, 'I would have sold it for three.' He smiled again, so that was two smiles in one day, and they were smiles worth waiting for, full of mischief and shared delight. He really would have made a very good pirate, based on his smile alone.

It had been a bewildering day. I walked home full of feelings. Some of them not worth thinking about further, others meriting great attention. The joy that I could not only type, but also sell furniture. The lingering wish that Mr Blackthorn was my detective. The unsettling feeling caused by the blonde woman who had exploded into his shop and been very affectionate and loving, even though he must have forced himself on her extensively, to produce such a flotilla of children. Life was very curious.

I wondered when I would sell my next item of furniture.

Chapter Eighteen

I had searched my mother's belongings thoroughly when she disappeared, as well as read all her letters, several times over. I had not found anything that cast light on her disappearance.

Until I was ten, we had lived near the Crystal Palace, south-east of London, before we had moved to Hastings for the peace and sea air, but no one from that time had written to her, or if they had, she had destroyed their letters. She had called it a fresh start, an escape from the dirt and crowds of the metropolis. There was correspondence from an aunt in Scotland, who had died several years before she disappeared, and letters from my grandparents, whom I had never met. There were even a few love letters from my father, but it did not feel right to read them and I had put them away again, after the first few lines. It was sad that those splendid marital hopes had dwindled to bitterness. They must only have been twenty or so when they tied the knot.

I had not taken part in the packing up of her belongings and their transportation to the attic. That task had been assigned to the servants without my knowledge, so I came back from

Sunday church one day to find her bedroom empty and any sense of her swept away, up into the rafters.

My mother had loved colour, and the house had been scattered with cushions, covers and muslin drapes in vibrant purples, deep reds, dark blues and burnished gold. They had all been removed, as had the glass paperweights with swirling patterns which I had loved to hold and stare into when I was small, my hands slowly warming the cold glass. She had insisted my father install a bathroom next to her bedroom, with taps and running water, and she had left behind soft soap and bottles of perfume, musky and sharp, a scent I sometimes thought I caught around the house, even though they had long been banished to the attic.

It was time to look again. Everything was stored in big trunks, and as our banshee activities did not stretch to the attic, they were covered in dust and fine spiderwebs. I brushed them off, one by one, and got to work.

She had not left much evidence of her secrets behind. There were none of the clothes she had worn in those salacious pictures. Her clothes had been simply but beautifully made, by a dressmaker in St Leonards. She had not needed to wear giant feathers in her hats, or rows of tiny bows on her dresses like some ladies did. She had been the ornament herself.

Reminders of her always hurt. I realised I was crying a little, and I had to breathe deeply through my nose and shake myself to stop. She had even left her hairbrush behind, pretty, silver-backed, engraved with flowers, a few of her golden sunset hairs still caught on the bristles. There were a few of her pen and ink sketches in a notepad. She had liked to sketch people, funny, delicate caricatures that caught people's expressions, their flow of movement. She had been good at everything.

There were many clothes, a few books. Gothic novels that my father had scoffed at. There was a vase, wrapped in brown paper, carefully glued together. She had once thrown it at my father, and it had hit the wall behind him. She had run to it and cried and picked up the pieces as if it was her child and it was his fault. She had not been without drama, my mother. And perhaps my father and I had not been as good as outsiders were, at worshipping her perfection before her faults.

I shook myself again, this time to get rid of uncharitable thoughts. It was nearly two o'clock, and I was starving. There was nothing of any significance that I could see in the attic. I bundled up a few things to take downstairs with me – a glass paperweight in purple and green; her letters, to read again; a scarf that still held her perfume; a box of inlaid wood containing her jewellery, which should have been given to me anyway – and went to beard Edith in the kitchen for some food.

'The thing is,' Edith said, looking militant, 'you haven't put our wages up in five years. And that's not realistic, what with cost of living being what it is. I didn't sign up to be a slave. It's not like your father doesn't have the money, with a job like his. Your mother would never have allowed it.'

She was right, and my father must earn a good salary at the bank, but the thought of arguing with him, with his complete incomprehension of what it took to run a household and keep servants, was exhausting. He was likely to blame my lack of financial acumen, my general girlish incompetence at managing servants, the price of haddock and the weather before he considered raising their wages. That was what he had done five years ago, before finally agreeing to put them up. It would be a long battle.

'You're right,' I said.

'Yes, I'm right, and I'm not going to stay silent any longer. There are other households in St Leonards that would pay better. I've been working my shoes off these past years, and sympathy is sympathy, but your mother's gone and I am not skivvying for nothing in memory of a ghost any more.'

It was a lurid statement, one that might lurk in the pages of one of my mother's gothic novels. I almost wished my mother was a ghost, will-o'-wisping her way around the house. She would probably still be good company, if she was in one of her happy moods.

'Fair enough,' I said. 'I shall look into the matter forthwith.' I needed to humour her, because she was standing over a loaf of bread with a knife, but not slicing it. I needed a sandwich.

'Do,' she said. 'I mean it.' At last she sliced the bread and made me a great pile of a sandwich with ham and cheese, slathered with some of weary Millie's homemade pickle. It was a small slice of joy, and I knew I needed to find a way to make them both happy, even if it meant pawning a painting. The horrible one in the hall might do, all dark brown paint and grey-bearded men in togas, even though it was a religious scene and I would go to hell.

After luncheon I went to my mother's bedroom.

It was empty of anything now, but a few sparse pieces of

furniture. We should really have thought of another use for the room, so that we did not look at its closed door every time we passed and remember its emptiness. But there was a faint, pathetic hope on my part that it might be occupied again one day and if we turned it into some other use, it might upset her. I knew it was foolish, but to change it into a music parlour or somesuch – and after all, what use would we have for one of those? – would make it my fault if she never came back.

I did not know what my father thought. He had not said anything before instigating the clearance of her possessions, and he never seemed to notice household matters, as long as his clothes were washed and he was well fed. It was only when I asked him for more money that such things suddenly became a concern.

So the space stayed empty, when people in the poorer parts of Hastings lived seven or more to a room. I was not blind to life's disparities.

I sat on the edge of the bed frame and looked around me. There was nothing here, either, and it did not hold any echoes of her any more. She had chosen the intricate wallpaper, exotic birds on a blue background below the picture rail, plain green above, and I noticed there was a patch on the far wall where the sun had faded it. I should close the curtains, but that felt too funereal, and she would have hated the darkness. She had loved the light in Hastings, agreeing with the artists who flocked here who said it was special, unearthly. One of the Pre-Raphaelite artists had married his muse in a church only a few streets away.

Could she have hidden anything in the very fabric of the room? In one of the Reverend Bartle's detective novels, a sharp-nosed detective had found a missing gold necklace hidden in a secret cupboard beneath a windowsill. In another story he had even discovered an evil villain scrunched up dead in a priest hole. I was not so keen to find an evil villain, but it was possible my mother might have hidden her secrets somewhere. I got down on my hands and knees and began searching.

Chapter Nineteen

I found a postcard, but it was likely nothing. The corner was sticking up by a millimetre, just above the gap between two floorboards, under her bed. I got my nail file and managed to prise it up and out.

It was a small card in a tattered envelope. On the front of the card there was a coloured illustration of three male frogs in striped swimsuits. Two of them were singing, holding song sheets, and the third was conducting them with a baton. It was postmarked Buxton, and it was addressed to my mother. Buxton? I knew nothing of it, beyond a vague impression of a spa town where people went for their health, much like they flocked to the seaside. It was much further north, Derbyshire perhaps, but we had no relatives or connections there that I was aware of, and my mother had never mentioned it.

On the back, it had just one line: 'I dream of your Bubbins. xx'

What on earth were Bubbins? It was all incredibly irritating.

I found nothing of any consequence, and at the end of an hour I was dusty and exhausted. Why was I paying Mr Knight to swan around in his assorted seaside attire, and doing all the hard work myself? It was ridiculous.

I went back down the stairs and Edith popped out of the drawing room.

'Why are you covered in dust?' she said.

'I have been cleaning my mother's room,' I said. 'With my skirts.'

Edith, unsurprisingly, looked at me as if I had lost more than one marble, so I went up to my bedroom and propped the frogs on my dressing table.

I felt even less inclined to go to church than usual that Sunday, but not going was not an option, if one was not to be considered a heathen. As my father had been called to London on business I had to go alone, never my favourite pastime. He inspired respect, even sympathy, especially among the widows of the parish; I inspired a strange mix of avoidance and disapproval that I didn't quite understand. Perhaps they thought I might disappear unexpectedly too, one day; perhaps even in the church itself, in a puff of smoke, during the Lord's Prayer.

The Reverend was in a good mood, though. He had found a sermon about lambs cuddling up to lions, or something along that vein, and I am sure he had tweaked the words to make it kinder, more loving. He strove to encourage goodwill and peace among his congregation, who in contrast mostly longed for something exciting to happen, even something as simple as gossip, so that they could rip it to pieces like crows fighting over bread.

I liked singing the hymns. If I listened hard, I could hear the other people in the congregation who could hold a tune and shut out those who couldn't. I was sure we all listened out desperately for each other, resisting the tidal wave of discordant sound, hanging onto harmony. My mother had been in the choir; after she had gone its membership had faltered, never to return to full numbers.

Mrs Withers approached me after the service. I managed to keep a pew between us.

'Your hat is very nice, dear,' she said. 'But would be better if it was at less of a jaunty angle. We are not at sea, here.'

Indeed we were not. 'Thank you for letting me know,' I said.

'Did I see you with a gentleman in the park, the other day, dressed in black?' Her own hat was a blowsy affair, pastel blue, covered in green drooping feathers and red cloth cherries, more suited to a woman of the streets. But she was married, with a monstrous opinion of herself, and therefore not to be criticised.

How had she recognised me in my half-veil? She must have the eyes of a goshawk.

'Yes,' I said. 'I occasionally wear mourning, in memory of those I have lost. He is a man in distressed circumstances. I am a member of the Hastings Society for Benevolent Benificence, as you know, and I was merely handing him a leaflet, so that he knows where to go for assistance with clothing and such.'

'As an unmarried lady you would be best to leave those charitable endeavours to others more suited, Violet. And men like that should not be frequenting public parks. They are a blot on the landscape. Does your father know of these activities?'

'Where should men like that be spending their time?' I asked.

'There are workhouses, in the old town,' she said, and actually sniffed the air, as if she smelt something unsavoury. Her husband appeared under her elbow. That was not quite true, as he was not that small, but there was something about him that gave an impression of a little goblin, shrunk by his wife's evil charm to a shadow of his former self.

'We must go, Wilhelmina,' he said, and his eyelid twitched in a way that could have been a wink or perhaps, just a twitch.

I stayed behind after the others to speak to the Reverend. He was still worried about my father's words about marriage.

'I was surprised that your father spoke so unkindly to you, Violet, when he knows how difficult life has been for you. You are a blessing in his household. He of all men should know how important marital harmony is and that the endeavour should not be undertaken lightly. I hope he has softened and is seeing things in a kinder light.'

'He is courting a woman,' I said. 'So he is in a much better mood.'

'A woman? But he can't. Your mother…' He dropped his sermon on the floor and it skated across the stones.

I picked it up for him. 'I know. But he seems happy and she seems… jolly.'

'Jolly…? Your mother is – could be – full of delightful humour at times. We laughed a lot, those evenings in your parlour. But jolly… no. I hope they are remaining… But they have not approached me regarding marriage and, of course, it is impossible…' he said. He looked up at the stained-glass window behind the altar, squinting worriedly. 'I can only assume theirs is a pure friendship, untouched by… And how can we resent him some solace, some tender innocent company, when his wife has been gone so long? I am sure all will be as it should be in the eyes of God.'

'Indeed.' I remembered their flushed faces, her giggles, his wandering eyes, and doubted it was chaste. But the gentle Reverend did not deserve to be shocked.

'Did my mother ever tell you...' But no. I could not ask him that either. He would never know about her other side, the wanton side. There was no point asking. 'Never mind. I am well, Vicar. There is no need to worry about me. I have my charities, and my painting.' I did paint, around once a year.

'Which charities is it again?' he asked, and as he was the one man I could not lie to because he might actually know them, I dropped my hymn book and then, in the kerfuffle of picking it up, forgot to answer his question.

'I must depart,' I said merrily, and kissing him on his cheek with affection, I left him by the altar.

Chapter Twenty

That evening, I found myself thinking about what Frank Knight had uncovered about my mother; the photographs; why she had called herself Evelina Joyce. What kind of performer could my mother have been? She could sing well enough. She wouldn't be so good at the rough and tumble, the coarseness, of comedy. I could see her perhaps as the assistant to a magician, being sawed in half or having knives thrown at her while the audience watched with bated breath.

How had she managed to have this secret life though, away from me and my father? She had not been absent from the house very often in the evening, maybe once a week or so. Many of her social gatherings had been at home. How could she have fitted it all in, without us knowing? It was all confusing, so I put it out of my mind and turned instead to planning my campaign to raise Edith and Millie's pay.

'We need to put up the servants' wages,' I said firmly to my father the next day, as he passed me on the way out of the door. He was whistling a merry little tune. I had chosen the timing carefully, because if he was on his way out to meet Mrs Beetling he might not linger so long to argue.

'Very well,' he said. 'I'll have a chat with Tilda – Mrs Beeton, I mean – and see what she pays hers. If it's more, we can up their wages. They do a decent job, after all. It would be a shame to have to search for new ones.'

He left me there, standing in the hall, struck dumb. It was A Good Thing that had just happened, but I lamented those lost hours of sleep I had spent in bed the night before, formulating arguments. I had a great bundle of them, all perfectly phrased and ready to wheel out, now rendered completely pointless.

I was still feeling nervous about Mr Knight. I dreaded to think of him, careering around town, turning up stones and uncovering secrets. How many people knew that he was looking for her? How many of my neighbours knew that the wife of a bank manager, instead of being stuffed full of moral rectitude, had behaved in a saucy manner? And even worse, looked happy about it? Because she had looked happy. There had been no shame in those photographs, no sign that she knew they were wicked, or that she would mind men looking at them with lustful eyes. It was immensely confusing.

I wanted copies of the photographs. Because she was still my mother, and possibly because she looked so joyful too. I wanted to remember her like that. Not scantily clad, but happy. I had thought she was. I had thought the bickering between my father and her had just been what married couples did. She had told me they were content together, that although marital intimacy had been brief, theirs was a contented partnership of like minds, kindred spirits. I had been foolish enough to believe her.

I decided to go to Farnham & Sons. It was in a cottage-like building on the edge of St Leonards, surrounded by bushes and the restless chatter of house sparrows. The bell pull did not lead to a ringing of a bell, but a dull clang, as if someone had hit a tin bath with a spade. The thin man who opened the door had a mildly panicked air.

'Do you have an appointment?' he asked.

'No,' I said. 'But—'

'Would you like one? Photos, is it? How about next Tuesday at two p.m.?' He looked from side to side, as if more than sparrows might jump out of the foliage.

'How about now?' I said.

'I'll have to look,' he said, disappearing inside. He left the door ajar, so I followed.

I had only had my photograph taken once, a family portrait when I was ten, and it suddenly came back to me that it had been here. The set-up had not changed, the draped camera in the corner, the seats, the curtains, the metal pole that children could be strapped to if they were likely to move and ruin the photograph. It was possible this was even the same photographer. My parents had been more pleased with life and each other then, and the photograph had been a happy time, a celebration of us as a family. I wondered where that photograph had gone.

'Yes, now will be fine,' he said, reappearing abruptly, and shutting the door firmly behind him. 'Full-length? Two or four? Backdrop? Props?' He pointed at a table, on which sat a group of strange items including a vase of fake flowers, a pile of books, a fan, a small marble bust of a gentleman and a stuffed cat, looking surprised it was not still alive.

'No, thank you,' I said faintly.

'Stand over there then,' he said, pointing to a velvet curtain, and he disappeared underneath the camera.

I went and stood, while he shouted muffled instructions from underneath his drape.

'Left! One step to the right! One step forward! Stay still! Cross your arms at the elbows! No, not like that!'

'I wanted to ask,' I said, and then he appeared from under the drapes again.

'You have to stay still,' he said. 'It will come out all blurred if you keep moving like that. I've never seen anyone move about as much as you do.'

He disappeared again, so I stood perfectly still. It was a novelty, I realised, to stand unmoving. I gained a whole new perspective on myself, as a generally fast-moving person. He mumbled and fumbled until the giant flash in his hand went off and then he popped out again.

'Right,' he said. 'That'll be it then. Come back in a fortnight. Thin, thick or extra-thick?'

'Sorry?'

'The card? What thickness of card do you want? And do you want your name on the bottom or the back? A frame?' he said.

'Please do as you see fit,' I said. 'My name is Violet Hamilton.'

'Aaahh. You are Lily Hamilton's daughter?' he said.

'Yes.'

'Ah.' He ran a hand through his hair. 'I thought you reminded me of someone.'

'We do not look alike,' I said. 'But I understand you knew her.' I sensed he was on the back foot and was determined to keep him there.

'Barely,' he said. 'I saw her once or twice, perhaps. A family portrait, the first time. You do look a little like her. She couldn't stand still either.'

'I understand she came a few times on her own,' I said, and waited.

'Do you want a copy of one? I was sad to hear of her disappearance, very sad. A striking-looking woman. The light on her cheekbones... made for photography. It was tragic.'

'You needn't dissemble,' I said. 'Mr Knight enlightened me. I know you took some licentious pictures of her. I should like to know if she posed for them of her own free will, or if she was forced into it.'

'Ah, goodness,' he said. 'Knight is working for you? I did not know that, otherwise I might not have shared them with him.'

'I asked you a question,' I said. I was furious in a way I had not allowed myself to feel since the months after my mother had first disappeared, when I first realised she might not come back. It was giving me a courage I didn't know I had.

'Of course she wasn't forced,' he said. 'It was her idea, she was more than willing. I gave her fifty percent of the profits. She enjoyed it, dressing up, dressing...' he paused. 'Won't you take a seat?'

'No. I want copies of all of them. All of the photos. Mr Knight was not willing to share. As her daughter I think I am entitled to them.'

'Very well.' He disappeared into the back of the shop and returned a few minutes later, carrying a small pile of card. 'Here you are. I am quite running out of spares.' He smiled and then quailed under my glare.

Two of them were the same photographs, but there was a third one I had not seen. In this one my mother was dressed in her chemise, coiled coquettishly on her side on a bed, her head on her hand. She was laughing at the camera again and stroking the stuffed cat from the table.

'Does Mr Knight have this one?'

'No, I didn't give it to him,' he said. 'I'm not sure why not. It's right that you should have all of them, anyway.'

'How many people in Hastings and St Leonards have these photographs, Mr Farnham? Did it go beyond, to Bexhill and Battle?'

'A few,' he said, rubbing his ear. 'A select few. I didn't sell them here at first, I sold them in London and Brighton, but word did get out a bit, and so when people came here and asked for them, I sold a few. Only the respectable folk, mind. I wouldn't go selling her picture to just anyone. And mostly only after she'd gone…' In the frozen pause that followed, I could see his face drop as he realised what he'd said.

'So you assumed she was dead and that her reputation didn't matter? Ghoulish of you, don't you think, to sell pictures of a woman who might be dead? And did you think, at any point, of the damage that would do to me? To my reputation?'

'I wasn't the one who posed for them,' he said. He was very thin and twitchy, as if he had ants crawling around inside his shirt. I saw the exact moment at which he decided he'd been craven to a woman too long and straightened his shoulders. 'I need to earn a living, and she was the one who was more than content to pose. She came here, she thought it was a great lark. And if she wasn't around, it couldn't harm her. And I hear you're quite capable of scaring off the gentlemen all by yourself. I'm not charging you for these photographs, let that be an end to it.'

'It is merely the start,' I said.

Then I put the photographs in my reticule, marched over to the table, took the stuffed cat and left. He didn't try to stop me.

The cat had once been white but was now yellow, and quite worn on top from people stroking it. Despite a lack of evidence, I decided he was male, and that he should be called Nigel. He was lying down, his paws outstretched, tail curled, his mouth almost, thanks to inferior taxidermy, smiling. His glassy stare was not unfriendly. He would do as a bedroom companion. I put him on my dressing table, next to the musical frogs.

It was liberating to be angry, I realised. With anger I became fierce, like Joan of Arc. Not usually. Mostly it just made me cry, like a weakling. But on this occasion, it had been useful, and I secured a photograph that Mr Knight hadn't got his hands on. And a cat, although I was not entirely sure why I had taken that.

It was clear, now, why the respectable women of Hastings and beyond gave me a wide berth, and why suitors thought I would be amenable to a groping. How many of them had seen more of my mother than they had of me? It did not bear thinking about. And how recently had Mr Farnham been selling these pictures? How could my father not know? Surely if he did, he would have stopped it. Why would my mother voluntarily *choose* to be captured by a camera in so little clothing? It could not have been her idea, surely.

I had a pain behind my left eye. Altogether it had been a terrible day.

'I have spoken to Mrs Beeton,' my father said at dinner that evening. 'And it's clear we should be paying the servants more. I'll increase your household allowance accordingly. It's important we are a harmonious household.'

I crumbled up my bread roll in my hand and thanked him, politely.

Edith and Millie were not grateful when I told them, because it was a pay rise long overdue, but Millie did smile and Edith bared her teeth slightly, which was a positive sign.

Chapter Twenty-One

The next time I went back to Mr Blackthorn's for the typing, it was possibly a little early at eight in the morning, but I had not been able to sleep. He was awake and dressed, however, and he let me in and then asked me to follow him out to the little stone yard at the back of the shop, because he was doing exercises.

He was doing it to bring strength back into his leg. He was fully dressed so it was all very respectable, but, all the same, it felt odd to be standing by while a man swung his leg about.

'I forgive you for your dawn visit,' he said. 'By now I shouldn't expect anything less. But give me a moment to finish these' – he was a bit out of breath from doing one-legged squats – 'and I've a favour to ask you.'

I stared at the sky for a while, admiring the fluffiness of the clouds.

'Right, done,' he said, standing straight. 'My left leg is thinner you see, the muscle wasted, because I haven't been using it properly.' He hoiked up both his trouser legs to below the knee and suddenly I was alone with a man who was showing me his legs. It was true, one was thinner than the other, and it had a red scar on it. But both of them were much bigger and more muscled than mine and covered in dark hair.

I looked quickly and then looked up at the clouds again. 'I see,' I said.

He harrumphed and pulled his trouser legs back down.

'This favour,' he said. 'There is another woman who keeps writing to me to ask me to take on a case. But she is on the shy side, and she keeps saying she wants to speak to a lady. Something to do with a suitor. She won't go to Frank Knight either. I wouldn't pursue it, except she's written three letters already and I sense she's in sore need of help.'

I felt breathless and giddy.

'Why would you take this on, when you have refused mine?' I asked.

'You've already got Knight,' he said. 'I do have a soft side, even though you might think me heartless. Life isn't always easy for people who are timid, especially women. And since you're here, and you like asking questions… One case doesn't mean I'm taking up the business again.'

'You want me to? Shall I go? I can go right away,' I said.

'If you can promise not to insult her, then I'll get in touch with her and arrange a time,' he said. 'Probably not today. But yes, it would be good if you could find out what the problem is. Ask questions, and don't sell her footstools. Her name is Miss Turton.' He smiled at me again, for the third time, although I was not counting.

Then I typed a whole letter for him, which he needed to send to an auction house, regarding several items of furniture that he wanted to purchase. It took seven sheets of paper but eventually there was a version I was happy with, with only two mistakes on it, and he signed it with a flourish at the bottom and I put it in an envelope and took it to the postbox for him.

Unfortunately, as I left the little alleyway that led from the square to the street, I ran into the Misses Spencer, my former schoolmates. They stared at me with horror, as if I was leaving a house of ill repute. I wondered if they spent their time tripping around, looking for scandal. But this was surely not the right side of town for ladies of their ilk, especially unmarried ones. I could be forgiven, because I was two years older and a spinster.

'Hello,' I said, but their heads spun sharply towards the sea and they were off down the hill.

'I was buying FURNITURE,' I said loudly to the air. 'But I didn't see anything SUITABLE.'

There was a seagull standing at my feet. Surely it could not be the same one I had seen before? It looked up at me, sympathetically.

I had an assignment. An actual assignment, and this time I would not blow it. But first I had to beard Mr Knight in his den again, because I had heard nothing from him, which felt more suspicious than hearing something.

Chapter Twenty-Two

'I have been thinking about why you suggested cancelling my services,' Mr Knight said.

'Indeed?' I said.

'Is it, perhaps,' he said, 'that you have developed a fondness for me?'

The suggestion was so alien that I carried on examining a hole in one finger of my glove for a second, before realising what he had said. I half fell off my chair and had to clutch the desk to save myself.

'Goodness, no,' I said.

'Really, Miss Hamilton?' he said. He was wearing a spotted blue and green necktie, and his moustache was shiny with brilliantine. He smiled, knowingly. 'I wondered if it was some delicate female modesty that might shy away from sharing personal details with a gentleman you… would like to have an affinity with.'

'No, absolutely not,' I said. I was not sure if my horror was showing in my expression.

'I am afraid I must let you down gently,' he said. 'Ladies do often develop an affection for me, but I am a man of steadfast loyalties. There was a lady, once, but… Since then… I have not felt the same about any woman. And you must recognise that there is a gap in our ages, even though you are no longer young.'

I looked at him, at his damp lips and his moustache like flat creeping ivy, and wondered which pagan gods I had offended, to be rejected by the last man on earth I would ever want.

'As well as this,' he continued, 'I fear we would not suit. I need a woman of a gentler, shall we say, less argumentative disposition.'

I weighed up my response in my mind. Was there any point in arguing with him? Any attempt to convey the truth would only convince him I was protesting too much. Even if I was driven to emptying the contents of my stomach on his lap, he would likely take it as flattery. I gave a deep sigh and set my pride to one side. The outcome, after all, was exactly as I might have wished.

'I shall attempt to contain my distress,' I said.

'Good,' he said. 'Good. I would like us to go forward in a spirit of honesty. Athough you are a little older than other ladies on the market, I am sure one day you will find a gentleman who will not mind your… eccentricities. Meanwhile I will do as I am employed to do and find your mother. I hope you are not too disappointed.'

'You are too kind,' I said. 'I will survive. Yes, by all means, let us move forward rather than linger in the mire.'

'I have spoken with the constabulary,' he said. 'They were very thorough at the time, it seems. They interviewed a lot of people, her friends, her family, the performers and the holidaymakers on the pier that night, and they took a lot of notes. But the actual substance is disappointing. She was seen around the pier, several times, talking with different people, but no one knows when she disappeared or saw anything useful. It is odd, for a woman so vivacious, to disappear so entirely without notice.'

'I know,' I said.

'They checked the passengers on the steam ferries, and she was not on any of them. I'll recheck the lists to see if there was an Evelina Joyce. She didn't leave the pier via the promenade, for the pier master admitted he admired her, and was looking to see her on the way out. So at some point between nine o'clock and when the pier closed at ten o'clock – probably closer to nine – she disappeared.'

'Yes,' I said. I knew all this. I had asked to read the notes, in the first year, when I was foolish enough to think I could find her myself. The constable was a kindly man and, even though I was a lady, he had let me.

'It is just as if she vanished into the air,' he said. 'I think we will not find out what happened here, until we understand her better.'

My heart sank, for he was heading in a direction I was not willing to go.

'What was she like, your mother? Was she happy in her marriage? Did she ever form other attachments? Is it possible she posed for those photographs to give to another man she admired, perhaps? Was she flighty, capricious in her nature?'

I could not do it. I could not let him get his paws on her in that way. He saw her as lightly, as superficially, as most men did, and he had not earned a single right to know her better. My memories were mine, and I did not want to hand them over for him to parcel up and label as roughly as he saw fit.

We had been close, as two females in our little family of three. She had shared her secrets and stories, thrown me advice, scolded with affection and hugged me more fiercely and freely than any other mother I knew. I had relied too heavily upon her, perhaps was not so far from childhood when she disappeared; and yet there had been something childish about her too, that had called on me to protect her in return. She had been kind, funny, loving, warm, flawed, and I still missed her desperately, even though she had been absent for over a third of my life. And even if it might lead to finding her, or finding out what had happened to her, I could not give Mr Knight an inch more insight into her than he already had.

'I am feeling a little faint,' I said. 'After your rejection. Do you think you might fetch me a glass of water?'

Mr Knight looked reluctant, but he went towards a dark corridor at the back of the shop to fetch me some water.

He would not listen to my excuses, it was clear, and I couldn't handle further interrogation. As soon as his back disappeared into the gloom, I stood up, shot towards the door and ran out of his cave.

On the beachfront I stood irresolute for a second, and then I turned and headed along the promenade to Mr Blackthorn's. I could have gone home, but I needed some light typing to distract me. It was odd, that one man's cave felt so intimidating and the other so much like a refuge.

Chapter Twenty-Three

So that Mr Knight couldn't spot me easily if he chose to give chase, I decided to walk not along the high promenade but on the beach. Luckily there was a path for most of the way, but the nearer I got to the old town the harder it became because it was all shingle, and walking fast on shingle was, I discovered, as quick as running up a hill of dried beans. I was very tired and cross by the time I made it.

When I got to the shop, it was closed, the door firmly locked. I stood there for a minute, unsure where to go next, and then a complete stranger came up behind me and began talking to me as if he knew me.

'Hello again. I've just been to the shops, so I locked up,' he said. 'Hold on a second and I'll get it open.'

'I am not here for furniture,' I said, and then he looked down at me and smiled and I saw it was Mr Blackthorn, with his crutch. He had shaved off his beard. It was terrible. He looked younger, handsome even. He had a firm chin. I had much preferred him with his ragged, matted coating of hair, had entirely relied on him to keep it there. How dare he?

'I know you're not, Miss Hamilton,' he said. 'Or Violet. Can I call you Violet, as we are working together?'

'No, you can't,' I said. 'It would ruin my reputation, if anyone heard you. Especially now you have shaved off your beard. Why have you done that?'

He looked startled. 'It might be the fashion, but it's actually not much fun to wear. It gets caught in your buttons when you're doing up your shirt, and sometimes it itches. It's a relief to get rid of it, frankly. Don't you like it?' He looked proud of himself, his face as naked as a baby's bottom. It was insupportable.

'No,' I said. 'It was a good disguise. Your beard was a good disguise for your detective work, and now you've shaved it off and you're all exposed to the air. How can that be a good thing?'

'I'm not doing detective work,' he said. 'I mostly sell furniture,' and suddenly I knew I had to flee, before I said anything else that was stupid.

'I have to go,' I said, 'I have a meeting at the Association for Alcoholic Animals,' and I ran off down the hill as quickly as I could.

He must think me such a fool, I thought, as I wandered up and down the beach again, trying to gather myself. And I had not cared, when he had a beard, whether he found me a fool or not. It was odd, how reassuring that beard had been. But now it was clear he was a man, rather than a hairy injured giant, and I would either have to deal with that, or stop asking him for help. None of it mattered anyway, with his affectionate wife and his enormous brood of hungry children, so why was I being so ridiculous?

***

A dull pain in my abdomen gave me part of the reason, and there was also the grave insult of Mr Knight imagining I might want his wooing, but I was not normally known for dramatics. I walked up and down the beach briskly for a while, hoping the sea air would bring back my good sense. It was busy today, the May weather attracting the tourists. The bathing carriages were lined up in the far bay and I could hear the shrieks and laughter of people as they splashed in the sea.

'Miss Hamilton,' a voice said near my knees. I looked down, and there was Mr Parchment, erstwhile suitor and seller of assorted goods, squinting up at me from a beach towel, his trousers rolled up, displaying white and pasty ankles. 'How fortuitous. My mother has gone to get ices, but you must wait and meet her.'

'That's very kind of you,' I said, 'but I must go—'

'I've been meaning to call on you,' he said, surging to his feet on the shingle. 'I've been thinking carefully about what you said, and I realise I may have given you the impression that I was wary of commitment. But it's just that the depth of our discussion, the speed of it, took me by surprise. On reflection, you were remarkably brave to tell me so much about yourself so soon, your vulnerabilities, your defects. I see now that you did it with the best of intentions, so that we might begin our relationship with honesty on both sides. I would be pleased if we can renew our acquaintance. Won't you join us? There is plenty of room on this towel, if we turn it sideways.'

His speech sounded as if he had been rehearsing it for days.

My cleverness had taken a holiday and I didn't know what to say, but I could see the doom of a doughty woman in orange marching across the stones towards us, with ices. I decided, against habit, to be truthful with him.

'Forgive me, no,' I said. 'We would never suit. And I apologise for not being kinder in telling you so. But it was wrong of you to think, as others have thought, that I am amenable to taking liberties before marriage. Is it because you think my mother's disappearance might make me – abandoned?'

I could not tell if it was shock or guilt on his face, but I thought it might be guilt. I nodded and began to move on, but unfortunately the orange lady had put on a spurt and reached us.

'I could only get vanilla,' she said breathlessly, 'because they have sold out of lemon sorbet, and strawberry as well. I know you're not so keen on vanilla, Jeremy, but oh! You are speaking to a young lady. How nice. Do introduce me.'

We stood awkwardly, while he made the introductions, and then she chattered on politely, while Mr Parchment stared miserably at his feet. It was a whole ten minutes before I could politely escape, and as I crossed the beach towards the promenade, I could hear her scolding him.

'That was a perfectly nice young lady, Jeremy, and all you did was stare at your feet. That's no way to go about courting. In my day, gentlemen were full of charm, full of *joie de vivre*. You'll never get anywhere if...'

Poor Mr Parchment. Apparently, I was not the only one with a tone-deaf parent.

Chapter Twenty-Four

The postcard was bothering me. Bubbins. There might be some great clue, some code, in the word, if I could find out what it meant. They might be a type of iced bun that I had not heard of, although I had not known my mother could bake. Was it even addressed to my mother? Goodness knew.

I took it to the Reverend Bartle. He knew a lot of words, because of his vocation. If there were Bubbins in the Bible, he would know what it meant.

'I have no idea,' he said, scratching his head. 'She had a lot of friends, though, as you know. Maybe it was a song she sang, at one of her evening gatherings? I wouldn't get too het up about it though, Violet. I doubt if it means anything.'

'But what if it is a clue, or hidden there because that person was important to her? Maybe she left it behind so that we could find her, if we wanted?'

'Sit, Violet, sit with me here,' he said, patting the pew he was sitting on. 'I am worried about you. This is not likely to be a clue or any kind of message from her. It has been almost ten years. It is hard, incredibly hard, but I think it is perhaps time for you to accept that she is not coming back.'

He had never said that before. He had always been the one who had seemed hopeful, upbeat almost, in trusting that she was alive and well somewhere.

'But you have always been so positive,' I said. 'Trusting that she was in God's care somewhere. I thought you hoped as much as I did.'

'I do. I did. But how is it helping us, to wait for someone who might not want to come back to us? This is about you and your life, Violet. You are the one who is still here. What do you want from it, this short time we have been granted on earth? How will you make the most of it? What would you be doing now, if your mother hadn't been wrenched away so cruelly?'

'I don't know. Most of the time I only know what I want to avoid. Being a fool. Living with my father forever. Marriage.' It was the first time I had said it out loud to someone who might care.

'Why would you avoid marriage, Violet?' He had that great, wondrous ability that good listeners have to make you think he truly wanted to hear your reply. He was not thinking about his new woman, my mother, the weather or a million other things that other people were usually thinking about when I came across them. I loved him for it. It did not mean I could tell him the truth, though.

'It seems a messy business,' I said. 'Full of emotion and arguments.'

'Your father and mother were not compatible,' he said. 'This does sadly happen in some marriages, no matter how tightly God has tied them together. Many couples have the fortitude to work through it, to count their blessings and work towards harmony. But your father is very traditional and your mother... was not always as giving as she could have been.'

'Giving?'

'Generous, with her time, her affection,' he said. Did he mean – marital relations? 'She was the centre of her own world, Violet. I loved her like a daughter, and I admired her immensely, but I was not blind to her faults. She was not always as thoughtful to those around her as she could have been. In your case, too, I noticed that often she put herself, her own joy, before yours. One of the greatest gifts of motherhood is the ability to nurture others before yourself, to accept that the selfishness of youth must be set aside, and that the self-sacrifice is worth it. She was not always able to do that, and I think, even if you did not realise, you suffered from it.'

He had never said these things before either. He had always been wholly admiring of her, wholly worshipful, as all her other friends had been.

'She might not be alive,' I said. 'Perhaps we should not talk of her like this.'

'If you want marriage, children, all it entails, you should not let the example of your father and mother taint that. You are more level-headed, more sensible than your mother, and I expect you would choose wisely. You have shown discrimination so far already, and you are to be commended for it. But if that is what you want, you must go for it, and let nothing stop you. And if it isn't, think about what else will bring you joy and comfort in the years to come.'

Did I want children? I did not feel an all-encompassing broodiness, or that sense of urgency that other women seemed to feel. Children were a nice idea, and I was sure I would be fond of them, but it was perhaps something I could think about seriously when other bits of my life had been lived, when I was sixty or so.

'I want to live,' I said, slowly. 'I want to find out about life, all of it, to understand, to know. I don't want to be protected from it or kept from it. I want to be out there in the world, learning about people and helping them, and having adventures, and doing something important, even though I am only a woman.' He was blinking at me, startled, and I knew I had strayed too far from his familiar paths. 'I should like to be respected, as well. Women avoid me in the street, and men—'

'But, of course you are respected,' he said, and I had touched on his blind spot. 'Everyone who knows you, loves you. How could they not? Anyone who does not treat you with the reverence you deserve, refer them to me and I will sort them out.'

I imagined a long queue of Spencers, Parchments and Withers queuing up outside the church to be firmly set in their place by the Reverend Bartle. He had already put Mrs Withers straight though, when she had claimed I should be wearing black after my mother's disappearance. He had given a sermon about tolerance and had told me the lavender dress I was wearing was beautiful and very appropriate, right in front of her. She had never forgiven me for it. I reached out and hugged him abruptly.

'Well, well,' he said, patting my back awkwardly. 'That's all good.' His spectacles had misted up. 'I was not lucky enough to have my own family, but I hope I can count you as an honorary daughter, Violet, if your father is willing to share you. And I hope you will forgive me, for, for… wanting the best for you.'

'Definitely,' I said. 'And if we are talking shares, I'm prepared to let you have seventy percent.'

There were two letters waiting for me when I got home. One was from Mr Blackthorn, the other from Mr Knight. Two letters from detectives, all in one day. Edith had never seen me so popular.

'I hope your animals are recovering well from their intoxication,' Mr Blackthorn wrote. 'I have heard from Miss Turton. Please pop by the shop at your leisure tomorrow to discuss it.'

'At your leisure tomorrow?' The man had a cheek. But I was strangely warmed by his letter and its rudeness. He had obviously not been seriously offended by my nonsense the other day.

'I will forgive you for *disappearing*,' Mr Knight scrawled. 'Please come to my office *at your convenience tomorrow*. I have found out some *very interesting facts*.'

Why did these people bother talking about my convenience, when everything was urgent? Politeness was a strange thing, as useful as froth on the top of a pint of ale. Not that I had ever drunk ale. I wanted to though, just to try it. Particularly the red gold kind that looked like sunset in a glass.

Had my mother been selfish? I was not sure she had. She had made life joyful. She had found fun in everything. A simple walk to the park became an adventure; a challenge to spot birds, to skim sticks in the river. She had played games far more exciting than hide and seek, where we laid trails through the woodland, leaving arrows made of sticks and leaves for each other to follow. She had taken me boating in the lake and we had splashed about shrieking, threatening to overturn the boat, until the man who owned them had rowed out to tell us off. Even the one time she had tried to bake had been hilarious, ingredients splattered across the kitchen while she dropped chocolate on the floor and decorated my nose with blobs of dough, the result a hard, sticky mess that we all ate anyway.

She had been moody, at times, and she had sometimes got upset when the attention was not on her. But was that surprising, when she was used to people finding her fascinating? A lifetime of being adored was likely to do that to anyone. It was probably the reason that she and my father had grown apart over the years, because he had got tired of worshipping her and treated her like an ordinary person.

But anyway, today was detective day. For it was clear, despite their chatter about convenience, that I might as well go and see both detectives in one day. Blackthorn in the morning, because he was a nicer start to the day, and Knight in the afternoon, by which time I would be more prepared to do battle and tell him nothing.

I turned up at the furniture shop just after ten o'clock and this time the door was not locked. I could hear Mr Blackthorn moving objects around at the back of the shop and when the bell rang as the door opened, he called out, 'Is that you, Miss Hamilton?'

'Yes, it's me,' I said. I was still feeling a little awkward about the previous day, when all he had done was shave off his own beard, as he was perfectly entitled to do.

'Hold on,' he said, and then there was some scuffling before he came out towards me.

He was wearing the most ridiculous fake moustache and beard I had ever seen. It was enormous, reaching to his waist, and might once have belonged to a badger. It was obviously hooked over his ears, and the moustache was so thick, I could not see his mouth.

'Hello,' he said, and I looked at him, then bent over and laughed until tears came to my eyes.

'Do I have to wear it for long?' he said. He might have been laughing under his beard too, as his eyes were crinkling at the corners, but it was difficult to tell.

'No, you may take it off,' I said, so he did, and threw it across the room so that it landed on the corner of a wardrobe and hung there. 'Hot,' he said.

'Thank you. I am sorry I was a little… strange the other day. You have a perfect right to – I was a little emotional about other things.'

'That's all right,' he said. 'I can understand that drunken animals are distressing. I hope you managed to sober a few up. Now, to business. Miss Turton's address. Can you visit her on Tuesday at two o'clock?'

He had sorted things for me, and made them easy again, and I was enormously grateful.

Chapter Twenty-Five

My meeting with Mr Knight was not so successful. I did not want to see him again, but I needed to know what he was up to.

He was sitting alone in his office, his desk so empty that it was almost as if he sat all day looking out of the window. Surely there must be other cases he was working on, that would need files? Paper? When he saw me, he opened his desk drawer and took out a single sheet.

'Ah, Miss Hamilton,' he said. 'That was a precipitate departure the other day. I will forgive you, as you said you were feeling under the weather.' He gave a sharp smile of annoyance that showed he had not forgiven me at all.

'I have got a list from Mr Farnham of those he can remember selling the photographs to, and I have spoken to Simon Wilson, the manager of the Pier Pavilion. There are some interesting developments. It's clear I need to get the complete picture from you too…'

'Who did Mr Farnham sell the photographs to?' I said, as a distraction.

'There are seven on the list. Sadly, they are among some

of the most respectable men in town,' he said, and my heart sank.

'Who are they?'

'I am not sure it will benefit you to know,' he said, pursing his lips. 'It may only give you a distrust for the men in your home town, and as you are already of delicate sensibilities—'

'Is that a mouse?' I said and, as he turned to look at his shelf, I lunged across the desk and grabbed the sheet of paper. For of course I had to know. He slapped his hand down too, but a second too late, and it hit the surface of the desk. I subsided into my chair and then made the mistake of looking at him. For a second his eyes were full of absolute fury and then he banked it and gave his small tight smile.

'That is no way to behave, Miss Hamilton,' he said. 'No way at all. I do not want to have to use force, but if you behave like a hoyden—'

'Edwin Pearsall, of Pearsall's Butchers, Captain Dalrymple, Edward Tolhurst from the Hatters & Tailors, Edmund Lint, preacher. Gregor Casey who owns the soap factory and Walter Field, the watchmaker. Dr Septimus Patmore,' I read aloud.

'Yes, it is disappointing, to find they are of questionable morality. These will not be the only photographs of indecent women they have purchased, I am sure.'

My mother was not an indecent woman. I knew Edmund Lint. He was a lay preacher who had once attempted to fondle my knee at a musicale. Suddenly the reason was crystal clear. It would have been deeply inappropriate even if there had been any inclination on my part to marry him, which there was not, as I had only met him that afternoon. I had flung his hand away so sharply that it flipped back and hit his own face, and he had yelped right in the middle of a Beethoven sonata.

'Is Septimus Patmore related to the poet who lives around here?'

'Coventry? A cousin, perhaps. But of a very different mindset, obviously. Coventry Patmore is the soul of moral rectitude. He funded the church at the top of the High Street and his poems are wholly respectful of women, adoring even. I doubt your mother could be described as "The Angel in the House".' He smirked, and I hated him, with a passion.

'I will go and question them all. The second thing I have discovered,' he said, drumming the desk with his hands, 'is that she performed the week she disappeared.'

'She performed?'

'Simon Wilson, the manager, wasn't there at the Pier Pavilion when she disappeared. But he let me look back through all their records of performances, and yes, Miss Evelina Joyce performed there for that first week of June, 1886.'

'But how could she have performed, in her own home town, without anyone knowing it was her? She would have been easily recognised. What did she perform?'

'It still doesn't say,' he said. 'It just says "the fragrant and popular Miss Evelina Joyce". There was no review in the *Hastings Observer* for this performance either. I am trying to track down the former manager of the hall, if he is still alive. He retired two years ago. He may be living in Bexhill.

'I had another thought,' he said. 'Your family moved here eighteen years ago, from London. Why did you move here? Was there a reason? Had she fallen for another man, perhaps? Did your father move you here to stop her returning his affections, for a fresh start?'

I stared at him, surprised. For a fresh start was exactly as my mother had described it. But it was not, as far as I could remember, because of her longing for a man. It had been, perhaps, to give peace to them both from the crowd of men who had longed for her. It had been sudden, our move, but she had talked about sunshine, the seaside, clean air and swimming, and I had not questioned it.

'There was no reason like that,' I said. 'They just wanted to get away from the pollution, the noise. There were the parks in Crystal Palace, but factories too, and more and more houses being built, and they said they wanted me to grow up near fresh air and the seaside.'

'Are you sure?' he said. 'Are you sure, you cannot remember any reason why your family should move to Hastings so abruptly? It seems odd, don't you think, for a man who was a successful banker in London to move to a seaside town?'

I had to give Mr Knight credit for being thorough, as much as I disliked him.

'I will think back,' I said. 'Although it is a long time ago. I will think back, and let you know if anything occurs to me.'

'Do that,' he said. 'Do that. And now, if you will excuse me, I have work to be getting on with.' I had put the list of names down on the desk and he twitched it back over to his side and around to face him again. He was apparently making some kind of point in dismissing me, so I left him, busily staring at the single sheet of paper on his desk.

It was windy on the promenade, a bracing wind that almost made you gasp for breath. I was grateful for it. It was impossible, when your skirts whipped around you and every step forward was a small fight against the elements, to hold onto old habits of thought. It was the freshest of fresh air, straight off the sea, and it drove through the muddle in my head and cleared it. 'Under the weather' was a foolish phrase for being unwell, I thought, when often driving rain or gusts of wind blew and washed away the sticky cobwebs and reminded you that you were wholly, vitally alive.

There had been an incident, I recalled. I had been returning home from school, a small girls' school not so far away from our house, and a man had come up to me, muffled, bowler-hatted, and thrust a small brown-paper parcel at me.

'Give this to your mother,' he said, and I had sensed anger in him – not at me, but at something, somebody – in the way he held out the parcel, in the thrust of his arm, with impatience, giving me no choice. I had taken it, told her about him, and given it to her, and later that day I had heard her crying in her bedroom, arguing with my father.

'That he should go through my Violet,' she was saying. 'That he should approach her in the street, like that, my child, our child. We need to leave, Lucas. We need to leave, and make a new start, somewhere else. We need a new beginning.'

I had forgotten that moment, somehow, until today. Because afterwards it had all been excitement, and packing up, and the glamour of the huge houses of St Leonards, and joy of living right next to the sea, like always being on holiday. I had loved Hastings and St Leonards when I first came, and today the elements had reminded me of it, even though my eyes and nose were running with its sharpness.

Could that have had anything to do with her disappearance, that small incident of eight years before? Who had he been, that angry man?

My parents had not kept in touch with their friends from before, and I had not been encouraged to correspond with mine. It had been a fresh start, and they had made friends in Hastings, my mother more quickly, because she had a warmth that made people flock to her. I had not considered, until now, how thoroughly we had left our old life behind, or why.

Chapter Twenty-Six

The first Tuesday in May was the day to visit Miss Turton.

She lived in one of the new big houses on the seafront, gleaming white and five storeys high. Once I had navigated her stiff-backed butler, I found myself in a pretty parlour, decorated with tall ferns and several large cages of budgerigars and canaries.

'They can talk, you know,' she said, after we had introduced ourselves and I sat down. 'Not as much as parrots perhaps, but they come out with words, every now and again. And their songs! I am teaching them songs.'

She had a pouffe of fluffy blonde-grey hair and a tentative smile that flashed out and disappeared too quickly.

'Have a biscuit,' she said, offering me a plate of shortbread, then whisking it away again and putting it back on the table. 'Oh… unless you don't like them, of course. Maybe you don't. Do you take tea? Do you like biscuits?'

'I do,' I said. 'I like them both. And your birds too.' I smiled at her, and her smile came out again and stayed a little longer.

'Oh, that's good,' she said, and she offered me the plate again, and poured a cup of tea.

'How can I help?' I said. 'Oh, that is exceptional shortbread. Is it lemon?'

'Yes,' she said. 'My cook is an excellent baker.' She took one herself, arranged it carefully on a small plate, and smiled again before she lifted it up and took a bite.

'So, your trouble, Miss Turton?' I asked again.

'Ah, yes,' she said. 'It is nothing, really. A small matter. I am most tremendously happy, you see. At my time in life – approaching my middle years – I did not expect – one does not expect – to meet a gentleman who wants to marry one. And yet, there he is, and he does, and it's so wonderful. So unexpected.' She put the biscuit back on the plate and frowned.

'I am so pleased for you. So, what concerns you?'

'He is so gentlemanly. So absolutely right and proper, in his courting. Never overstepping in any way, but complimentary in exactly the right way. Knowing how bewildering this must be for me. Gentle, in his approaches. Romantic, in the sense of small kindnesses that ladies appreciate.'

'Indeed,' I said. I sensed she needed encouragement.

'He is very respectable, an ornithologist, and he is an expert in the preservation of birds too. He mounted Delilah for me.' She pointed at a small stuffed yellow bird in a glass case. 'He has been so supportive of my passion for birds, and we have so much in common. Really, my life is about to change in such a magnificent way, and I have no reason, no reason at all, to doubt.'

She was no longer eating her shortbread, and her smile looked as if it had been sewn on with tight thread.

'Tell me about it,' I said.

'It is only – I am alone in the world now, since my mother

died. I spent a lot of years caring for her, you see, and before that, my father. I didn't get the opportunity to meet young men, really, but I have always been quite prosaic. I know that if I had, they might not have taken to me anyway.'

'I am sure that is not true,' I said. I looked at the little yellow bird in the cage and realised that her unknown suitor had not done a very great job of stuffing it. Its head was lumpy, and it had an expression of squint-eyed angst.

'I am most enormously grateful to Mr Prout for choosing me. I know how lucky I am. I am not beautiful, you see. I never have been. When I was younger people used to talk about plain girls letting their inner beauty shine out, so I used to try, but really, what does that mean? Do men want to see my innards? Should I blow champagne bubbles out of my nose? Outwardly beautiful women may have inner beauty too, so do I have to try three times harder than them?' She stopped abruptly.

'I'm sorry. I tend to get passionate about certain subjects. My point is, I am finding it hard to believe that Mr Prout truly holds affection for me. He has professed it so very much, so very thoroughly, that I am really quite convinced, almost completely in fact. I was almost overcome with his tenderness when he proposed. It is just...' She raised her hands, helplessly.

'You want me to find out if he loves you?'

'No, no. I am comfortably off,' she said. 'So, I just want to make sure – although I am sure, really – that he is all that he says he is. Just to check his background a little, to make certain. Of course he will be entirely respectable. All his behaviour, his patience with me, tells me so. I met him at the opera, he knows so many of the important people in town.

It's just as my father used to say – women can be so very foolish, at times. I want to make sure I am not being foolish.'

'Please, do carry on eating,' I said. 'Of course, I will help you. You are very wise to make sure of a suitor. Not because of your looks, because I disagree with your opinion of yourself, but because any sensible lady should do so. Can you let me have your fiancé's name and any other details, and we will investigate him for you? Discreetly of course.'

'Oh, please, never let him find out,' she said. 'I would never want him to know I doubted his affections.'

I left Miss Turton's house feeling pleased with myself. I had not insulted her, I had listened well and got the right details, and I had eaten some very fine biscuits.

Her suitor was a complete bounder, I was certain.

Not because of the way she looked, because she had a lovely warm friendly face. It was because of that ugly lumpy stuffed monstrosity. He had taken something she loved and made a mockery of it.

There were definitely days when Mr Blackthorn looked larger than others. There were days when he loomed, and days when he didn't. Today was a large day. He seemed to take up a lot of space with the breadth of his shoulders and his height, and I wondered how often he hit his head on low doorways.

He had given me some invoices to type after I had returned from Miss Turton's, as if I was an official lady typist. I was getting better at it. My forefingers had ached after the first two sessions, but now they felt stronger, and I was hitting the keys quicker, making fewer mistakes. There was only one smudge on my cheek.

After I had finished my typing for the day, I went to say goodbye. He was sanding down a cabinet in the back yard, sitting on the ground with one knee bent and his injured leg straight out, his sleeves rolled up, and I could not help but notice his efficiency. He really was a very hands-on kind of giant.

'I'll do a bit of asking around about Mr Prout,' he said. His fingertips must be rough, with all that sandpapering. 'I think I've heard of him, but nothing bad, particularly. He's an ornithologist, yes, but also a taxidermist for the museum, and he owns a gunsmith's in town as well, I think. A man of a few trades, but then many of us are.'

'Can I help you with enquiries?' I said. The idea filled me with a feverish kind of anticipation.

'It's easy enough for me to do,' he said. He ran his hand across the cabinet's curved doors, checking for smoothness. Then he threw the sandpaper down, put his hand flat on the cabinet and eased himself up onto his feet, simultaneously reminding me that I was a fairly short woman. 'Probably best done by asking a few people I know. If there is anything untoward, I'll find it.'

'Whatever you discover, I should like to be the one to tell her,' I said. 'I think she trusts me.'

'Fair enough,' he said. 'It might be best for you to handle it, as she asked for a lady in the first place. Give me a week or so, and I'll update you. I'm glad my last case is an easy one.'

'Why do you not want to be a detective any more?' I asked. 'Was it really because you got beaten up?'

'My father was the detective,' he said. 'I was in the navy for many years, and I helped him out when I was on shore leave, but it was his passion, his calling. He was a good man, who put his life in his job because he wanted to help people. Then he was murdered on a whim by some drunk fool smuggling cheap gin and cigars.' He ran a weary hand over his face, and grimaced.

I looked at him in shock.

'It doesn't work, to be a detective with principles,' he continued. 'You have to get as down and dirty as the people you are investigating to do it well, and it leaches your soul. I am like him, and I don't want to be like some of the scum we had to investigate. There's no halfway road. I'd rather keep my principles and hock furniture.'

'I am sorry about your father,' I said. 'I did not know. Did they catch him, this evil man?'

'I did,' he said, 'I caught him, and took him to the police station without flattening his face into the ground even though I sorely wanted to. He got his sentence.'

'It must have been terrible for you,' I said. I understood now why he had given it up. It would have been surprising if he hadn't, after such tragedy.

'For all of us,' he said, and I remembered his wife and all his children who must have suffered too. They did not seem to visit him very often, so I hoped I could be forgiven for forgetting them, this once. 'You were right, when you asked if he would have wanted me to give it up. The answer is no, he wouldn't have, but I haven't had the stomach for it since.'

'Are you sure there is no compromise? Where you keep most of your principles and your honour, but bend the truth a little to get what you need?' I was not thinking of my occasional white lies.

'I don't know,' he said. 'Maybe. People don't seem willing to leave me in peace to pursue my new career, that's pretty clear. There's you, a constant firework in my ear, and Maria Monk, and Miss Turton, and now others are harassing me to take on their cases as well. If Frank Knight would get his finger out and start doing his job, I'd be extremely grateful.'

'No one has ever called me a firework before. What are the other cases?' I said.

'No,' he said. 'No. I haven't agreed to take them on, and I'm not telling you anything about it. I have sandpapering to do. Sandpapering. And chasing information on Miss Turton's fiancé. Now if you will excuse me, Violet. Miss Hamilton. This cabinet needs a good hard rub-down, and I must be left in peace to do it.' He ran his hand over the surface again, firmly, caressingly, and a strange warmth went through me that I couldn't identify.

I left the shop a much wiser woman. I could see now how bleak and dangerous detective work was, why Mr Blackthorn had been so resolute in his intent to give it up. It was not a profession to be chosen lightly.

I felt his pain, at an unexpectedly deep level, but I could not be entirely sad for long. Even though he had told me to go, he had called me Violet by accident, and he was allowing me to carry on with Miss Turton. And oh, I did like a man with firm principles.

Chapter Twenty-Seven

I had to go back and see Mrs Monk, of course. There was no escaping it, as I was not content to let the insult lie. There was, however, a certain amount of girding my ladylike loins to be done. I thought long and hard about it, and then I went to the bookshop and bought her a book on fossils. It was a pretty thing, with hand-coloured engravings. It was much easier to buy books than borrow them from the library, thank goodness, as I had not yet rebuffed the bookseller in marriage.

I called on her early on Saturday afternoon, but she did not receive me, so I left my card, a short note of apology and the book. It was not Mackenzie who answered the door but a young maid, who had been warned that I was evil, and was impressively expeditious in shutting the door.

I got a note back from Mrs Monk later that day, though.

'One would think you might have learnt to avoid making hints about age,' it said. Her handwriting was beautiful and slanted, but there was definitely a sharp edge to some of her letters. She signed it 'MM'.

Oh, for goodness sake. Now she was actively looking to take offence. It was ridiculous. There were three churches not far from her house, and as a respectable woman Mrs Monk was sure to be at one of them. The next day I feigned sickness to my father and then, when he had left for our church, I dressed in my finest and went on a religious expedition.

The difficulty about going to a new church was that I was a novelty. If I didn't want to stay for the whole service then it was important I remained near the back, but people had established themselves in their pews and in their curiosity might be keen to usher me to the front, so that they could stare at me during the sermons. And if I was too friendly, they would have me renting a pew in no time.

In the first church I was late and able to sidle in and perch on a rear pew, slipping out during the Lord's Prayer without the entire congregation turning round to look. Mrs Monk was not there. But at the second church I was early, and the congregation was small and so avidly over-welcoming that I felt I was committed to attending for the next forty years at least and ended up in the very front pew. How was I supposed to spot Mrs Monk from there?

Things got worse when I saw that in some strange twist of fate, the service was to be led by Edmund Lint, preacher of the wandering hands.

His pale face flushed strawberry red when he saw me, and then he spent a considerable amount of time flipping through his papers before he spoke.

'I was going to speak about Jesus and the fishes, but I think instead today I will speak about misunderstandings, and how easy it is for us to deliberately misinterpret those around us when they are purely and innocently trying to spread the word and the love of God. His ways are infinitely mysterious and holy…'

It was a long sermon.

There were very few reasons one could leave a church service from the front pew in the middle. As I saw it, one could cough, feign sickness, or create a scene. I thought through them all and decided, sadly, that the final was the quickest and most effective.

I said an inward prayer to apologise to the Lord, and then I shrieked, seconds before Mr Lint started a prayer about humility. Everyone turned to stare.

'M-Miss Hamilton?' Mr Lint said.

'A rat,' I said, pointing behind him, very close to his feet. 'There is a rat. An evil, dirty rat. God, save me!'

I shrieked again, and then ran down the aisle clutching my skirts, looking frantically from side to side to see if Mrs Monk was present. I could not see her, just the stares of the tiny congregation. The door was heavy and hard to wrestle open, but it slammed behind me with a satisfying thud.

I ran to the next church quite quickly, in case anyone should come after me. I had not known I possessed the courage to make such a scene, but apparently it took the sober words of Edmund Lint to drive me to it. At least public shame would ensure I need never return.

The third church was the biggest, stone-built and gothic with more than one gargoyle peering down from the roof, and I could not face going into it. I lurked outside in the churchyard instead, reading gravestones and wondering about the lives of the people under them.

Mrs Monk was one of the first to come out and she was alone, walking fast, as if she had no time to wait and speak to the rest of the congregation.

'Mrs Monk,' I said, and she glared at me, but she stopped, so there was hope. 'Can I speak to you?'

'Not here,' she said. 'Walk with me.' She took off at pace, up the steps that led to the street of white cottages called Tackleway, then up a steep path through gorse and bracken on the side of East Hill. I had to run to catch up with her.

'You know I am sorry,' I said as I ran. 'You know I meant the book as a peace offering, because you were looking for fossils when I met you first. I was foolish, and I can't apologise any more than I have done already, but I really, really, want to help you.'

She stopped abruptly and turned to look at the vista of Hastings and St Leonards spread out below us. There were the rooftops of the houses in the old town in reds, yellows and browns, the black fishing huts, and then the white promenade stretching into the distance against a haze of dull sunshine breaking through the clouds and, framing it all, the blue-grey sea.

'You are persistent, I'll give you that.' There was no sign of the worn-out woman she had seemed the first day. She was all patrician splendour, the kind that some women acquired with age, when their faces said they were less likely to put up with nonsense.

'I am new to this, but I'm learning,' I said. 'Won't you forgive me, and tell me your problem?'

She looked at me briefly and then back at the view.

'Very well,' she said. 'Can you do it today? I left a piece of jewellery at a house, but I can't go back myself. Will you go and ask them for it?'

'Today? Of... of course,' I said. 'Where? Will they give it back freely or do I need to persuade them?'

She laughed, short and sharp. 'They might be slow to understand, so do be crystal clear as to what it is I want, but I'm sure they will be happy to oblige.' She pointed down the hill. 'Do you see that street of houses there? All Saints Street. It is the yellow house, number forty-three. Ask for Mrs Tibbs. She'll help you, I'm sure.'

It seemed odd, for her case to be so simple.

'Are you sure that's all there is to it?' I said.

'Absolutely,' she said, and then she described the jewellery for me, carefully. 'I might have left it in the blue bedroom on the second floor,' she said, 'if it's still blue. I lost it in the bed, so worth looking there.'

'How long ago was it?'

'A very long time,' she said, 'but that's of no matter. If they have it, they'll have it. The most important thing is for you to go this afternoon. I need to go home now. But do keep me informed.' She swept off up the hill, disturbing a wren which flew chattering from the brush, and I was left alone on the hillside.

Something was not right, but I could not work out what it was.

Chapter Twenty-Eight

Despite the slight oddities, it seemed like an easy case, so I decided just to sort matters myself, so that I could tell Mr Blackthorn I had solved a case quickly, all on my own.

The house was not hard to find. All Saints Street was one of the oldest streets in Hastings, full of cramped houses, some of them looking as if they had been built when Queen Elizabeth sat on the throne and never since repaired. It was a noisy, bustling thoroughfare, full of shouting from windows, doors slamming, animals bleating and the rumble of barrows and carts. Number forty-three seemed to be the only quiet house among them.

I rang the bell pull and heard it ringing within. There was a shout from an open window above.

'Christ, sod off,' it said. I had never heard a woman use those words.

The door opened to a very burly woman with big fists, who looked like a boxer.

'Yis?' she said.

I had prepared everything I was going to say carefully, down to the last detail, and it all fled from my head, instantly.

'My name is Mrs Tibbs, and I am looking for Violet Hamilton,' I said. 'I mean – the other way around.'

'That's me, but we don't take callers on Sunday morning,' she said. 'Come back tomorrow.' She tried to shut the door on me, and I tried to resist, and because she was built like a bull she naturally won.

I rang the doorbell again.

'For fucking hell's sake!' The cry came from above. At least I would go home with a richer vocabulary.

She opened the door again.

'I don't know what you're about,' she said. 'But my girls are sleeping. I said to come back later.'

'I have come on behalf of Mrs Monk,' I said, 'and I just need two minutes of your time inside. Just two minutes, and then I'll be gone and I'll leave you in peace, I promise.'

'Mrs Monk?' She was still primed to fight, but she stood back reluctantly and let me in.

She led the way into a drawing room, clean and bright, and the couches looked to be covered in calico. There was a vase of cheerful flowers on the mantlepiece, and the decor was one of wholesome good cheer. Maybe my task would not be so difficult.

'Well?' she said. She did not invite me to sit. 'It's a long time since I've heard from Maria Monk.'

'I understand you were kind enough to let her stay with you several years ago, when she first came to Hastings. She says she left a piece of jewellery behind, and wonders if you would be kind enough to return it.' I couldn't see this frightening woman returning anything of value, but I had to try.

'Ha! Yes, she stayed here all right. A right fancy guest she thought she was too,' the woman said. She put strange emphasis on the word 'guest'. 'But as to whether she left anything behind, it was over thirty or forty years ago. If she was foolish enough to leave it, it won't be there now. And we wouldn't keep anything we found. If you're thinking of making accusations, I'd watch who you're talking to.'

I did wonder what would happen if she decided to hit me with one or both of those giant fists. It would be the end of me, no doubt, and then would anyone be able to make sense of why I was there? Mr Blackthorn, perhaps, but even he didn't know I had come here to solve his case. A small pang shot through me, as I imagined him denying all knowledge of me as I lay dying.

'She left it in the blue bedroom on the second floor,' I said. 'If it's still blue. She says she lost it in the bed.'

'Sounds like a load of old balls,' the woman said. 'She always did give herself airs, that Maria, but she wouldn't have had anything worth anything in those days. That's what you get like, when you think that what you have in your bloomers is more special than everyone else. Although it's done her good now, so I hear.'

I stared at her in shock, while she stared into space for a second.

'We can go and ask Hildebrand, I suppose,' she said. 'She stays in the blue bedroom, though it's green now, but I imagine the bed is the same one. They're built to last.'

She stomped up the stairs at great speed and I followed, terrified.

The room was a mess, scattered with clothing, the curtains still drawn. It smelt of cigars and alcohol, and a certain mustiness. There was a very large bed on the left-hand side of the room and on it I could make out a huddle of sheets and blankets and the possible shape of a woman. Mrs Tibbs marched over to the window and flung the curtains wide.

'Your room's a pigsty, Hildebrand,' she said, and going over to the bed, she shook the woman roughly by the shoulder. 'Wake up.'

'Go 'way,' the woman said.

'Hildebrand, wake up. I need to talk to you. Hildebrand, don't make me shake you properly,' Mrs Tibbs said.

At that, the girl sat up. Her hair was flowing loosely over her shoulders and the strap of her chemise had fallen down over one shoulder. She would have been pretty, if she hadn't looked so exhausted.

'I'm tired,' she said. She yawned and spotted me. 'Who's that? I don't do ladies.'

'Don't be rude,' Mrs Tibbs said. 'Out. Out of bed. Madam wants to look at it to see if there's some jewellery hidden in it. Though if there was, someone would have found it by now.'

'There's nowhere to hide anything in that bed,' Hildebrand said. 'Sadly, or I'd be hiding in it myself.' She giggled.

'Out,' Mrs Tibbs said, and she threw the covers onto the floor and started to remove the mattress from the bed before Hildebrand had fully climbed out of it. Hildebrand scampered onto the floor and wrapped herself in the coverlet, shivering.

'I'll be expecting a reward, milady, if we find it,' Mrs Tibbs said, looking at me. 'What does it look like?'

'It's just a pink pearl,' I said. 'A small pink pearl. She said she lost it here, but that it might be possible to find it in the bed.'

Mrs Tibbs dropped the mattress back on the bed abruptly.

'Maria Monk said she lost her pearl here,' she said.

'Yes. It wasn't attached to a chain or in a setting, just on its own, and she said she didn't intend to leave it behind, because it was worth its weight in gold, but she had to. Perhaps it might have rolled somewhere?'

Mrs Tibbs started laughing, the loudest, most aggressive laughter I had ever heard, clutching her belly and her bosom, tears streaming from her eyes.

'She lost her pearl,' she said to Hildebrand, and Hildebrand starting laughing too, although it seemed more because it was expected of her.

'I don't understand,' I said.

'Oh boy, oh boy,' Mrs Tibbs said. 'I don't know what you did to Maria Monk, but she doesn't like you. She doesn't like you. It's not here, milady. She lost it a long, long time ago, and she ain't getting it back. In fact, she sold it about three times over, if I remember right.'

This was a very strange household. Hildebrand was still smiling, but it was not a real smile, and I didn't like the flash of fear in her eyes when she looked at Mrs Tibbs. Hildebrand looked as if she needed more than one good night's sleep.

'Can you explain, please?' I said.

'Tell Maria Monk she's entertained us today,' Mrs Tibbs said. 'Very funny. Very funny indeed. I think now it's time for you to leave.'

'But...'

Mrs Tibbs flexed her hands, and I changed my mind about staying. I was down the staircase and out the front door in seconds.

'Well, there we go,' Mrs Tibbs said from the doorway. 'Funfair over. Final word of advice... don't mess with Maria. Goodbye!' She slammed the door so hard she nearly sliced off my nose.

***

I worked it out, in slow, painful steps, because I was not entirely stupid. Mrs Monk must have found my ignorance very funny. I realised quickly enough that the house full of sleeping girls was most likely a house of ill repute. Mrs Monk had sent me there knowing it might destroy my reputation. How much must she dislike me, a woman she had barely met?

I guessed what the joke might be, that a pearl was linked somehow to a woman's innocence, but it was, as always, a guess. The truth lay under shadows and darkness. Nobody I knew would ever tell me honestly, and no librarian would ever hand me a book to explain.

Why would she choose to reveal something so personal to me about herself, when it meant, if I was so inclined, I could share it with the town and ruin her?

I knew that women did things like this. I did. I knew that brothels existed, and that men visited and women were paid for entertaining them. How awful must it be, for women who were not married, to put themselves through all that pain and torment, purely to satisfy men's lust? At least in marriage you could put a stop to it, especially after babies.

Maria Monk must have intended for me to feel foolish, and I did, wholeheartedly. I flushed with shame all day, on and off, thinking of how little I knew.

But underneath, a resolution was forming. It was no good, constantly tripping the line between innocence and scandal, without knowing exactly where scandal lay. It was like being forced to make meals, without knowing which ingredients were poisonous.

The worst part was that I had visited a den of iniquity for

the first time and not even known until afterwards. I had not had the chance to look about me with a clear eye and gain any sort of useful knowledge at all.

I had to discover a foolproof method of finding out all I wanted to know in life, without destroying my reputation.

Chapter Twenty-Nine

For his own reasons, my father had instantly assumed my mother had left us. He had been stony-faced at first, disbelieving, stoic in the face of shock, and he had not said much at all to anyone except the constables. Then one day he had come home and put one hand on my shoulder, so firmly it had hurt.

'She has gone, Violet,' he said. 'She has left, and we need to carry on without her. She has chosen a life without us, and we must make the best of it. You are old enough now, to take on the house. You are the funny one in the family, you must bring back the joy, the laughter. We will get along well enough. I need… I need a clean shirt.' His voice had cracked. It was a lot of emotion for him and after that day he had packed it up tightly, never to be seen again.

It distressed me, thinking of those first, empty hours when no one realised she had gone. When anything might have happened to her. She might have been distressed, drowning, under threat of violence or looking to escape some awful fate and no one, no one who loved her cared, because they did not know she was missing.

I had stopped cracking jokes a long time ago. There were not bucketloads of things to laugh about, and besides, my father had no sense of humour.

You would not have thought that though, the following Tuesday. I remained discreetly out of the way, but from the gales of female laughter coming from the parlour, you would have believed he was the finest comic to walk the earth.

'Your father wants you downstairs,' Edith said, appearing at my bedroom door. Her knock was almost a thump, and she was scowling. I was glad to see that extra money had not changed her essential character.

There was nothing to be done but straighten my frock and go and meet Mrs Beetling's five daughters. Five daughters! I wondered if they were all as ebullient as her. I felt like taking an umbrella, in case I needed to protect myself from the cheer.

'This is Ada,' Mrs Beetling said, 'and Mary, Annie, Harriet and Amelia.'

They were all lovely. I could not fault them. Large, cheerful daughters aged roughly between six and twenty-four, who did not flinch at meeting me, enquired politely after my health, remarked on the weather and asked if I played the piano. Had my father been unmarried, I could have had no objection to their joining our family at all. The littlest one was sweet, round-faced, with red curly hair and big eyes that stared around the room in wonder.

They were a little loud, of course, but they were not as loud as their mother, and they were full of such goodwill, such determination to please, that I felt churlish for wondering why they were there.

'Which charities do you assist with? I may know some of the ladies at them,' Mrs Beetling asked. I sensed the trap just in time, even if it was not intended.

'I was volunteering at the Society for Suppressing Mendicity for several years,' I said, 'but I feel I have done all I can do there. Mendicity is very difficult to suppress. For a while I helped out at the Blanket Lending Society also, but I am currently in between charities.'

'You should join mine,' she said. 'I volunteer weekly at the District Visiting Society.'

Oh God. It sounded like a real one. 'I should be delighted,' I said weakly. 'Who do you visit?'

'The poor,' she said cheerfully. 'We take soup, and clothing, and medicine, anything we can think of that they might need. I don't know if it helps them for long, but it helps them.'

She was a nice lady, with nice children. My father looked happier than I had ever seen him. I could see him sneaking looks at her as if he could not believe she was sitting there in his parlour, so much warm flesh and joy.

Maybe those big arms, that soft chest, would not mind that he was still married, and that his missing wife was quite possibly, almost definitely, wanton. Mrs Beetling looked like she had a big heart that could embrace the world.

'Mrs Beetling,' I said, 'do you—' But my father shot me a glare so furious I jumped in my seat.

'It's Beeton, Violet, Mrs Beeton,' he said.

'Mrs Beeton,' I said, wishing I had not started on the question, 'do you cook?'

'I do love to bake,' she said. 'Although the servants do most of it now, I'm afraid, with so many girls. But every now and then on a Sunday afternoon, we all get together in the kitchen, and we make scones. Or crumpets. Everyone likes crumpets, don't they? And buttered teacakes. We get flour everywhere, but no one minds. It's a lovely way to spend the day.'

Her daughters all nodded happily, and my father looked at her as if she was a teacake herself, dripping in butter and slathered with jam.

I had to escape.

'You must excuse me,' I said. 'I need to write to the coal man urgently. About the coal. He has been dirtying the coal bunker with… his coal.' Even my lies were falling apart.

'Can he read?' my father asked. 'Can't you just speak to him?'

'I believe he can,' I said. 'It is always better to put reprimands down in writing.' I escaped to my room, and I don't think they missed me.

Chapter Thirty

I didn't tell Mr Blackthorn about what Maria Monk had done. I was frightened he would laugh at me or ban me from helping him ever again. I had a certain determination that my dealings with Mrs Monk were not over, but it had become a battle between the two of us. The next move was mine.

'Mr Prout is exceptionally dull,' Mr Blackthorn said when I visited the next day. He was re-upholstering the worn armchair I usually took, so I was perched on top of a country-style sideboard of weather-beaten pine. 'I've asked round my usual sources, and no one can tell me anything bad about him. He is late to getting around to marriage but hasn't left a trail of broken hearts or seem to have any dark proclivities. Doesn't have a mistress. He records rare birds and sends details to the Society of Ornithologists. He does most of the museum's taxidermy for their natural history collections, at a discounted rate. He is respected in hunting circles, sells high-quality equipment. His finances seem solid, he doesn't spend more than usual on gambling. I think we need to tell Miss

Turton that her beau is a good catch. She presumably won't mind that he's dull.'

'I shall let her know,' I said.

As a terrible taxidermist, Mr Prout should be giving his stuffed specimens to the museum for free.

'Can you type up an invoice for her?' Mr Blackthorn said. 'I've scribbled it out there, but it could do with the professional touch.' He smiled at me. He was smiling a lot more these days, and it seemed as if the sadness that had hung around him when we first met was lifting.

'Of course,' I said. 'But… this is too much, surely?' It was for five whole pounds.

'Standard rate,' he said, 'taking into account the time worked. I sent her our list of fees at the start.'

'Can I see your list?' I said. He rooted round in a cabinet, and I scanned it carefully. It needed typing out for a start.

'But…' I said. 'But Mr Knight has only charged me three pounds. And he has been working on my case for weeks already. Why would he work for so little?' I was stupid, for not knowing how much a detective cost, for not understanding money the way a man would. Mr Knight did not seem to be a person who would underestimate his own worth. 'Does he plan to charge me an outrageous sum at the end?'

'I wouldn't think so. That doesn't sound fair practice. But he should be completely clear about what he's charging upfront. I would have a word with him, get it straight.'

I nibbled on my thumb, worriedly. Was it possible Mr Knight was charging me by the hour, when I had been having so many doubts about him anyway, and had even tried to cancel him at the beginning? He was not anybody I wanted to owe money to.

'Don't worry about it,' Mr Blackthorn said. 'If it looks like he's overcharging, I'll have a word with him. We have a professional reputation to uphold as detectives, after all. How is he getting on with it?'

'Please may I have a coffee?' I said. Because I had decided to tell Mr Blackthorn some of the truth, about my mother and about Mr Knight. And I needed strong coffee to do it.

It did not take long, because Mr Blackthorn listened well, and because I only told him what Mr Knight knew. I wanted to see how that went first, how Mr Blackthorn would react, before I told him anything more.

'So your mother posed for some racy pictures,' he said, thoughtfully. He didn't leap to denounce me or her as a handmaiden of Satan, which was hopeful. 'I wonder what she wanted the money for. Was your father tight with her allowances?'

'No,' I said. 'He was very generous with her.' It was only after she had gone that he had got more careful, perhaps because I was his daughter, and had not managed a household on my own before. Or perhaps he regretted his generosity, if it had meant my mother could leave.

'I doubt she was an actress,' he said. 'It seems too far a stretch in her home town, to me. I can do a bit of rooting around, see if I can find out more about this Evelina Joyce. There might be a clue there, though I don't think they are the same person.'

I smiled at him, mildly, although my insides were jumping

up and down. Because it looked as if he was going to do a bit of investigating for me. If I handled it right, if I didn't make it too formal. If I just gave him titbits, and intrigued him, maybe he would get involved and then solve it for me, with discretion and valour, like a proper detective.

Chapter Thirty-One

'Well, that's wonderful to hear,' Miss Turton said.

She presented me with a plate of petits fours, specifically lemon millefeuille, filled with Chantilly cream. She was getting ready to go on a trip, but she received me anyway and produced some very fine tea.

'I am going to the Hydropathic Establishment,' she had said. 'For two nights, and I will stay there, even though it's only up the road. They have all sorts of water treatments to invigorate the health. Some of them may not be entirely pleasant – I hear they direct hoses of cold water at you very early in the morning – but I am certain to come back refreshed.'

She looked happy and excited, but when I told her the good news about Mr Prout, her smile fell off her face again.

'I am so relieved to hear that,' she said, though. 'I always knew he was a man of good character. That is such a tremendous relief! Thank you for looking into the matter for me. I am so delighted. I can marry him now without any worry at all.'

She had put her millefeuille down again untouched even

though they were absolutely delicious. I was already on my third.

'Are you quite happy with the result?' I asked.

'Of course!' she said. 'Of course! Am I not lucky, to meet such a worthy man? I know how fortunate I am, at my age, no longer in the flush of youth, to be swept off my feet by such a very devoted suitor.' She looked at the lumpy bird again and made a minuscule grimace.

Talking to Miss Turton was a peeling away of layers. I made general conversation with her for a little longer. We talked about her birds, and she told me about some of the charities she supported.

'Of course, my husband may not want me to be so active outside the home,' she said. 'But the marital state has so many other attractions.'

I did not like to think of her, gentle as she was, facing the extreme horror of a wedding night.

'It must be very exciting,' she said, 'working as a Lady Detective. Investigating people, uncovering things, following people – oh!'

'Oh?'

'That's it!' she said. 'For my peace of mind. You see, I cannot quite... relax about Mr Prout. I think if you could follow him, just for a short while – see where he goes, who he meets, that kind of thing – I think if you could do that, and he does nothing out of the ordinary way, I think that would quite put my silly mind at rest.'

'I will ask Mr Blackthorn,' I said. 'But I don't see why not.' She had called me a Lady Detective, and a wonderful warm glow travelled from my forehead to my toes.

She picked up her petit four again, and all was well with the world.

That evening I patted Nigel, the stuffed cat once also patted by my mother, with approval. 'You may be ratty,' I said, 'but at least someone loved you enough to stuff you properly in the first place. You should be proud.' He glinted glassily back at me, with affection.

Chapter Thirty-Two

'We can do it for a week,' Benjamin said. 'It's man-heavy, but doable if she's willing to pay. To his office and back home again, to his club and back again, so that we know exactly where he is at all times and can work out if he is visiting a fancy woman or gambling all his money away. But it still might not turn up anything.'

'I can help,' I said.

He frowned. 'It's not really a job for a respectable woman. I've got a man called Davies I can ask, who can cover him most of the day, and I can put a few of Agnes's brood on it when they are not at school – people never notice children dawdling along behind them. I can't hobble along after him yet. My leg is getting better but I think there's a few weeks in it before I can get back to normal.'

I did dislike men who referred to their own children as the responsibility of their mother.

'I can help,' I said again. 'Who would suspect me? I am fit, and I can scurry along behind him like a little brown mouse.'

'You have a lot of vivacity, Violet. People can't help

but notice you when you're in the room. You are not as inconspicuous as you think.'

There was a compliment in there, I was sure. I would have to think about it later. Vivacity? Surely that quality was my mother's.

'Nobody knows what I'll be like, as we've never tried it,' I said. 'Give me the opportunity, and I'll show you.'

He stroked his jaw. 'Maybe you could cover a couple of shifts. You could just wander along and see what he's up to. But it's really not a suitable way for a young lady to spend their time.'

I wanted to do it. I wanted to follow Mr Prout more than I had ever wanted anything in my life, apart from finding my mother. More than typing, more than riding a bicycle. I wanted to follow someone, surreptitiously.

'I am certain it is quite suitable for me to assist a lady in distress,' I said. 'But I want to know how to follow him well. I want to know how I can make sure he doesn't spot I'm following him. I want to do it properly.'

'It's not an art,' he said. 'Most of the time it's pretty boring. Just follow them, at least the length of an omnibus behind, best to vary it. Most people don't think they are being followed. Try not to burn holes in their back with your eyes. If they feel they are being followed and turn around, don't dart into doorways or fling yourself into a bush. Just keep on walking, right on past them, because remember, you are going somewhere that doesn't involve them. If they go into a shop, wait behind a tree until they come out. A lot of it will be waiting, to be honest. Perhaps take a book. If you suspect something is amiss, come back and tell me before you do anything else. We are looking for a mistress, or anything that he hasn't told Miss Turton about that looks shifty.'

Take a book, indeed. He did not know me well enough. For me it would be an art. I would be the best follower of people in history. I would stalk with the slick sleekness of a tiger after its prey.

I was good at it, I discovered, although admittedly Mr Prout was not expecting to be followed and was therefore oblivious. In the mornings he worked at Hastings Museum, where he had a taxidermy lab. In the afternoons he went and opened up his gunsmith's shop, which sold a range of shooting and hunting equipment. He usually either went for a walk or straight home, Davies said, and on Thursdays he usually went straight to his club, at the end of Ponsonby Avenue. But there were gaps in the schedule. I was the first person ever to follow him on a Wednesday.

Miss Turton had given me a photograph of him. He was a tall, thin man, in his late forties, with a small handlebar moustache. He locked up his shop in St Leonards abruptly at five o'clock, charging out the door as if hyenas were on his heels, and set off across the street at a spanking pace. Due to the proliferation of hills and valleys, it was no mean feat to keep up with him. I stayed a discreet distance behind him, remaining as insignificant as possible.

He did say hello to the Misses Spencer, who materialised out of nowhere in that slightly creepy way they had. He had no choice really, because they stopped in the middle of the path and simpered at him. When he had carried on and it was my turn to reach them, I tried a new approach. A second before they noticed me, I turned my head abruptly to the left and gave them the cut direct before they did. It worked until they had passed by, when I unfortunately made contact with a lamppost. It was not severe though, and once I'd recovered my wind, I set off doubly fast in pursuit of Mr Prout.

He was fond of walking, it seemed. He charged out of town and up East Hill towards Ore at a pace more suited to a runner, and I was quite out of breath by the time he reached the top. I sat on a bench for a while and drummed my heels, looking at the seagulls swooping across the bay.

Mr Prout took out a pair of binoculars and looked at the view for around ten minutes, then turned abruptly and walked all the way down again, rendering my marathon completely useless. I had to be careful as I followed him down. If I ran too fast, I faced the very real prospect of gaining momentum, tripping over my skirt, and somersaulting down the hill right past him. At one juncture I was forced to grab a tree.

When he got to the bottom, he took a sharp left towards the seashore, where he bought some fish, possibly haddock, wrapped in brown paper and string. He seemed to know the fishermen well. And then he turned around and walked all the way to his home in St Leonards, which involved more hills.

By the time he got home, I had given up trying to hide. I attached myself to the spear-headed railings of a front gate a few houses along from his and hung there, sweaty and gasping for breath, as he ran lightly up the sweeping path, leapt up the steps to his front door and handed his haddock to a servant.

It had been a disappointing mission, but at least I knew I could do it. And by the time we found out if he was morally suspect or not, I would have the wiry physique of a greyhound.

Chapter Thirty-Three

After my first adventure following Mr Prout, I went to Mr Knight's office. Unusually, there was someone else there. It was a man wearing a coat with a giant fur collar, odd in May. He was arguing, and Mr Knight was shaking his head.

'No, no, I'm sorry,' he was saying. 'I have an immense portfolio of cases on at the moment, and I can't take on any more. My apologies. No, there's no one else in town just now. I would try a London agency. They sometimes second agents here if it's important enough.'

The man gave up, and turned towards the door, his shoulders hunched, and I realised the coat was balancing out a very narrow person.

'Try Mr Benjamin Blackthorn,' I said to him, out of the side of my mouth, as he left, and he looked at me startled.

'He's given it up,' Mr Knight said, hearing me, but the door had already closed and it was just the two of us.

'You have filled your shelves,' I said, because it was true, his shelves were full of gentlemen's shoes and boots. It was very peculiar. They looked new, and the shop smelt strongly of leather.

'Yes,' he said, looking cross, as if it was impolite of me to ask. 'I like them.'

There was a whole shelf of very small shoes, I noticed, and I wondered if he had made friends with a few elves in the course of his detective work. But it did not seem the time to question him about his oddities.

'I wanted to ask about payment,' I said. I was feeling braver, these days. 'Are you planning to charge me more when you have solved the case? I must be honest with you and say that I do not have any more money. If you are expecting it, I must ask you to drop the case.' *Drop it, drop it*, I begged him silently. I almost had a Blackthorn working for me, and if Mr Knight gave up I was sure I could persuade the better detective to take me on.

He was spreading his hands out on his empty desk again, like starfish.

'I am a generous man. I saw the moment you came in, you were a lady in distress,' he said. 'For that reason, I decided not to charge you as much as I would in normal circumstances. This is a complex case. If your mother is found alive, my reward will be your rosy, happy cheeks.' He frowned heavily, undermining all he had said. 'Although if you find more money, I think it incumbent on you to give me it. Your father is a wealthy man.'

Why did I not believe him, for a second? Everything he did made me suspicious, instead of reassured.

'Very well,' I said, and I rose to go, but he had not finished.

'Remember we talked about why you left London?' he said. 'Have you thought any more about that, about reasons? About any... temptations to stray?'

'There was a man,' I said, 'in a silk muffler. Who gave me

a parcel in the street for my mother, and it made her cry. It might have had something to do with him. She seemed to want to move after that.'

'Did she,' he said. 'Did she. Now that's interesting. And how did she react when she got the parcel? At first? Was she crying at first, or was that when she spoke to your father?'

'She just took it from me,' I said. 'I didn't hear her cry until later.'

'And would you recognise the man? If I were to find him, to track him down, would you recognise him?'

'I don't think so,' I said. 'Because he was in a muffler, and a bowler hat.' It was hard to read his expression, but it was possibly excitement.

'We might have something there,' he said. 'We might have something.' And abruptly I regretted telling him, because I didn't trust what theories he might come up with, and it didn't feel like the right avenue to go down.

'I'm not sure,' I said, but he was playing power again, and he picked up his pen from his desk and started twirling it.

'You must excuse me now,' he said. 'I have other cases to be getting on with and I need to go out.'

I was mildly curious to see which pair of shoes he chose to wear, but mostly, I was glad to leave.

Chapter Thirty-Four

I arrived home, looking slightly the worse for wear from my professional need to follow Mr Prout, and of course my father was in the parlour with a gentleman.

'Violet, is that you?' he said, as I tried to tiptoe past. 'Please join us.'

He had not given up, then. I took off my hat and coat, wiped the sweat off my brow with my arm and went into the parlour to meet my fate.

The man sitting by the fireside was the best of the bunch my father had offered me. He was handsome, at least, and young, and there was something very clean and freshly scrubbed about him, as if he had only just completed his ablutions.

'This is Dr Septimus Patmore,' my father said. 'He is an ophthalmic surgeon. He has agreed to look at my eyes to see if an operation might help with my eyesight. Septimus, this is my daughter, Violet Hamilton.'

'Dr Septimus Patmore?'

'It is a pleasure,' said the man who had seen my mother in her nethergarments. He rose from his chair and bowed over my hand. Did his lips linger half a second too long? 'A pleasure to meet you, Miss Hamilton.'

'Violet, is that a bruise on your cheek?' my father said. It felt a little sore, and I realised it might be from my encounter with the lamppost.

'Yes,' I said. 'I was helping out at the mission today, and I had to go to the attic to fetch some blankets for the poor, and I accidentally walked into one of the eaves.' That sounded far more plausible than my usual lies. Detectiving might be finessing my falsehoods, too.

'How distressing for you,' Dr Patmore said. Was he looking at my bosom? Perhaps not. It might be that I was just naturally inclined to think his every move was inappropriate.

'It is fine,' I said. 'I am as strong as a horse.' I saw my father wince. He would have preferred I was as delicate as a bluebell. But it was best to warn Dr Patmore, in case he got any ideas.

My father did not need an operation. He just needed to wear his glasses more. But I could understand why, with a new woman in his life, he might be looking for another reason not to.

I could not look at Dr Patmore without imagining him poring over those pictures of my mother. Perhaps in his bedroom, alone, late at night, in his nightclothes. Any potential handsomeness had evaporated as soon as I heard his name.

'Is there a great deal of training involved, to become an ophthalmic surgeon?' I asked.

'A great deal,' he said. 'Enough to make my own eyes very tired. But we men are made for such things, are we not? The academic study, the late nights, the intellectual challenge, that dogged pursuit of a higher goal. I should imagine ladies' brains would explode were they forced to go through a similar rigour. But we humble men could not cope with all the effort required for domesticity, so there we are even.'

'You are so right,' I said, 'and talking of exploding brains, there is a danger that mine might do so at any moment. It is exhausting, folding blankets. Will you excuse me, while I repair to my room and tend to my bruise?'

'By all means,' Dr Patmore said, swiftly. Perhaps he did not want to help clean up the detritus should the worst happen. My father rose, and I could tell he was not happy with my performance.

Well, so be it. He had tried to matchmake me with a man who had bought rude pictures of his wife. As sons-in-law went, it couldn't get much worse.

My father shared his discontent at dinner.

'Dr Patmore is one of the most eligible young men I have had the pleasure of introducing you to and you hardly spared him the time of day. You are fast gaining the reputation of a woman who is fickle, and you should not underestimate the gravity of the stain on your character.'

'I am not fickle,' I said. 'I am consistent in not wanting to marry Dr Patmore, or any of the others. I do not like them. Is it imperative, absolutely imperative, that I marry?'

He put his knife and fork down.

'Of course it is. What other avenue in life is there for a young woman? Why would you want to take any other path? God forbid –' he looked horrified '– God forbid you take after your mother. Even so, surely you want your own home, your own children? Security? I cannot understand you, treating life as if it is some frivolous game, while the years tick away and your chances shrivel.'

'How would I take after my mother?' I asked. I watched his face darken.

'It is not… things were not. There was a coldness. It is not something that is appropriate to discuss with you.' He shook himself. 'We are talking about your reputation, and while we are on the subject, more than one person has commented that they have seen you walking around town alone. It is not suitable behaviour. I have been more lenient with you, perhaps, than I should have been, because you have not had a mother's influence. But in the future, you must take a chaperone with you.'

'Who has said that?' I asked.

'Acquaintances,' he said. 'It does not matter. The point is I will not allow you to go wandering around on your own any more. Take a servant, or a female acquaintance. No, Violet, I am firm on the matter. Take a chaperone, or you shall not go out.'

Chapter Thirty-Five

I decided that my father could not reasonably expect me to find a chaperone immediately. Putting it into practice would require some considerably annoying effort, so I decided it could wait until Thursday at least, and meanwhile I would have to wear a disguise again. I had to go to work for Mr Blackthorn.

He was good with customers, I noticed. He had created a little enclave of furniture for me and the Remington, so that I was mostly hidden, and I tended to quieten my typing when they came in, but I could see what was going on.

He handled people easily, assessing them as they came in, and then treating them in a matter-of-fact, straightforward way that meant they left feeling satisfied, even if they had not bought anything. The worried mother-to-be frightened her crib might rock too wildly; the dandy obsessed with finding a scarlet deep-buttoned chaise-longue. He dealt with them adroitly, calmly, and usually they went away having purchased more than they intended, but happy with it.

It would make a good quality in a detective, that ability

to manage. I watched and learnt, because it would be a good skill to have in life as well.

The Misses Spencer entered one day and I scooted under my desk so that they wouldn't see me. I wondered if they had come in because they had once seen me here. They fussed around the shop for some time, ostensibly looking for a rocking chair, but after a while it became clear that their requirements were too exacting. Mr Blackthorn showed them what he had, patiently, and then finally he recommended that they ask a furniture maker to create a bespoke one for them, and suggested a couple in town, and they went away, talking excitedly.

'They won't commission one,' he said, looking after them. 'It's just talk, to fill time. There's something not right about those girls' home lives. They are forever scampering about town looking for something to do, and they are outside from dawn till dusk. I hope whatever it is, they sort it one day.'

I looked at him with wonder, because I had been thinking of them only in relation to myself, all this time, and he had seen them clearly in seconds, as souls in trouble. I made up my mind to reach out a hand in friendship to them one day, if they would take it. And I made a vow to try to look at people clearly, as he did, without being hampered by my own insecurities.

I had plenty to be insecure about, to be fair. For one thing, I was forever embarrassing myself in front of him. There was the mortifying time, for example, when I shut myself in a box.

He had played a joke on me, with his badger beard, so it seemed only fair I should return the favour. I decided that I would wait until he had gone out and then when he was due to come back, I would leap out of an item of furniture and surprise him. It was not a very sophisticated joke.

A small wardrobe near the back of the shop would be best, I thought, because I could open the double doors at the same time and say, 'Ta-da!' like a performer on a stage. But it seemed wise to try out a few options, which went well, until I climbed into a blanket box, and after I closed the lid I couldn't get it open again.

It was a fairly heavy lid, but it seemed to have locked itself. Possibly the top clasp had fallen over the bottom one and secured it. After some minutes of pushing and struggling, I remembered a scary legend about a new bride who had played a game of hide and seek in a country mansion and never been found again.

The wood in the blanket box was very thick and it was possible Mr Blackthorn might not hear me. And also, what on earth would he think of a lady typist hiding in a blanket box? I was such a fool.

He took much longer to come back than I expected, so by the time I heard a tentative 'Miss Hamilton?' – because of course I could hear through the box – and I knocked on the lid, and he opened it, I was not a respectable sight. My hat had fallen off, and there may have been a slight dampness around my eyes.

'Hello,' I said.

'Miss Hamilton,' he said, and he gave me his hand so that I could stand up. 'What an unexpected surprise. Were you taking a nap?'

I mumbled something, crossly. 'Please assist me out,' I said, and he put both of his big hands around my waist and lifted me out, easily, and I rushed to the little outhouse in the yard to put my hat back on and, frankly, use the necessary, because that had also become a concern.

When I got back, he was examining the lock on the box, and he handled me as masterfully as he handled everyone else, by not questioning my idiocy.

'It might be useful for you to know how to pick a lock or two in life,' he said instead. 'Here, lock me in.' And without ado he climbed in, and shut the lid on himself, and I could have hugged him for it, if there wasn't a lid between us. I made sure the clasp was closed, and then waited. In seconds a very thin metal tool came through the lock, and he twisted it and pushed it until he was able to push up the top half of the clasp, and he opened the lid with a flourish.

'There,' he said. 'Try it.' So I climbed back in the box and he gave me his special set of tools, a ring with thin metal implements dangling from it, and he taught me how to unlock it from the inside. And then he showed me a few other locks too, and although it would take me a long while to be as expert as he was, it definitely made me feel more confident.

It was necessary to be fairly close to him, as we examined locks together, and at one point we were nearly cheek to cheek, and there was no beard any more. I ignored whatever that made me feel, of course, because he was married with a multiplicity of children.

'I have a spare set,' he said at the end, and he gave me one to keep that easily fitted in my skirt pocket.

It really was a shame that he had chosen to give up being a detective.

Chapter Thirty-Six

I was going back to see Maria Monk. She had thoroughly trounced me and, even more, landed me in a situation which could have led to my rejection from polite society forever. I did not owe her anything, but I could not leave matters as they were. Loveday Brooke, even though she was entirely fictional, would never have allowed herself to be made such a fool of. I owed it to myself, as a real person dipping my foot into the waters of investigating, to prove that I was not always a numbskull.

My mother had a dark purple satin dress, a little like a widow might wear, which I thought might give me an air of dignity for my return visit to Maria Monk, so I spent an evening taking it up. As with the mourning dress I'd worn to meet Mr Knight, it did not fit me very well, being a little long in the skirts and tight across the chest. The tightness across the chest was not so noticeable, so I left it, although it made it harder to lift my arms. It had a nice little hat to go with it, though, with a short veil of black net which hid the upper half of my face beautifully. Surely, in such a disguise, I could get away with one more solo excursion.

Saying a small prayer for forgiveness I then took the pointed end of my metal nail file and hacked into a mourning brooch that had belonged to an unknown great-aunt. It contained a lock of her hair arranged into the pattern of a fleur-de-lis, surrounded by a border of black velvet and tiny old seed pearls. It was a very ugly brooch, but I hoped my great-aunt was not watching me from heaven as I prised out one of the pearls.

Mrs Monk received me this time. She was sitting in a wicker chair by a big bay window that looked out onto the sea. I was shown in by the maid who had shut the door on me before. Mrs Monk turned her head only reluctantly from the view and then looked me up and down before raising her eyebrows.

'I have brought your pearl,' I said, sweeping back my veil, and I marched over and put it down firmly on the glass table in front of her, where it rolled a little and then stilled.

She looked down at it, and then back at me.

'It's very small,' she said.

'That will be four pounds and sixpence for solving your case,' I said.

She smiled a little, and then rang the bell for the maid. 'Rose, please bring my cheque book and a pen from the study,' she said. She turned her head and looked out of the window again. 'Stormy day,' she said, and indeed the sea was grey and wild, buffeting the rocks below.

When Rose came back, Mrs Monk picked up her pen.

'And two pounds for unnecessary distress,' I said. 'That makes six pounds and sixpence in total.'

She sighed and put the pen down. 'Sit,' she said. I crossed my arms and stayed standing.

'Please sit, Miss Hamilton,' she said. 'Rose, please bring us some tea and cake. The simnel cake.'

I did not sit but I turned and looked out of the window until Rose brought the tea and cake and left.

'I was… not kind,' Mrs Monk said. 'I am sorry. You seem so young, and cosseted. It angers me that one half of the world's women are exposed to the worst of life, and the other half so protected from it. But you are not to blame for that. You offended me, but I was a little harsh in my revenge.'

'I am twenty-eight, and not untouched by life,' I said. 'I might be ignorant, but it is not by choice. I don't seek to be ignorant. I want to know everything. I have always wanted to know everything, even though my reputation depends on knowing nothing.'

'Did Mrs Tibbs behave?' she asked. 'She did not threaten you? She had enough sense to know you are respectable, I hope.'

'She laughed at me, that was all,' I said. 'She told me to tell you it was a fine joke. Did you find it funny, too?'

'No,' she said. 'I was, I confess, a little guilty about the risk for you. I hope you were not seen. I am glad you are fierce with me. Please, sit, and take some tea and cake.'

Because she had asked three times, I sat and angrily ate cake. It was very good, with marzipan icing.

'If you can put our contretemps behind us,' she said, 'I do have an actual need for a detective. And I am beginning to think you might be someone I can trust. I think you have gumption.'

It felt good to be regarded as a person of courage. I could almost forgive Mrs Monk for sending me to a house of ill repute out of spite. Almost.

She must be a lady who had rolled in the gutter herself. Did I mind working for someone who was so full of sin?

I would decide that later. She had obviously risen in the world and was passing herself off as one of the many respectable ladies who moved to Hastings for their health. She had entrusted me with her secrets, however maliciously. I would wait and see what she had to say.

'I have not had an innocent life,' she began, 'so if that bothers you, or you think my truths might tarnish you, best run away now.'

'I am listening,' I said.

'I was born on the wrong side of the blanket, in the kind of poverty you can never imagine, even though my father owned a considerable portion of East Sussex. My life has not been… comfortable. My mother died when I was barely eleven. People have betrayed me, through desperation or selfishness, and I have come to be where I am now only because I have worked hard and fought. I have fought, with all the weapons that a woman can have, to be where I am today, to be living here, in comfort. Eating the finest cake, drinking tea from china cups.'

'Goodness,' I said.

'I have had protectors,' she said. 'I lived in France for over twenty years and I was sought after by many gentlemen. I worked my way up. I was the best. Men desired me, fought duels for me. I was given jewels, houses, clothes, horses, whatever I wished. Sometimes, it was snatched away again, or I was hurt. But always, always, I survived, and those that crossed me lived to regret it. Do you know what it is, to fight to your last breath to survive?'

'Possibly not,' I said. 'It sounds exhausting.' I was not

entirely sure what she was saying about herself. Had she been a courtesan? A mistress? I wished people would not speak in half-truths. She had the same overdramatic air as my mother.

'Well, I fought,' she said. 'I have faced brutality, and I have been abandoned in the direst of circumstances. There are very few people I trust. One of them was a naval architect called James Narbeth. He designed some of the world's finest ships, but he had worked his way up from a shipwright apprentice at Portsmouth Dockyard, so he understood about life. We understood each other, I think. There was a peace between us, when we were together.

'He always said that when he died, he would leave me everything. But of course, he had a wife, an unloving, flat-footed creature, and when he passed seven years ago, she got everything. If they had had children, I would have left things as they were, but I know he wanted me to have at least some portion of his estate.'

I could see why men would adore Maria Monk. She had a magnetism when she spoke that drew you in, and she told fascinating stories. I was still wondering whether she had once been a naughty nun, but it wasn't the kind of question I could ask.

'He told everyone that his will was on his last ship, the SS *Ortara*, in the captain's mess. They assumed it was hidden somewhere, built into the walls perhaps, and they searched it from top to bottom, but they did not find it. And a year later it sank, to the bottom of the Black Sea.'

'But,' I said, 'if the will is at the bottom of the ocean, how can we possibly help you? Mr Blackthorn doesn't do deep-sea diving, as far as I'm aware.'

'James sometimes travelled on his ships and collected

objects from across the world. He bartered with natives and brought back a Tahitian cloak, shells, ceramic pots. When he died his wife sold it all to Lady Brassey, who owns the Brassey Institute, and now some of the best pieces are on display in the museum.'

'I don't understand,' I said.

'His wife also sold them a model of the SS *Ortara*,' Maria Monk said. 'She does not know her ships and she sold it to Hastings Museum as the SS *Fairwind*, even though the name is there on the prow, clear for anyone who looks closely enough. The will is inside it. He showed me a secret drawer.'

'So you want us to ask them for it?'

She smiled at me, and I wondered again how those teeth were possible, so pearly and white. 'Of course not,' she said, 'I want you to break into the museum and steal it for me.'

It was a ridiculous idea, of course – as ridiculous as sending a stranger to a brothel to reclaim your innocence.

'I asked them if I could have a closer look at the ship,' she said, 'but I could not tell them why, so they would not let me. Perhaps if I had a husband with standing in the town they might listen, but they are all men, the Trustees, the manager, the curator, and used to ignoring requests from females. I am tired of flattering people to get my way. I feel that breaking in would be the simplest option. I can lend you Mackenzie to help, if you like.'

'I am just an emissary, of course,' I said. 'I will take your suggestion back to Mr Blackthorn and see what he thinks of it.'

'Ah, cowering at the first hurdle? I am disappointed.'

'Mr Blackthorn is a splendid detective,' I said. 'If anyone can advise in this matter, he can. If he thinks it is a good idea for me break into Hastings Museum in the middle of the night, I'll do it. But I'm not solving cases for you on my own again.'

'Very well,' she said. 'Do what you must.' She looked very remote and empress-like again. I left speedily, in case she decided to send me to an opium den for her amusement.

Chapter Thirty-Seven

As my father had omitted to hire me a paid companion, there was no other option but to ask Edith to be my chaperone. She was an exceptionally cross person to have to spend time with, but I needed her.

'It isn't my job,' she said immediately, when I asked her to come out with me.

'It is for today,' I said. 'Don't you want a break, a nice walk in the fresh air? We can take the chance to get to know each other.'

She pursed her lips like the end of a withered lemon but put on her hat and coat and followed me out of the door, muttering.

'Where are we going?' she asked.

'For a walk,' I said. It was true, although the direction of it would be mildly dictated by the direction in which Mr Prout walked. At least the sun was out, and the wind off the sea was not too sharp.

I had the late afternoon shift, so we walked to his gunsmith's shop, down a small alleyway off George Street. He had not yet locked up, so we loitered by Butler's Emporium, admiring the metal buckets and mops and other useful household items in the window and piled outside.

'What are we doing here?' Edith said.

'Do we need a mop, do you think? Or some new scrubbing brushes?'

It turned out we did, and a metal bucket too, so we had to go inside and buy them, and all the while I was peering out of the window to make sure we didn't miss my target. He passed the window just as I was paying, so I had to throw the money on the counter, grab the mop and run.

'If you had waited we could have had them delivered,' Edith said, puffing after me. She was carrying the bucket. 'Why are we hurrying?'

'I am feeling exuberant,' I said. Mr Prout was going his usual route, so although he was quite far ahead, I had not lost him.

'Is it necessary?' she asked. 'Are you on a health regime? Wouldn't it be better to take these things home? Where are we going?'

'No. Just where the fancy takes us,' I said, but at that moment Mr Prout veered sharply to the right down a street I had not expected him to take, so I was forced to slow down abruptly and then do the same.

Edith was intelligent, so it was no surprise that after a while she caught on. She stopped abruptly in the street and faced me. 'Don't stop!' I said.

'Are you,' she said, catching her breath. 'Are you following that strange gentleman?'

'Of course not,' I said. 'That would be ridiculous.' I calculated that if we stood here for a very short while I could still see the route he was taking, although it might take a sprint to catch up.

'Miss Hamilton, this isn't proper,' she said. 'I don't know what you are doing, but it doesn't seem right. I'm not paid enough to watch you chase men all over town. And you're carrying a mop.'

'It's only one man,' I said. 'And I'm not chasing him. I'm just… oh, there isn't time. Later. We have to go.' I set off at full pace again, and she ran after me, but I could tell she wasn't happy, as she lagged behind and slowed me down.

He went home, of course, just by a slightly different route, and once the door had closed behind him, I stopped and turned to face Edith again.

'Right,' I said. 'That's enough exercise for the day. Shall we go home?'

'I don't know what you're up to, but I don't like it,' she said.

'I confess I am on an exercise regime, Edith. The doctor advised that I find a different person every day and follow their route. It's completely harmless, as they will never know, but it helps to keep me enthusiastic, and they always go places I don't expect.'

'I wasn't born yesterday,' she said. 'You've always been a little odd with the gentlemen, but if this is your way of finding a husband, I'd advise against it. Men don't like to be chased.'

Edith wasn't working out very well as my chaperone. I'd have to find another strategy. I couldn't very well take her along when I broke into the museum.

Chapter Thirty-Eight

I had to wear a disguise again when I visited Mr Blackthorn, and I didn't like it. This time I chose a very large hat, which by chance meant I was being very fashionable. I didn't like being fashionable. I was very glad that bustles had faded away and I refused to wear one again, even though they were threatening to come back as whimsically as sails in wind.

'That's an impressive hat,' Mr Blackthorn said. He was looking fit, and happy with the world. Today he was bringing in a delivery of furniture, carrying in bookshelves and cabinets with ease. He still had a limp, but it was definitely healing. I wished he was not always doing physical things when I saw him. It was so distracting to speak to someone when they were always moving about, flexing muscles.

'Thank you,' I said. 'I went back to visit Mrs Monk and she has forgiven me for accidentally insulting her. She would like us to steal a model ship for her from Hastings Museum.'

He laughed, a great rumbling laugh that seemed to come from his boots.

'I think she may have mistaken detectives for hired thugs,' he said. 'We don't break the law. Mind your hat.' He circumnavigated me with an umbrella stand. I perched on the sideboard, where it seemed safest.

'Well, not exactly the ship,' I said. 'A will that is hidden inside it. She has tried to get closer to it by asking, but they wouldn't let her. And if she told anyone the reason, she is worried they might decide to get rid of it rather than share it.'

'Do you think you might consider taking your hat off?' Mr Blackthorn said. 'I am sure it is in fashion, but I can't see your face. It's hard to see what you're thinking, and with you, it's always best to know.'

'That's not very polite,' I said, but I took it off and hung it on the umbrella stand.

He was manoeuvring a bookshelf to the far wall, walking it on its corners.

'Can you stop shifting things about, so that we can talk properly?'

'Anyone would think,' he said, shoving the bookcase against the back wall, 'I ran a coffee parlour. God forbid that I should move furniture about when I run a furniture shop.' But he went to the small room at the back of the shop, made us both a coffee, and then propped his hip on the far end of the sideboard to listen, so I considered that small battle won.

I told him Maria Monk's story. Not the bit about the brothel, because I still didn't quite know what to make of it, but all about her hard life, the architect and the will.

'If someone has a protector, does that mean they are a courtesan, or a mistress?' I asked.

'I'm fairly blunt, so if you ask me questions, I'll likely answer them,' he said. 'Are you sure you want answers to questions that ladies shouldn't ask?'

'I wouldn't ask questions if I didn't want them answered,' I said. 'Are you suggesting I am not a lady?'

'God, no,' he said. 'Anyone with a hat your size must be. If a woman has a protector, she might be a courtesan, a mistress, a fancy-piece, a doxy or one of several other names. The rules aren't written down, as far as I know.'

'Should we be helping a woman who has a wanton past?' I said. He laughed again, but this time at me, so I didn't like it so much. Also, I realised I might be insulting my own mother.

'This world has a few double standards,' he said. 'If I've learnt anything through detective work, it's that real life is far less black and white than the church-going masses would like. I've no problem with helping her, as long as she's honest and can pay. I have more of a problem with the way she's asking us to do it.'

'Do you know anyone we can ask to get access to the ship?' I said. 'Mr Prout is a taxidermist at the museum – do you think we can ask him?'

'Best not muddle our cases,' Mr Blackthorn said. 'Although, you can tell Miss Turton that we've followed him for over a week, and nothing has come of it. He's a boring man, that's for sure, and he doesn't have any peccadilloes we can unearth. The most adventurous thing he does is stand on hills and birdwatch, and I do mean birds.'

I should feel happy at the thought of sharing the good news with Miss Turton. She was free to pursue her great romance. It was odd, but I had a strange inkling it was not what she wanted to hear.

'I shall let her know,' I said. 'But about the model ship. Wouldn't it be the simplest thing, just to break in and get it? Mrs Monk says that security is very lax.'

'No, it would be the very hardest option. Have you ever broken into a building? I'd like not to get involved in criminal activity, if I can avoid it. I'll ask around, make a plan. Leave it with me.'

Much as I liked Mr Blackthorn, there were times when he lacked a certain urgency. He had not yet done anything to find out about Evelina Joyce for me, and Mrs Monk had been waiting years for the will to be found. Surely the role of detective required a bit of impetus, of drive?

'Very well,' I said. 'But meanwhile, I shall go to the museum, and paint.'

'Paint?'

'Yes,' I said. 'Did I not tell you that I am an artist? And I happen to know that next Thursday is the day when people can go and sketch the exhibits. I shall go and examine the museum for you.'

'You surprise me each and every day,' he said. 'Very well, as I can't see how you can possibly get into trouble sketching. Go forth and sketch.'

I considered I could visit Miss Turton in my half-veil, without a chaperone, because it really was a splendid disguise.

'Well, that's marvellous,' she said, blinking back tears. 'I only cry because I am so happy. So... reassured. I am very grateful to you, for putting my worries to rest. Now I can marry Mr Prout in six months – goodness, is it only six months? – with all my worries quite laid to rest. So happy.'

A tear dripped onto her ginger snap biscuit, and her mouth was all turned down at the corners.

'Are you sure, Miss Turton, that you want to marry Mr Prout?'

'I am very aware,' she said, 'of his generosity in choosing me. Of course I want to marry him. Doesn't every woman want to get married? It is their dream. Of course I do. Now, how much do I owe you?'

And despite all my gentle encouragement, I could get nothing else from her but miserable delight.

Chapter Thirty-Nine

'Where did your mother go, the night she disappeared?' Mr Blackthorn asked. I was typing out some invoices for him, my fingers clacking speedily across the keys.

'We don't know,' I said. I explained she had said she was going to her friends for a recital but, when the police interviewed them, they said she had not arranged to meet them and they had gone to the Isle of Wight for the weekend.

'So where does the pier come in?'

'She was seen on the pier a few times that evening. But no one could quite tell who she was with. It was very crowded that evening, as they had fireworks on the seven hills, so everyone stood on the pier to watch them. Mrs Withers said she saw her with a woman. She didn't know who she was. Someone else said they saw her laughing by the bandstand with a man, later during the fireworks. But all we really know is that she didn't come home.'

'What kind of weather was it?'

'There was a beautiful sunset, people remarked on that. And then the night stayed fairly warm, and clear. There was no particular squall in the sea, it was all quite calm. The boats came in at the normal time with no trouble.'

'People have drowned off the coast,' he said. 'But not normally on a calm day. It's usually further along the coast, when those giant waves come in and catch you off guard, or if you're doing something stupid and leaping off places you shouldn't onto rocks. The idea of a fully dressed woman just falling off the pier without a splash or a shriek, no matter how busy it was, doesn't seem feasible. And there is that point about a body never being found, pardon me for saying it.'

'I know,' I said.

'And there's that bit about her being beautiful. It's odd that not more people noticed her. I imagine she had her fair share of admirers, as well as people who knew her. It seems odd that not more people noticed her that night.'

'Yes.'

'Was she unhappy, before that night? Would there be a reason for her to leave?'

'She was happier,' I said. 'In the last few months, she had seemed much happier. Before that she had been frustrated, I think. My father and her had not got along all that well, for several years before that. She wanted more out of life, I think, than being the wife of a bank manager in a small town.'

It was the first time I had said that last out loud, but of course it was true.

'Do you think she had met another man?' he asked.

'No, I don't think so,' I said. 'I don't think she would have had an affair.' I couldn't tell anybody why, but I knew in my heart of hearts that she wouldn't have wanted to go through the same torture again with a new man. He would have had new expectations, new demands.

'Why not?'

'She wasn't like that,' I said. Although from all the evidence, it would surely look as if she was. Had she lost her senses in those last months? But she had just seemed happy, and excited. A bit like my father was now, in fact, as if life had added sunshine to it. And my father's joy could be solely attributed to Mrs Beeton.

'Although,' I said. 'Thinking again about the happier part of it, it could be something to do with an affair. There could have been another man, I suppose. It's just...' Maybe this man had agreed to a platonic relationship at the outset, or somehow overcome the horror of it for her. He would have to have been a very understanding man indeed.

'Was there anyone you had seen her with, whom it could have been?'

'I don't think so,' I said. 'Why are you asking all these questions?'

'Just curious,' Benjamin said. I wondered for a second if he was developing the same fatal obsession as Mr Knight but, when I looked at him, he didn't have the same frenzied air.

'I've done a bit of searching about Evelina Joyce,' he said. 'I don't know the reason her name was on those photographs, but we can be reasonably certain she's not your mother. She's an actress, who tours around the country doing repertory theatre, vaudeville. She hasn't toured as much in the last few years, though, and annoyingly, I can't find a longer-term address for her. I'll keep searching.'

'Thank you,' I said. I resisted the urge to take his hand and shake it firmly in gratitude, like a gentleman. 'It is so strange. Do you think my mother wanted to be an actress like her?'

'Possibly,' he said. 'But I feel as if Evelina is the clue to all of this. Give me time.'

I would give him the time, because I knew he would use it well. 'I think that is the invoices done,' I said.

'Thank you,' he said, and his smile was so genuine I felt I had climbed a mountain.

As I was leaving, he gave me a pound note. 'What is this?' I said.

'It's payment,' he said. 'For the job you are doing. You work for me, you get paid.'

'You are giving me a post in your detective agency?'

'That might be taking it too far,' he said. 'I haven't put you on the books and I'm still mostly selling furniture. But let's call you a temporary assistant.'

It was good. It was definitely good. As I walked home, with my first payment from my first real employment in my pocket, I felt ten feet tall.

I wanted more, though. The knowledge came crashing over me on that mundane walk home, with the force of a giant wave, that I wanted nothing more in the whole wide world than to be a Lady Detective.

Chapter Forty

I was not satisfied with the outcome of my first case. It had left a bad taste, but what could I do? I could not force Miss Turton not to marry Mr Prout and his haddock, if she was so determined.

I concentrated instead on packing up my art equipment and visiting the museum. There, too, I felt I could quite safely travel without a chaperone, as wardens were there, ensuring everyone behaved.

Hastings Museum shared the same building as the public library, just across the hall. It was three floors of galleries. There was no particular order to the displays, but the ground floor was largely populated with stuffed animals. As Mr Prout was responsible for mounting them they each had their own slightly nightmarish quality, from goggly wild eyes to lopsided bodies.

The ship was on the ground floor, though, thank goodness, in a glass case towards the back wall. I spoke to the warden on duty on the floor, a blue-suited gentleman in a flat cap, to inform him of my intentions. Although sketching was permitted for everybody on a Thursday, it tended to be gentlemen who usually took up the mantle, so he huffed and puffed a little before reading out a formidable list of rules, which included keeping lead pencils well away from exhibits and not removing my bowler hat. Eventually, I set up my easel and sketch pad and got out my pencils.

I chose for my subject a cheetah set on a stand just slightly to the left of the ship. Its sad eyes told the shame of its stuffing. The ship, by contrast, was beautifully made and it was easy to imagine the real one, sailing the ocean waves. I tried to work out where the secret drawer was, without looking too directly at it.

I was a quick sketcher, so within half an hour I had got the cheetah and the ship on my page quite well. But then I realised I should be sketching a wider, landscape view, to include the curved stairwell in the corner that ran down to the basement, and the windows, so I crumpled the first one up. It was a plan of the gallery, of sorts, that was needed. I got to work.

There were no other people around today, on this floor at least, and not many visitors either. The warden wandered past at around eleven o'clock.

'Ah, that's...' he said, looking at my sketch. 'That's...' and then he walked off again and didn't come near me again all morning. I thought he demonstrated a lamentable lack of artistic appreciation.

Mr Blackthorn came too, at around twelve o'clock. He wandered in and around the gallery with his hands in his pockets and then stood slightly at right angles to me, so that it was not obvious we were talking.

'It's in a glass case,' he said. 'If it was on open display, maybe, but how would we get it out of a glass case?'

He was showing a low level of detective-like behaviour.

'It is locked,' I said in a low hiss. 'You can see the small lock on the side of the case, there. You would just need to pick a lock. I believe you can pick a lock?'

'Of course I can pick a lock,' he said. 'I'm just not sure it's worth getting arrested for. My God, what on earth are you drawing?'

'It is quite obviously a plan of this corner of the gallery,' I said. The warden was at the opposite end of the gallery, but he looked our way, so I made sure my back was turned to Mr Blackthorn and muttered through my teeth. 'Look, there's the ship and there's the cheetah.' I pointed with my pencil.

'Right,' Mr Blackthorn said. He turned his head and leant so that he was looking at the painting almost upside down. 'Is that a window?'

'No, that's the floor, quite clearly,' I said and then the warden appeared.

'Is this man bothering you?' he said.

'Yes, a little,' I said. 'He doesn't understand art.'

Mr Blackthorn didn't stay much longer after that, and part of me worried that I had been too pert with him. But his presence had been more of a hindrance than a help, and I had a job to do.

Chapter Forty-One

May was heading fast towards June, and it was hotter in town. The seafront was overflowing with flushed and burnt people, beset with a frenzied determination to enjoy themselves. I liked this time of year, when there were so many new people in town who did not know me. I was an anonymous lady, who could be judged only on the tilt of my hat on a particular day, and not on a great lumbering burden of a past. There was freedom to it.

'I plan to place an advertisement in the *Hastings Observer*,' Mr Knight said without preamble, as I entered his office. I shut the door quickly.

'An advertisement?'

'It is coming up to the anniversary,' he said. 'The tenth anniversary of her disappearance, the third of June. It would be a good idea to put an advertisement in the paper, asking if anyone knows anything. It might bring up some new leads, when events are less fresh. Tempers have cooled, things have moved on. People are more prepared to talk.'

'No,' I said. 'That isn't a good idea.'

'Or an article. I'll speak to the Editor, see if he would run an article, refresh people's minds. Publish her picture, talk about what happened. Not the private pictures, of course.'

'I have always said I wanted you to be discreet. That wouldn't be discreet. I don't want my father to know.'

'Ah, yes,' he said. 'Your father. Don't worry, I don't plan to tell him about you. You needn't be connected with the article in any way. It would be entirely normal for a newspaper to want to run an article on a ten-year anniversary.'

'I don't want you to,' I said. 'My father wouldn't want it. This is not what we agreed.'

'We are not partnering in this enterprise though, are we?' he said, with the small smile I was beginning to hate. 'You have hired me, as an expert, to find out what happened to your mother. The knowledge, the decisions of how to proceed, are all mine. You have no experience in these matters. Your role here is simply to trust me, purely to listen and to trust.' He stroked the corners of his desk, as if it was a pet.

I didn't trust him one iota. I wished I could tell him that I did have experience and I could likely pick a lock better than he could, but his supercilious expression was apparently welded to his face.

'Have you talked to the men who bought those photographs yet?'

'Yes,' he said. 'They did not say much that was useful, and I am no longer sure it is the right road to follow. The photographs are perhaps merely sad confirmation that your mother's character was not what it should be. I feel that the answers may lie in the reasons you left London. But either way, a piece in the newspaper will stir things up a bit, get people talking about her again. My instinct, I am afraid, is that she was murdered.'

Outside, I could hear a child screaming. It was a shame that so many children were brought to the seaside to have a pleasant time and then screamed when they got here.

'No,' I said. 'No, I don't think you are right.' I had thought about it too many times, but in my bones, or my waters, or whatever one liked to call it, I did not think she was dead. I felt there was something that happened to photographs of dead people, that you could see in their eyes, a dullness which showed their souls were no longer on this earth. In all the photographs of my mother she still looked vibrantly alive. I could not share something so fanciful with this detective.

'I think,' he said now, 'that if she were alive, she would have gone to this great love of hers, the one she had in London, that you mentioned. I don't suppose you have a name?'

'The man in the muffler? No, no name,' I said. 'But I have never said he was a great love. He was a nobody.' I was going on instinct again, rather than fact, but I was fairly certain that whatever burden this man had placed on my mother, it had lifted as soon as we moved to St Leonards. Why did Mr Knight think otherwise?

He frowned. 'Again, I am the detective here. I would ask you to stop leaping to conclusions like an untethered goat. This case needs my full focus and resolve, and so far you have proved more of a hindrance than a help. It is almost as if you do not want me to solve it.'

He was absolutely right. I didn't want him to solve it at all. He would ruin my reputation and my life along the way, and I could not bear the idea of the preening parrot he would become. I wanted Mr Blackthorn to solve it, a fine, upstanding detective with morals and a big smile, who listened to my ideas. The two detectives were as different as chicken soup and stewed tripe and I would choose chicken soup every time.

Chapter Forty-Two

I needed to speak to Mr Blackthorn. Unfortunately, when I arrived, he was in conversation with Mr Parchment, my erstwhile suitor. I came in the door, clocked them both and shot off to the left to hide behind the furniture. I was not in the mood for the Parchments of the world.

'Did someone come in?' I heard Mr Parchment say. He sounded puzzled.

'No,' Mr Blackthorn said. 'The door does sometimes blow open in the wind.' He went to close it. From there he had a direct line of sight to me, flattened behind a wardrobe. He raised his eyebrows and I shook my head at him, frantically.

'Can I ask,' Mr Parchment said, 'if you sell any fish in glass tanks, or animals?'

'No,' Mr Blackthorn said. 'Occasionally I do, but it depends on what comes through. My stock comes from auctions, house clearances, that kind of thing.'

'How about gout stools?'

'Gout stools?'

'For putting your feet up, when you have gout,' Mr Parchment said. 'They are shaped to accommodate the foot.'

'No, I do not have any of those.'

'Billiard accessories? Cue-racks, billiard balls, the like?'

'Not at the moment.'

'Bootscrapers? Those fancy ones, with the combination scraper and brush?'

'Mr Parchment,' Blackthorn said, 'am I right in thinking you are not looking to buy anything here, but are just working out what I don't sell, so that you can sell it yourself?'

I could almost hear Mr Parchment puff up. 'We are both businessmen. I am sure you will be looking for gaps in the market yourself. How about fenders?'

'I think you will find that due to the nature of my shop, if I sell any of those things, it will be a one-off and, quite likely, not new. You can rest assured there is plenty of room in East Sussex for both of us. Now, if you will excuse me, I am quite busy.'

'I am courting,' Mr Parchment said.

'Excuse me?'

'I am courting Miss Violet Hamilton, and I have heard that she has been visiting your shop. I just wanted to check if there is any understanding between you, any prior agreement. I will step aside if there is.'

'You seem somewhat misled,' Mr Blackthorn said. 'I believe Miss Hamilton may have visited my shop only once or twice, to select some furniture. Beyond that, I have no contact with her. Who told you this, out of interest?'

'It does not matter. It is only… I should not like to tread on toes.'

There was dust on the back of the wardrobe, and it was threatening to make me sneeze.

'No toes are trodden,' Mr Blackthorn said. 'But anyway,

it is no business of mine. I am expecting a delivery, at any moment, so it would perhaps be best to leave before you get trapped by furniture.'

'You didn't answer my question,' Mr Parchment said.

'Which one?'

'About fenders.'

'We have one for sale, cast iron, not cushioned, a little rusty. Now time for you to go,' Mr Blackthorn said, and I could sense him crowding out Mr Parchment like an advancing army until there was no option for him but to leave. The bell clanged again, and the door shut.

I fell out from behind the wardrobe and sneezed until my eyes watered.

'That's no way to treat a suitor,' Mr Blackthorn said. He sounded amused. 'Can I take it he's not top of your list?'

'We are not courting,' I said. 'I have put him off, twice now. How dare he say that we are. How dare he monitor my movements. How dare he.'

'It's clear this can't go on,' Mr Blackthorn said, thoughtfully. I stared at him, my heart in my mouth, as everything crumbled.

'You'll have to come in through the back yard,' he said. 'I'll give you a key. Try to be more inconspicuous. Wear your giant hat.'

'Thank you, Mr Blackthorn,' I said.

'I have another case for you,' he said. 'It's about wool, but hopefully you won't get in too much of a tangle.'

I am sure I looked like a labrador waiting for a treat.

'There's a small knitting shop on the corner of Cumberland Gardens and Dane Road, and the owner thinks that one of her customers is stealing her balls of wool. But she can't work out who it is. I wondered if you might want to go and work there for the day?'

'In a shop? Work in a shop?' I asked.

'Yes,' he said. 'Is that too low-class for the Lady Violet?'

'No,' I said. 'Is it another of Mr Knight's cast-offs?'

'Very good,' he said. 'Very good. Top points. Yes, it is. I don't know what Mr Knight is doing these days, but he's certainly not solving cases.'

'What day do you want me to start?'

'Thursday would be good. Her name is Mrs Cherry. Maybe pop along at around ten o'clock.'

I beamed at him in delight.

Chapter Forty-Three

'I realised we have never spoken properly about your mother's disappearance,' my father said that evening. It was just after dinner, and I had known all the way through it that he was planning to speak to me about something. He had spent it looking at me then at his plate, clearing his throat and frowning.

Ten years seemed a little late.

'It is my belief, it has always been my belief, that she tragically died,' he said, and I stared at him in shock.

'That isn't so,' I said. 'You have always been absolutely certain that she left us. You told me so, just a few days afterwards, and you've repeated it ever since. You said that she was bored by her life here, that she had not been a good wife and mother, and that the most likely scenario was that she had run off with someone else and left us. That's why you wouldn't speak of it.'

He shifted slightly uncomfortably in his chair.

'Underneath that,' he said, 'I have always been entirely convinced she is dead. I don't think she had the gumption, the ability to organise, to leave us. Plus, although I am perfectly aware she felt no deep attachment to me, I do think she was very fond of you. I don't think she would have left voluntarily. I think the thoughts of the police at the time, that she may have fallen in the sea and drowned, are entirely correct.

'I didn't want to upset you at the time,' he continued. 'Death seemed so much harder to bear.'

I narrowed my eyes.

'You want to get married,' I said. 'You want to marry Mrs Beeton.'

He coughed. 'It might be on the periphery of my consciousness. That has nothing to do with the fact that it is time for us to move on. You show an alarming propensity to hang onto the past, Violet. If she has left us – died, I mean – there is no reason for us to freeze our own lives forever. I have always said that we need to move on. If she died, would she want us to be mourning her forever? I do not think anyone would ask that of us.'

'But you can't. She might still be alive,' I said. 'You may still be a married man.'

'There is a procedure of getting someone declared dead,' he said. 'It might take a little while, but it's possible after ten years. They might reopen the investigation for a bit, make sure there are no new leads to be uncovered. I think we are safe there, though. I don't think there is anything new to find.'

'But if we do that,' I said, 'aren't we letting her down? When she might be out there, hoping we will find her?'

'You have to let her go,' he said. 'I have. I let her go before she left. Don't ruin it for me, Violet. She was no good for either of us. We both have a chance of happiness, but we can only do that if we lay the past to rest. I'm going to speak to a solicitor tomorrow, work out where the land lies.'

At least he was talking to me about it. A few months ago, he might not have. Mrs Beeton was having a good effect on him, making him human. I could easily see why he would want to grab a new chance at happiness with her.

The difficulty was that I had already unleashed whatever demons lay in his past, in the form of Mr Knight.

Chapter Forty-Four

Thursday came, and I hoped to spend it gently unravelling the problem of wool. Mrs Cherry was a lovely lady, but possibly aged around a hundred and three, so it was not a complete surprise that someone had been stealing from her.

'The police won't help me,' she said. 'They've said they'd have to police the shop all day, and they can't do that. It's just that it's some of my best wool, the alpaca, the angora, and in such lovely colours too. Purple, dark green, sage, rose pink, yellow gold. I try to keep an eye on things, but my legs get tired, and I like to make a cup of tea in the back and rest them.'

'I am here to sort things out for you,' I said. 'Rest assured, if anyone can solve your case, I can. I am very nearly a Lady Detective, you know.' It was not quite true, but I hoped she wouldn't tell anyone.

'Well, that's nice,' she said. 'Would you like a cup of tea?'

It was the best kind of day. She talked me through all her wools, and told me where they came from, and then she showed me how to knit. I was terrible at it and made a great lumpy patch of nothingness, but then she gave it to me and told me to use it as a doily, and I was enormously proud. She was knitting a very intricate jumper, in a Shetland pattern, and her needles moved so fast they were almost a blur.

It was a fairly busy shop, with people coming and going. Most of them she seemed to know. I stationed myself near the door, lounging casually, until Mrs Cherry said I looked a bit threatening, looming over people like that, and wouldn't it be better if I sat on a stool by the counter near her, and knitted. That was when she taught me to knit.

Most of the people who came in wouldn't dream of stealing from her. They had known her and shopped there for years, and it was obvious they cared about her. Some stayed and chatted about their families, others asked for her advice on their patterns. Most of them I could rule out for that reason, although I still watched them like a hawk. I asked Mrs Cherry to elbow me in the ribs if anyone who hadn't been coming for years came in, which she could do quite easily while knitting, without arousing suspicion. There were several new people, but no one showed any sign of thieving tendencies.

She closed the shop at twelve-thirty and made me lunch, ham and cress sandwiches and a piece of carrot cake, and then we went back on surveillance duty at one-thirty on the dot.

Nothing suspicious of any kind happened until four o'clock, when Hildebrand, the girl from the brothel, came in.

I didn't realise it was her at first because she was dressed – in a dark woollen gown and jacket. Mrs Cherry elbowed me in the ribs, which was getting painful, as her elbow was quite sharp. It was not until Hildebrand turned in the light from the window that I recognised her face.

'Have you seen her before?' I hissed in Mrs Cherry's ear.

'A few times over the last few months,' she whispered back. 'She bought a few balls of the blue lamb's wool.' It was a strange sensation, having someone whisper so many 'b's in my ear.

Hildebrand wandered around, picked up balls of wool and put them down again. She didn't see me. She perused a knitting pattern of baby clothes, I noticed. There were a few other customers in as well, so I was keeping busy watching them all, but I watched her the most. I felt guilty for suspecting her, just because I knew what she did for a living.

She did it so quickly, I nearly missed it. She picked up two balls of red merino wool and put them inside her jacket, in front of her bosom, one on each side, so that it just made her more well-endowed, and then she strolled towards the door as if she had all the time in the world.

I got there first. I shut the door with my back to it, and locked it, and then it was just me, Hildebrand, Mrs Cherry and five other puzzled customers trapped in the shop.

I took her arm and marched her to the back. 'You can let the other customers out now, Mrs Cherry,' I said, once she was safely cornered behind the counter. Mrs Cherry got up and let them out.

'Show me your bosom,' I said to Hildebrand, who sniggered. 'I mean, open your jacket and show me the wool that's in there.'

'Aren't you the girl who came about the pearl?' she said. 'Do you work here now?'

'I am almost a Lady Detective,' I said. 'And I have caught you in the act of stealing wool. How much have you stolen in the past few months? How could you steal from a little old lady who has loved and supported this community for centuries?'

'I'm not that old, dear,' Mrs Cherry said behind me.

'I apologise, Mrs Cherry,' I said. 'For decades. Have you been pawning this wool too?'

'No,' Hildebrand said, 'I've been knitting. A blanket. I am sorry, Mrs Cherry,' she said, looking past me. 'I used to knit when I was a child, when life was happier, and it always comforts me. I don't get enough money for wool, where I work. I didn't mean to keep stealing, it was only a ball or two at first, but then – it's a blanket, so you need more, don't you. I'm really sorry. It's the only good thing I do in life, knitting.'

I thought back to Tibbs, and those fists. 'How does Tibbs treat you, Hildebrand?'

'Very well, she protects us all,' she said, but there was that look in her eyes again, that I didn't like.

'I tell you what, Mrs Cherry,' she said. 'The blanket's nearly done. How about I bring it back, and then you can have it, and everything's even? The knitting is the bit I love, for me. I don't need the blanket. It's just something I do, to take my mind off.'

'Off what, dear?' Mrs Cherry said.

'Off… life,' Hildebrand said. She shrugged her shoulders, as if she didn't care.

'That sounds like a good deal to me,' Mrs Cherry said. 'Do you need those last two balls of red? Here you go then, and I'll expect you back soon.' She was obviously too soft to run a shop. She handed back the wool, and Hildebrand's eyes filled with tears.

'Thanks,' she said. 'Can I go now?'

'You can go, if you promise not to do this again,' I said

severely. I was not sure of my authority now that my client had given the criminal some free wool.

'I promise,' Hildebrand said, and then she went and let herself out of the shop.

'You'll never see her again,' I said. 'But I do know where she lives.' Not that I relished the thought of going back there. Mrs Cherry smiled at me.

'Thank you for solving my case,' she said.

'Will you let me know, if she comes back?' I asked.

'Of course,' she said. 'I'm glad it was a nice girl, and not someone nasty.'

Chapter Forty-Five

Breaking into the museum was seeming easier every day. There was no security guard at night, Mackenzie had discovered, perhaps because nobody wanted to steal tortured animals. There was also a window with a broken latch on the ground floor at the back. He was proving to be a good ally.

For the first time I had a small contretemps with Mr Blackthorn.

I had found a day when he was in a good mood, which to be fair was most nowadays. Another aspect I liked about him was that he did not indiscriminately fling his moods about, as other people did. If my father was in a bad mood, for example, it was likely he would create a storm and expect other people to weather it out. Or if he was happy, everyone around him would be expected to laugh along, no matter if they were feeling rotten themselves. Even if Mr Blackthorn was having a tough day, he kept his moods to himself.

'No,' he said. 'We are not doing it that way. It's not the way my father would have done it. Following people, yes; breaking and entering, no.'

'But we are not actually stealing anything,' I said. 'We are just removing something that no one knows is there anyway.'

'I'll put an official research request in to the Trustees to examine the object,' he said. 'I can tell them I'm studying ships, or something. It might take a few weeks, but that'll be the best way to do it. Then I'll see if I can be left alone with it for a while.'

I was very disappointed in Mr Blackthorn. He was showing a lack of forward momentum. Mrs Monk had been waiting years, and it seemed only reasonable that we should solve her case quickly, rather than keep her hanging about.

'You are a respectable, unmarried woman, Violet. This is not something I can allow you to do,' he continued. 'Imagine if you were caught inside the museum? Imagine if you were arrested, or came to some harm? I would never forgive myself.'

'It just seems so easy,' I said. 'A matter of slipping in and out. No one will ever know. And if I'm dressed as a man, no one will think that it could be me, Violet Hamilton, spinster of this parish. And if, by any unlikely chance, I was caught, I could just say that I had lost my wits and had a passion for exploring museums. No one would call me a thief. I want to try this. I want to do this. Please don't try to stop me.'

'Violet.' He ran his hand over his face, put his head in his hands, and I waited, holding my breath, until he lifted it, his face wearing an expression of grim resolution.

'You are going to do this foolish thing, aren't you?' he said. 'Whether I say yes or no?'

'Yes,' I said, in a very small voice.

He had read me correctly, as always. Because this felt like the adventure I needed, to prove myself. It was linked to feeling as if I was a useful sort of person, who could achieve things.

'You are the most infuriating female I've ever met.' He gave a great sigh. 'You have exploded into my life and… very well. Very well. If you want to do this blasted thing and make yourself a criminal, we will do it together.'

'Oh, Mr Blackthorn, thank you,' I said, and I picked up one of his big hands in both of mine and kissed his knuckles, like a page to his liege. I had not thought it through, admittedly, and neither of us had gloves on, so I gave him his hand back quite awkwardly afterwards. He stared at me, momentarily.

'Let's do it quickly, before I change my mind,' he said. 'Tomorrow night, I'll meet you at midnight. Do you need clothing?'

'Mr Mackenzie said I could borrow his,' I said. 'As we are roughly the same size. You will be too big for me.'

'You've planned it all,' he said. 'Make sure your shoes are good for running in. Bundle your hair securely so it doesn't fall down. Christ, I must be going insane.'

Chapter Forty-Six

Mackenzie's clothing consisted of brown worsted trousers, a shirt, a tweed jacket and a flat cap. They all smelt faintly of cigarettes. I thought I made quite a good man, after I had swaggered up and down my bedroom a few times. A little on the short side, perhaps, but then so was Mackenzie, and it was better for burglary. Mr Blackthorn with his great loomingness had more to worry about.

I crept out of the house by the back door, not worrying too much about being seen. Even though our stairs creaked, my father usually slept heavily. It was a cloudy night, which felt good for the task. The streets were empty and I enjoyed slinking along them, keeping close to the houses and feeling like a spy. I was slightly terrified, but I kept reminding myself that detectives had no room for fear.

We had arranged to meet at the North Lodge, the gothic tollgate that spanned Upper Maze Hill, not far from the crescent where I lived. As I arrived an owl hooted, and I jumped out of my skin, before scolding myself severely. If I was going to be a man for the night, I would not ruin the opportunity by startling at shadows.

That said, I was hugely relieved when Mr Blackthorn appeared out of the darkness silently and nodded grimly at me. 'Let's to it,' he said, and he led the way downhill, zig-zagging smoothly from street to street so fast I had to run to catch up with him.

'Slow down!' I whispered at one point, and he stopped so abruptly that I careered into the back of him. He was wearing a woollen coat that smelt of coffee, sawdust and a clean-spice essence that must be him. He reached back and pulled me alongside him, then he took my hand.

'Stay with me,' he said, and he kept hold of it all the way.

It was possible to reach the museum from the back via a little alleyway. We could see enough, despite there being no moon. He had brought a crowbar as well as other assorted tools, and although it required clambering up onto the wide windowsill first, it was an easy enough job for him to prise up the window Mackenzie had told us had a broken latch. It opened with a slight screech, and a crow or a jackdaw shot off from the roof above us into the sky, cawing with indignation. We froze for a second, but all was silent.

I climbed in first, with Mr Blackthorn giving me a gentle shove up. I tried not to notice his hands on my person. It was pitch black, and I landed on a wooden floor. He landed behind me, quiet as a tiger. I heard a spark striking, and eventually he managed to light a small lantern. We were in a back corridor of the museum, and there were three doors off it, which hopefully all led to the ground-floor galleries.

I chose the middle one. It opened as loudly as a door would

in the daytime, and I clutched Mr Blackthorn's arm. 'Stay calm,' he whispered. His breath tickled my ear. We waited and again all was silent. It was not far to the case holding the ship. I gave a small yelp when I came face to face with the cheetah, as it looked even more anguished by the light of a lantern.

'Shh,' Mr Blackthorn said, and then he set about picking the lock on the case. In only a few seconds it was open, and I had access to the ship. I set to work trying to prise open the secret drawer, but it proved surprisingly difficult.

'The captain's mess is aft, Mrs Monk said,' I hissed to Mr Blackthorn. 'Which end is aft?'

'The other end,' he said.

There was a great crash and we jumped. I found myself clutching his arm.

'It's only thunder,' he whispered, and there was a flash of light and another crash.

Mrs Monk had told me that the key to opening the door was to stick a pin in a tiny hole in the ship, but it was proving difficult to see. 'I'll need to turn the ship around,' I said. Luckily it wasn't fixed to its stand, but it was quite heavy for a ship. It might have been the fake guns on the deck. We rotated it eventually, and then by the light of the lantern and the lightning I found the tiny hole, took out a hairpin and manoeuvred it in. Like a miracle, a flat section of the ship swung out from the hull.

'There!' Mr Blackthorn said, and sure enough there lay a small envelope. It did not look very big, for a will. I hid it inside my inside jacket pocket anyway, and then I shut the drawer and we closed up the case as best we could. It was not possible to lock it again.

I patted the cheetah on the head on the way out.

'I'm sorry,' I whispered, 'for all that was done to you.' It was possible it looked a little less upset.

'Haste yourself,' Mr Blackthorn said, and then we were out into the corridor again and climbing out the window. It wasn't possible to close that properly either, as it seemed to have wedged itself open, but it didn't really matter as we were free and clear.

The heavens opened, and we were soaked in seconds.

'Run!' Mr Blackthorn said, and he took my hand again and we sped all the way to Mrs Monk's house. I kept my hand over my inside pocket to keep the letter dry. It was a glorious run, even though it was uphill and we were drenched. I felt free and alive and full of a heady elation that came from beating the elements and committing criminal acts without being caught.

'I am so, so grateful to you both,' Maria said. Rose had brought towels for us and I was drying myself by the fire. Mr Blackthorn was waiting in the hall, as Mrs Monk was not dressed for visitors.

'The letter isn't very large for a will,' I said. 'But I hope it contains what you need.'

She looked the most relaxed I had seen her, in a red velvet dressing robe. She smiled.

'It isn't a will,' she said. 'It's a love letter. I have all the money I need to survive. But he always said that he would leave me his heart, and now I have it here. I will not read it until you have gone, if you will forgive me.'

'You lied to me again,' I said.

'Lying is not one of the seven deadly sins. I did not think that people would help me so readily for something as trivial as a love letter. Maybe that is just my cynical view. But this means far, far more than any will. I can make money however I have to. It is much harder to find someone who loves you. He did, and now I have this to remind me, I am content.'

'My mother found it very easy to be loved,' I said. 'Everyone loved her without asking. She often found it funny.'

'Well, perhaps for that reason she valued it very much less than I do,' Maria said. 'One is enough for me. And you, Violet – are you loved?'

'Definitely by the Reverend Bartle,' I said, 'in a priestly, fatherly way of course. Beyond that... beyond that... I must be getting home, before it starts to get light.'

'Please thank your detective for me,' Maria said.

'He isn't mine,' I said. 'I have another one. But I do like Mr Blackthorn better.'

Mr Blackthorn walked me home, slowly this time, as he confessed that his leg still wasn't used to all the exercise. 'I'll regret it in the morning,' he said.

I wouldn't regret anything. I was suddenly deliriously, wonderfully happy. It had been the best night I had ever had in my life. I felt powerful, adventurous, daring, and alive.

'Do you think I could be a Lady Detective one day, Mr Blackthorn?' I said, as we reached the end of my street.

'I think you can be anything you like,' he said. 'And call me Benjamin in private, for goodness sake. I won't tell anyone, if you don't.'

If anyone heard us use our first names, they might think we were lovers. It was a truly shocking lapse of formality. It felt dangerous, and illicit. I realised I didn't care.

Chapter Forty-Seven

After that excitement, church seemed a terrible chore. But with the likes of Mrs Withers in the world, it was impossible not to go. There were scores of churches of different denominations across Hastings and St Leonards, so I toyed with the idea of pretending I was attending the Holy Redeemer Catholic Church, or the Greek Orthodox Church of Saint Mary Magdalene, but that might upset Reverend Bartle. To be fair, I liked him and his sermons. It was other members of the congregation I wanted to avoid.

The hymns were nice though, as always. My father was there, with his big deep baritone, and there were a few others around me with loud voices too, so I gave 'Onward Christian Soldiers' my full fighting power and squeaked a little to reach the high notes in 'Amazing Grace', particularly the part about sparing wretches.

During the sermon I noticed Dr Patmore sitting across the aisle from us. I was sure I had not seen him here before. There was usually another family there, although I could not remember at all who they were or what they looked like, even though I had gone to the same church all my life. One of them may have had a squint.

I liked Dr Patmore least of all the men who had been thrust upon me. It was perhaps because I had briefly thought him handsome. He should have no need to buy dirty pictures of my mother. He should have the decency to go out and find his own, real woman and ask to see her in her undergarments once they were married. He turned his head round and smiled at me and I pursed my lips as tightly as a raspberry and turned my head to the front.

Mrs Withers got me trapped at the end of my pew after service. My father had escaped, but I was sure she had told some ladies at the other end to hold their position so that I could not.

'Miss Hamilton,' she said. 'You look tired. I hope you have not been taking too much fresh air.'

'Fresh air is good for you,' I said. 'Is it possible to have too much?' She frowned in a way that could not be good for her wrinkles.

'It is only that I could have sworn I saw you running, the other day, through town. Was there some calamity? Ladies do not usually run.'

'Mrs Withers,' I said. I looked from side to side and then stepped back further along the pew, as if inviting her to share a confidence. She followed me in, and then by good fortune a group of people stopped at her end, preventing her from leaving. It was tit for tat.

'You saw my mother on the night she disappeared, didn't you?'

'Yes,' she said. A spasm that almost looked like nervousness flashed across her face.

'Can you remember who she was with?'

'Why do you ask?'

'Just idle curiosity,' I said. 'It has been on my mind, as it has been nearly ten years, you know.'

'She was with a woman, arm in arm,' she said. 'A woman with lots of paint on her face, no better than she should be. They were walking along the pier, happy as anything, the pair of them, laughing at goodness knows what, not a thought to say hello to anyone they knew. They passed me by as if I was nobody.'

'Was that her crime, not saying hello, or was it that she was happy?' I said. Her end of the pew became empty and her husband materialised at her side. He would have made a good war spy, I thought.

'Manners cost nothing,' Mrs Withers said sharply. Her husband pulled at her elbow and she turned to go.

'Rudeness is also free,' I said, but they had gone, the pair of them, down the aisle and out the door. Mr Withers was good at making his wife disappear.

As I watched them depart, a dark figure loomed over me. Apparently Dr Patmore had crossed the aisle. He bowed with a flourish. 'Miss Hamilton,' he said. 'Delighted. How is your mission?'

What did he know about me? What had he found out?

'My mission?'

'Yes,' he said. 'You said that you hurt your cheek when you were working at the mission. I am pleased to see it has recovered its bloom.'

'Ah, yes. I am fully recovered, thank you.' I had absolutely nothing else to say to him. Any conversation we could have was not suitable for church.

'Can I just say,' he said, 'and I hope you will not be offended, but... you look like your mother. I was young when she disappeared, but I do remember her. And you have the same beautiful smile she had, the same turn of your head.'

'No,' I said, 'I don't.'

'You do,' he said. 'She had very fine, arched eyebrows, and I see you do too. I hope it will comfort you to know that.'

'No, I don't, and it doesn't,' I said. How much was he trying to compare below the neck too? Maybe he was about to say I had a larger chest.

'Forgive me,' he seemed puzzled. 'Do you not take it as a compliment? It must please your father, to see so many echoes of his wife in his daughter.'

There was so much wrong with that, I didn't know where to start.

'Dr Patmore,' I said. 'Please stop. I don't need any compliments from you. At present, we are wholly unconnected with each other, beyond my father's wish for you to look into his eyes. I would prefer it remained that way.'

I curtseyed sharply at him and left the church. He no doubt thought me very odd, but it did not matter. He had ruined any chance I had of finding spiritual succour.

I found the Reverend Bartle heading towards his garden. He was in cheerful good humour.

'I planted a whole row of cabbages,' he said, 'and most of them have survived this year. The trick with slugs is to bury a glass with half a pint of beer in it at either end of the row and then they fall into it and drown. And I also went out a few times at night with a candle and plucked them off. Would you like some cabbage?'

'No thank you,' I said. My loathing of cabbage was not

widely known in society. 'What do you think my father would say, if I took employment?'

'It depends on the type of employment,' he said. 'What are you thinking of?'

'Oh – this and that. Lady typist, perhaps.'

'Well, your father may not mind in the short term, but it is more a question for your husband, when you get married. I think most men find it acceptable for their wives to have some small, useful employment before marriage, but would prefer they give it up afterwards and concentrate on the family,' he said. 'Some husbands are happy for them to continue, if it does not impinge on the household. It really depends on the person you marry, Violet, so do choose wisely, and discuss this with your intended before you head to the altar. But if he is a modern young man, he can have no real objection in your helping to ease the burden of income before the advent of children.'

I had not factored a husband into the equation at all, but some concepts, like voluntary spinsterhood, were too much for my gentle friend. I left him to his cabbages.

Chapter Forty-Eight

The article covered a quarter of a page, on the bottom right-hand corner, three pages into the *Hastings Observer*. There was no way my father could miss it. I saw it myself, from upside down, as he was reading it over breakfast. It was the photograph of her in the giant feathered hat, with the fox fur. Perhaps my father would not recognise her.

It was a foolish hope. I saw his face change, tighten, and he spent an eternity reading it, while my insides dissolved into dust. Then he stood up and flung it aside.

'I'm going to kill him,' he said. 'Violet, there is a filthy article in the paper about your mother. I'm going to kill the Editor. There is no reason at all to be raking up the past, no reason at all. He didn't even speak to me before running it.'

'Ah… what are you going to do next?' I said.

'I am going to speak to the Editor,' he said, 'and find out what this article is about. And why he didn't consult me.'

'That's understandable,' I said. My father glowered at me, picked up the paper and began to charge out the door.

'Do you need that, to wave at the Editor? There will

probably be plenty of copies in the newspaper offices too,' I said. 'Would you let me read it?'

'Have it,' he said, throwing it on the table, and then he was gone out the door, with barely enough time to put on his coat and shoes.

I sat back and drank my coffee. I had switched from tea to coffee these days. It was a more businesslike drink.

I was surprised I was so calm, when my life might topple at any moment. There was very little, in fact, that I could do, except read the article.

There was something heartfelt and lyrical about it. It talked about the tragedy of her disappearance, her beauty, her kindness, the eternal pain of the husband and young daughter left behind. She would have been heartbroken to leave. There was very little in the way of new facts, beyond a plea to contact the newspaper with any information. The article itself did not cause me any difficulty. The Editor was unlikely to tell my father much, because I had written it for him, on pain of absolute confidentiality.

I had not been prepared to let Mr Knight get in first with whatever idiocy he planned to run. I wanted to tell the story of my mother's disappearance in my own words, show her for who she was and not who he thought her. If it was in my words I would not need to worry about his. And the Editor had asked me to write it a couple of months back, after all.

I was quite proud of my first published article. Perhaps there was hope for me as a writer yet. My only niggling concern was how Mr Knight might react to being pipped at the post.

Chapter Forty-Nine

It was around this time life got a little more complicated.

I hadn't felt quite myself since my night-time excursion with Benjamin. I had been having night-time dreams, and daytime imaginings, about an unavailable man that were not what I should be having at all. There was definitely flesh-to-flesh contact involved, more so at night when I was asleep and not in control of my thoughts, but also sometimes during the day, when my brain should know better. It was disturbing and confusing, because my brain didn't know exactly what to dream about, so it was all sensation and waking up in a hot sweat, wanting more. It was hugely unsatisfactory and beyond wicked. It had to stop.

Accordingly, a few days after the adventure I went for a great long walk up West Hill. Every time I thought about Benjamin, I made myself do some form of vigorous exercise – swinging my arms about, jumping up and down – until I stopped. Self-punishment, I had decided, was the only way I could get my wayward self under control. If that didn't work, I was going to go to the Hydropathic Establishment and get them to direct a cold hose at me for as long as it took.

Today, there was quite a bit of vigorous exercise required, so when I reached the top I was completely out of breath and needed to sit down. Unfortunately, Septimus Patmore was sitting on my bench. I had seen him at church only the day before when he had told me I looked like my mother, so I did not relish seeing him again so soon.

It was not my bench, I suppose, but it was the one that I had sat on for three days in a row when I was stalking Mr Prout. I could not help but think Dr Patmore had known I was heading up here, and had somehow managed to get ahead of me, but he did not look out of breath.

'Miss Hamilton,' he said. 'Do join me.'

'How did you get up here?' I said.

'I took the lift,' he said. It was so like me to forget that there was a lift that took you right up the hill in approximately five minutes.

'Ah,' I said. 'Well, must carry on. Still more hills to climb.'

'No, join me, Miss Hamilton,' he said. He looked a little like a comedy villain you might see on the stage, all in black with a green velvet waistcoat and his shirt collar points turned upwards. He was still handsome, but of course I could not see that aspect any more.

'I—'

But he rose, smoothly, and blocked the path, so I had no polite option but to sit next to him on the bench.

'You look very fetching,' he said.

Fetching what? 'Thank you,' I said. 'Well, time waits for no woman…'

'Your shyness is endearing,' he said. 'Your innocence is enchanting. You, are, I think, in sore need of wooing by a man who knows how to woo.'

He looked deeply into my eyes and quirked up his mouth in tender affection, leaning forward with intent. I shot backwards to the end of the bench.

'You needn't be frightened,' he said. 'I have honourable intentions. I am a very successful surgeon.'

'Are you going to operate on me?' I said, and he shook his head with irritation.

'No, I mean I have good prospects. Come here. You look like a woman who needs to be soundly kissed. I will kiss all your nonsense away. Come.' He slid along the bench towards me, and I leapt up.

'Stop that right now,' I said. 'Be warned. I've quite had enough of you. You are – you are a deviant.'

'So, the apple doesn't fall far from the tree, does it?' he said. He sat back on the bench and spread his arm along the back, quite at ease. 'Did your mother teach you that insult?'

'No,' I said. 'I read it in a book. If you do not let me go, now, without any fuss, then I shall tell my father about your behaviour. I know you bought private photographs of my mother.'

'Actually, I didn't buy them,' he said. 'Mr Knight gave them to me. He thought I might like them. I do. But I'd quite like to sample the real thing, too. And I'll gladly tell your father exactly what your mother got up to, if you're going to be difficult about it.'

'He gave them to you?' I sat back on the bench in shock. 'Why would he give them to you? When?'

'A few weeks past,' he said. 'He owes me a few favours. He's fond of a bit of cocaine now and then, and I get it in bulk for my eye operations. It numbs the pain. Mind you, Farnham orders more, and if I'd known I could have gone direct.'

That explained Farnham's twitchiness. I had read in the paper that too much cocaine made you feel like you had ants running under your skin. It didn't sound like a drug that should be legal. But that meant… that Mr Knight was betraying me, betraying my mother. I had to fire him, properly. He couldn't stay working for me if he was showing her photographs around indiscriminately, sharing them for titillation. He had to be stopped.

'Well, thank you for letting me know,' I said, standing up again. 'I must decline your request for more.' Was it marriage or something illicit he was asking for?

'Violet,' he said, and that was completely out of order, because we were definitely not lovers and never would be. 'You are not in a position to set the rules here. You'll go when I'm ready for you to go. I realise now it was unnecessary to court you in the proper way. You're not suitable for a wife. But I'd like to see if you're as saucy as your mother when you get going, so I'll have a bit of bed sport instead. I'm a handsome chap, you'd like me well enough once we got between the sheets.'

Bed sport? What was that? Did people do sport, in bed, before they actually did whatever it was came next, with the mushrooms? What kind of sport? I could feel my ignorance overwhelming me. Would I ever understand?

'I am not inclined to partake in any sporting activities in a bed,' I said. 'I have to go now. I will not waste time cogitating on what you have said. I think perhaps it would be best if you found yourself another woman, who actually liked you.'

'I like a challenge,' he said. 'I'm bored of paying women to be biddable. Rest assured, you'll be in my bed before long, for free, and if there's a bit of wrestling in it, all the better.'

Wrestling? Next he would bring tennis into it. It was all too much. I left him there on the hillside. He did not seem bothered by my rudeness. He stayed seated on the bench, looking out across the vista of Hastings and St Leonards below. He was right about himself, in that he was a very handsome man. It was a shame he was a complete bounder as well. What on earth was I to do about him?

Chapter Fifty

When I got home, Mr Parchment was in the parlour with my father, who was looking very confused. They had obviously been making painful conversation for some time.

'I don't know a great deal about waistcoats,' my father was saying, 'but your range does sound impressive. I did not know they could come in so many colours and patterns. I shall certainly consider your vest for golfing.'

'Ask for the single-breasted woollen golf vest edged with braid,' Mr Parchment said. 'That is the height of fashion nowadays. Or the Newmarket collarless checked waistcoats. Both are good for the outdoors.'

'Violet, you are back,' my father said. 'This young man is here to see you. I did not know you were still… acquainted.'

'Apparently so,' I said. I sat down on a chair, folded my arms and frowned at Mr Parchment.

'Well, I'll leave you two young people to it,' my father said and, good as his word, he was gone.

'Why are you here?' I said.

'I feel our acquaintance has been beset with misunderstandings,' Mr Parchment said. 'I thought perhaps we could renew our friendship and start again, on an honest, open footing.'

'I am not my mother,' I said. Things couldn't get more open than that.

'Yes, I know that,' he said. 'I am greatly sorry for your loss, but I do feel you are a little... obsessed with her. It might not be entirely healthy.'

'Obsessed? Me? It is you,' I said. 'It is you who is obsessed with her. You only courted me in the first place because of her.'

'That isn't true, Miss Hamilton,' he said. 'I knew of your mother's disappearance, of course, it is well known. But why would that affect my courting of you, except beyond a natural sadness for your loss?'

'You thought I had loose morals,' I said. 'Perhaps you have seen the pictures.' I suddenly felt less certain of myself. He seemed, today, not quite so ridiculous as he had at times. There was a dignity about him.

'I have never thought any such thing,' he said. 'And I do not know about any pictures. Your father invited me over, with the intention perhaps that I meet you. I was quite taken with you, although perhaps a little nervous at first about the speed at which things progressed. Your mother has very little to do with it, apart from my concern that you talk about her every time we meet. Do you think, perhaps, you are not quite recovered from her loss?'

'What are necessary things?' I said.

'I beg your pardon?'

'When we first met, you said you sold necessary things. What are they?'

'There are many necessary things for ladies,' he said.

'Sewing kits, shoelaces, buttons and suchlike. Many of them are for sale in our haberdashery department.'

'Not bloomer elastic?' I said and when he blushed red and shook his head, speechless, I knew I had done him a great wrong. But still—

'When we went for a walk that first day, where were you taking me?'

'Just to the promenade,' he said. 'I thought I might buy you an ice.'

'Mr Parchment,' I said, 'Mr Parchment,' and I wanted to cry, because I had done him a great disservice, and the contrast between him and the evil Septimus Patmore was too much to bear. I realised I had read Mr Parchment's shock on the beach in the wrong way. He had not known anything bad about my mother, and had not thought I might be free with my favours because of it.

'Miss Hamilton,' he said, his eyes as worried as the Reverend Bartle's, 'are you feeling distressed? Is it that... is it that I have a rival?'

'No, of course not,' I said.

'I did go to Mr Blackthorn's shop,' he said, 'because my mother said she had seen you go in there twice. But it was foolish of me to be jealous, just because she said you would prefer a taller man.'

'Your mother is not kind to you,' I said. 'Mr Parchment, I am sorry. I am sorry I have treated you badly. I am not a very good candidate for marriage, really, I am not. I am extremely foolish, and I am really not very domesticated. Sometimes, I pretend to do charity work, when I have never done any in my life.'

'You keep telling me of your defects,' he said. 'I am not convinced.'

He was so earnest and straightforward. Part of me wanted desperately to please him, because he was good, and I had been awful to him, and because if he didn't care about my mother, then that must mean he cared about me. About me, alone. Which was a wonder in itself.

But there was no attraction. And as I was currently fighting bewilderingly warm feelings for somebody else, which might, perhaps, be classed as attraction, I could not waste that chance on Mr Parchment.

'We would not suit,' I said. 'I have a lot of things to work out in my head, and I am not sure yet if I want to get married at all.'

It did not look as if that was going to work, so I took the final step. 'It is also my ambition,' I said, 'to become a Lady Detective.'

I think that helped him. I hoped it helped him. He went away slightly less upset, I think, after that.

Chapter Fifty-One

If Jeremy Parchment had liked me for me, then how many other men had I maligned over the years? It did not bear thinking about. I realised that for a long time I had always thought of myself in terms of what I was not, rather than what I was. I did not have my mother's melting green eyes, her cupid's bow lips, her lean elegance, that luxuriant red-tinged hair. Looking in the mirror the next morning though, I still had all the component parts of a face. It was not unattractive. And although my mother was beautiful when her face was in repose, it was the fleeting expressions that had crossed it – the winsome smiles, the sideways glances – that had made it more appealing. I had never seen my face in regular motion.

If I even had a sliver of my mother's charm, it opened up… possibilities. There was a power in it. I had watched her wield it on more than one occasion. How much more effective could I be in detective work, if I could add in a dose of charm as well? I thought of Cleopatra, wooing Caesar, and Salome with her veils. It was wondrous, and frightening. I might need to practise a bit at first, because for too long I had regarded myself as a wooden doll beside my mother. I would need to think about who I could practise on.

Edith was unhappy with me. I realised this because she was supposed to be polishing our shoes but left them in a giant pile at the bottom of the stairs instead, so that I tripped over them.

I found her in the laundry cupboard, smoking. When she saw me, she dropped the cigarette on the floor and ground it out with the heel of her boot.

'Ah Edith, I did wonder why our linen was smelling a bit odd,' I said.

'You can't run a household,' she said. 'You and your father never notice if things are clean or not, and you take no pride keeping a proper house. You're always out, running about, chasing the men.'

'Yes, that's true,' I said. 'Apart from chasing men. I only follow them. But surely, it's easier for you, that I don't care so much? Other women might work you to the bone from dawn till dusk, and we only have a proper clean once every two months.'

'That's it as well. That's no way to do things. It upsets me, that you don't take pride in keeping your home. That's not how a proper woman should be. It's unnatural. I wouldn't normally talk so, but you're not even annoyed that I'm here, smoking in the laundry. I have standards, I need to be kept to them.'

'I apologise,' I said. 'I've been a bit busy recently. I'll endeavour to change.'

'It's no wonder you're not married, when you couldn't

offer your man a spotless house to come home to. And you never make an effort to look good at all.'

'Absolutely, yes,' I said. It was hard to argue when it was all fundamentally true.

'Stop agreeing with me,' she said.

'What you say is very sensible,' I said. 'I do like a cleanish house, but I'm afraid I'm never going to be the kind of person who examines the skirting boards for dust. As long as there is good food on the table, I'm mostly happy. Do you think you can live with that?'

'No,' she said. 'No, I can't. I'm leaving. I've got a job with Mrs Withers.'

My heart dropped at all the gossip she would take with her, but it was clear that Edith and I were not made for domestic harmony.

'She'll be perfect for you,' I said. 'Congratulations.'

She gave me two weeks' notice. The big pile of shoes stayed unpolished.

That left me with a vacancy.

'Yes, she did come back,' Mrs Cherry said. 'Look!' She unfolded a blanket made of vibrant slices of landscape; sunrises, lakes, forests. 'It's like a work of art. I'm going to put it in the window, to attract customers. She said she would make more, if I gave her the wool.'

'When you see her next, can you ask her to come and see me?' I said. I gave Mrs Cherry my address. 'I have a proposition to put to her.'

* * *

When Hildebrand came the next day, I knew my instincts had been right. She looked far too tired and miserable for someone so young.

'I didn't mean to steal,' she said. 'And I've given the blanket back. Are you going to charge me?'

'Goodness no, I'm not a policeman,' I said. 'Do you like cleaning?'

'I don't mind it,' she said, 'but you saw my bedroom. I just get tired when I'm working.'

'I have a vacancy,' I said. 'If you want to come here. As a maid of all work. I'm not very good at managing a household, though, so I might be annoying to work for.'

She smiled at me, hopeful for a second, but then her face dropped. 'Tibbs would never let me leave,' she said.

'Just come,' I said. 'Just get your stuff and come here, and if you can't carry it all at once, make a few trips. In the morning when everyone's asleep, if need be. Climb out the window, whatever you need to do. Once you're here, we'll look after you.'

'Tibbs will come and try to get me back.'

'I'll deal with that when it happens,' I said. I did not have a clue how.

'I won't be good for your reputation.'

'Reputations are overrated,' I said, although I was not sure I believed it.

'Thank you.'

'That's quite all right,' I said. 'Perhaps you can teach me how to knit.'

After solving that problem, I was on a high. I was a woman who Sorted Things, and the rush of it led me to believe I might survive visiting Mr Knight and attempting to fire him again.

He had sent me a terse note demanding I call on him, but I had avoided going near since the article had been published. But I was tired of putting up with his ridiculous behaviour. How dare he give photographs of my mother to Dr Patmore? Who did he think he was? It was insupportable, and I was going to stop him.

Chapter Fifty-Two

Unfortunately, when I visited Mr Knight's office, something had changed. The gold lettering on his window had a big wooden sign propped over it that said, 'Scutts Boots and Shoes, Made for Marching the Miles'. It was not the class of shop usually situated on the marina, and as I approached a lady scuttled past, her head averted, frightened by the possibility of being associated with ready-made footwear.

Inside, Mr Knight was nowhere to be seen. There were shoes everywhere now, even propped in rows on a rack on top of his desk. Mr Scutts was there, though, according to his apron, and he looked very ready to sell.

'Shopping for your gentleman? What's his size?' he said with a wink, as if discussing the size of men's feet was salacious. He looked very sad when I asked for Mr Knight.

'Mondays and Tuesdays,' he said. 'Knight has the office Mondays and Tuesdays, and I'm here the rest of the week. Except Wednesday mornings, that's when Smith sells umbrellas. You can leave Knight a message, he comes in and picks up his post.'

I wrote out a message for Mr Knight on headed paper that

was emblazoned with sketches of hob-nailed boots skipping across the bottom of the page.

'Are you sure,' Mr Scutts said as I departed, 'your gentleman doesn't need any shoes?'

I wanted to tell him to move to Hastings, where his shop would be more appropriate, but as I was not a man of business, he would not listen, so I told him instead that my gentleman had giant feet and would not fit shoes that were not made especially for him. I did not tell him that the gentleman I was thinking of was not my gentleman at all.

Later that day I had an odd little note in return from Mr Knight, which demanded I meet him under the pier the next morning at eight o'clock.

'It is the only time I am free as I am going to London immediately afterwards, and as my office is occupied, I would suggest this is a good place for a private conversation as I have severe concerns about your cooperation on this case.'

The underlining was so extreme that I wondered whether it might have been easier for him to keep his pen in a straight line and underline everything. It was an early start to the day, but I determined it would be the last time he ever demanded anything from me. After tomorrow, hopefully, I would never have to see him again.

I was so set on firing him, and preparing my speech, that it was only when I reached the pier, struggling across the shingle, that I realised it was not the best place to share bad news. The pier was built on cast-iron struts, and the combination of the iron pillars and the underside of the wooden slats made it a dark, cold space where sunshine never reached. Lichen had grown up the sides of the pillars, green slime across the wood, leaving a sense of dankness and neglect. It was high tide, and the sea was quite wild against the pillars that were under the water. Tide times changed every day, and I realised I had forgotten to check them on the little weather station that sat on the pier.

Unsurprisingly, no one else was around. Mr Knight was sitting on a wooden crossbeam that was half buried in the shingle, and he stood up when he saw me. I decided I would let him speak first.

'You wrote that article for the newspaper, didn't you?' he said. 'The Editor wouldn't tell me, but I knew he was protecting a lady. Anonymous for reasons of delicacy, he said. Ha. Reads exactly like a daughter who's trying to keep her mother on a pedestal. You knew I planned to write one. Why did you do that? Has anyone contacted you with any leads? Share them with me.'

'Good morning,' I said. 'I hope you slept well. Yes, I wrote an article, because she is my mother, and I should have the right to write it if I want.'

'Was your mother,' he said, with sudden cruelty. 'Was. I think she was murdered.'

I took a deep breath. 'You have said this before, and I don't agree with you. I will share with you, though you must keep it to yourself, that she was not entirely content with my father, or with her life here. The likelihood falls more strongly towards her leaving us, than that she was harmed. My father has always said she left us.'

There had always been a streak in her; wilfulness perhaps,

I could not call it selfishness. She might have thought leaving without a word was the only possible way to escape. And it was much easier to think of her alive and happy, forgetting us, than dead. I had never been able to face the thought of murder.

'But that's the point, isn't it?' Mr Knight said, his protuberant lips twisted in triumph, and I realised instantly I had shared too much. 'That's exactly the point. She wasn't happy with your father, they move to Hastings because of a man, they try a fresh start and, eight years later, she disappears, never to be seen again. And your father tells everyone she has left. What does that lead you, lead any reasonable person, to think?'

'No,' I said. 'No, you are wrong. My father had nothing to do with this. He would not harm her. He would not harm anyone. You have got it all wrong.'

'Well,' he said. 'We'll see. But I think it's possible your father is a murderer.'

The waves seemed fiercer and wilder here under the pier, lashing against the cast iron. I wondered if the tide was still coming in and if it might trap us here. I did not like the thought of drowning in Mr Knight's company.

'I think you are wrong.' I took a deep breath. 'My father would never harm anybody. But I have already decided that I do not want you to investigate this case. I want you to stop. I will not pay you any more, it is taking too long. I am ending your services.'

I had practised my speech several times in the night, and it still sounded as weak as it had done the first time I tried to fire him.

He gave a short sharp laugh.

'Oh, Miss Hamilton, we are back there again, are we?

Running from the truth? I'm sorry, I don't stop investigations halfway. Especially when I'm gaining ground. I don't run cases for your convenience.'

I backed a little towards the sunlight; it felt too dark under the pier. My feet sank into the shingle at every step.

'Dr Patmore said that you gave him the photographs of my mother. He didn't buy them from Farnham, you gave them to him, and now he is blackmailing me with them. That is not ethical. You are not an ethical detective. I am firing you. Or I will go to the police.' I took another step backwards, because now he looked furious.

'You want to go to the police? You really want to? Do it then. Do it. I will tell them about your father. And then he can spend the rest of his life in jail. It's pleasant there, he'll like it.' He was snarling now, and coming towards me across the shingle, and I backed further away onto the beach.

'You do not even have a proper office,' I said, hoping to distract him, and he shrugged.

'I don't need one,' he said. 'Yours is my only case at the moment. I can't afford to keep an office for one case. I've sublet it. If you paid me more, I wouldn't have to.'

'But why…' He was behaving so oddly. 'Why are you only investigating my case? Why did you not take on others?'

He looked towards the swirling water, which did seem to be washing higher up the shingle than it had before.

'I want to solve this one,' he said. 'But you're aggravating me. Because you do know things, don't you? Secrets that you haven't told me. You've been spending a lot of time with Blackthorn too, haven't you? Whoring around, just like your mother.'

I stared at him in shock. 'I haven't… she didn't,' I said,

speechless, because no one had ever spoken to me like that before.

'This is my case,' he said. 'My case, and you have no right to stop me, or to hand it over to anybody else. No right at all.' He came towards me again and I knew it had been a mistake to come alone.

It was ridiculous, surely, to think he planned to hurt me, in broad daylight, but I continued to back up anyway, towards the little wooden steps that led up to the promenade. There were fishermen out to sea, but they were too far out to see what was happening on shore. I had never seen a look like the one on Mr Knight's face now, angry, relentless, and it reminded me of someone, but I could not think who.

There were seagulls whirling and swooping around the sky and abruptly one of them swooped low over Mr Knight, and a stream of blue-white landed on his straw hat.

'For Christ's sake,' he said, stopping, and he took off his hat and looked at it and swore some more. I was still backing towards the steps, slipping in the shingle, and it gave me precious seconds to reach them if he started towards me again.

Thankfully there was a man coming onto the beach, walking a pair of horses towards the bathing carriages to pull them to the water's edge.

'You mustn't be upset,' Mr Knight called to me. 'I have nothing but your best interests at heart.' He was all geniality again and he clapped his hat back on his head, bird excrement and all, and smiled at me as if we were having a summer's day out. 'Come and see me, soon, and we'll get all this sorted out.'

I had started to trust my instincts, in recent weeks. They had been clamouring for me to run from him since the day we met. Now I was prepared to listen.

Chapter Fifty-Three

Unfortunately, Benjamin sent me a note the next day saying that he was shutting up shop and going to London for a few days, so I could not go and tell him my fears. And the vagaries of fate, of course, threw me a picnic with my father, his paramour and her three youngest offspring, which I could not avoid. I had made too many excuses on previous occasions and run out of them.

Even the weather was against me, the sun shining bright and the sky azure blue and cloudless. It was back at St Leonards Gardens, where I had once met with Mr Knight. This time there were no marauding ducks, but there were little baby ducklings and coots pottering around on the lake, under the panicked eye of their parents. Mrs Beeton's youngest child almost threw herself in the pond to get close to them.

I had asked Millie to bake us a cake, and she had made carrot cake, bursting with raisins and covered in thick butter icing. The main offering came from Mrs Beeton's quarter, though. She had brought sandwiches, stuffed with ham and cheese, a meat pie, a blackberry and apple tart, lemonade for the children and ale for us.

Ale? Mrs Beeton was annoyingly likeable. Even though just about the whole park could hear our conversation, it was a happy one. She poured the frothing ale into small glasses and gave it to my father and me.

'I know we shouldn't,' she said, 'but my dear departed was such a lover of ale. Put your hand around the glass and no one will know what it is.'

'Violet hasn't drunk ale before,' my father said with a frown, but Mrs Beeton just giggled.

'Every woman should know what good ale tastes like,' she said. 'There's hardly any alcohol in it. It's only a small glass.'

It tasted mellow and wheaty and it was cooling on such a hot day. Her children ate quickly and then ran off to play, even the oldest joining in some game that seemed to involve defending a small hill from invasion. My father stretched out on the picnic rug on his elbow, and Mrs Beeton relaxed with her back against a tree. The seagulls seemed quieter than normal, and it was peaceful under the rustling leaves of the tree. If my father had not been in line to become a murder suspect, I might have felt a sense of calm beginning to warm my bones.

'I've been talking to Mrs Beeton about you and men,' my father said. She cast him a worried glance and shook her head, but he carried on. 'She thinks I've been too hard on you; tried to push you down the aisle before you're ready. I did it for you, Violet, to see you settled, but she's explained that you might have been scared without a female around to advise on what's what, see to your trousseau and such. She's willing to help you get on the horse, so to speak, do all that's necessary to get you married off.'

I watched her face as she worked out how to unmangle what he had just said.

'What Lucas means,' she said, 'is that he understands now that marriage is a big enterprise for a woman, that it needs to be approached with delicacy, and that you should not be rushed. And should you meet a young man with whom you share common ideals and affection, and you wish to settle down together, I shall be happy, in the sad absence of your dear mother, to provide a helping hand.'

'Did Patmore not suit?' he asked.

'No, Patmore would never suit,' I said.

'He was not a sight for sore eyes, then,' my father said, and laughed uproariously. He was surprisingly mellow about my latest suitor. It was possibly the rosy glow of Mrs Beeton. He was also on his fourth small glass of ale.

'Can I ask,' Mrs Beeton said, 'if you have an idea in your mind what man might suit you? Do you have in your daydreams, perhaps, a romantic ideal of a young man? Sometimes it helps, to think about the sort of man you would like and, before you know it, up they pop.' She beamed, genially, and slapped my father on the knee. He clasped her hand and squashed it tightly before letting it go.

'I should like a man who likes me for me,' I said.

My father laughed again. 'Who else would he like you for? That's a funny thing to say. You always were the comical one.'

'My mother,' I said, and a breeze came across the park, flapping the edge of the blanket and upending some of the picnic plates across the grass. Mrs Beeton gave me a startled look and then scrambled to rescue them, her bottom firmly in the air.

'Don't ruin it,' my father said under his breath, watching

her. 'Don't ruin the atmosphere. We came here to have a picnic, and everybody is having a good time. There is no need at all for you to ruin it.'

'That is very true,' I said. 'So please don't ask me about marriage.'

Things were a little more sombre after that, but it was maybe because the clouds came scudding across the sky and the effects of the ale were wearing off. The children came back, full of good cheer, and then it started to rain, so we gathered everything together and threw it in the picnic basket. They were such a happy bunch, I felt guilty for saying what I had in front of Mrs Beeton. But she had asked me a question I had never been asked before, and I had given an honest answer.

Was my father a murderer? Knowing him, it seemed unlikely. He was not a man for drama of any kind. He was a man for routine, respectability. He liked the prestige, the order, of working at the bank. My mother and I had annoyed him, often, but he had never lifted a hand against us, and he had been patient with her, loving towards her, for many years, even when she must not have allowed him near her for his manly needs. Beyond that, I could not credit him with the imagination or the impetus. And at the heart of him – quite deep inside, admittedly – he was kind.

What was I to do now that Mr Knight was heading down this ridiculous alleyway? How could I stop him, when he had never listened to me, and was now on some great crusade of his own? For the first time I understood why my skin had crawled the day I met him. There was an anger in him that I did not understand.

The only solution I could think of was to persuade Mr Blackthorn to find out the truth first. Because the truth, surely, had to be more palatable. And perhaps if I were to help Mr Blackthorn, to investigate a little myself, to rake up any clues I could think of, perhaps if I were to give him all the information I refused to share with Mr Knight, we would get there first? It had to be the best way.

Chapter Fifty-Four

Hildebrand came to live with us, in stages. Edith did not live in, but we had a decent-sized attic room opposite the one that was filled with my mother's possessions, and I helped Hildebrand to get it set up. Edith was perennially grumpy now, but she agreed to train Hildebrand before she left. I did not share any insight into Hildebrand's background.

'Did you check her references?' my father asked, and I told him yes, of course, and she knitted too, so he could expect woolly hats in winter.

She was quiet at first, and worried. 'Tibbs will come,' she said. 'She doesn't let her girls go easily.' I put the poker by the front door and waited for Tibbs to come, but she didn't. Maybe she had other females to fry.

'Stay out of the way when Dr Patmore comes, just in case,' I said. I felt he was the type of man that might have frequented her former place of work. 'I don't suppose you know a Mr Prout?' I added. 'Did he ever happen to visit for a… visit?'

'Bernard Prout?' she said, and when I nodded, 'No, not him. I know of him, but he never came to us.'

'Ah that's disappointing,' I said.

'We called him Bernie Bird Bollocks,' she said. 'On account of all the bollocks he makes up about his birds. Apologies for the language.'

'I beg your pardon?' I said.

'It's well known among the fishermen. He orders dead rare birds from France and Germany and pretends that he's spotted them in Hastings, sends details to the British Ornithological Society, drawings, etchings, details of what they are, stuffed specimens, all of it. He writes books about them and gets paid for it. He's considered one of the best in the country and, according to him, Hastings has more rare birds than anywhere else in Britain. But it's all bollocks, of course. We used to laugh about it. It's a good scam.'

'Hildebrand, you are a treasure,' I said.

The expression of dawning joy on Miss Turton's face was a sight to behold.

'But that's awful,' she said. 'That's criminal. It is presenting a false picture of the bird population across the whole of Britain. I cannot possibly marry a man like that.'

'I know,' I said. 'I'm sorry to break it to you, but I don't think he is a suitable match.'

'I will not be able to tell him why,' she said. I could see she was thinking rapidly. 'But I will know, and that will give me the moral fibre, the righteousness, to break it off. Oh! I am so glad that you have told me this about him. It is tragic, of course, but I cannot possibly marry him now.'

It was only later, when we had eaten a most spectacular selection of biscuits, that she opened up a little.

'I spent a long time looking after my parents,' she said, 'and it is so lovely to have a little independence now. I love my charities and going on trips like the one to the Hydropathic Establishment, and eating exactly what biscuits I like, and making plans for small holidays. I like my birds and my hobbies. I know that I am not supposed to want to be alone, and these are all very trivial things, but really, I am having the loveliest time. I am flattered, and so grateful, but I could not see a husband accommodating all the many things I want to do. Is that very shallow?'

'No, not at all,' I said. 'I am of a similar mind, at times. I am very glad to have been of help, and I am pleased you are not too upset.'

'I am devastated, of course,' she said, with the happiest, widest smile I had ever seen on anyone. 'But really, morally, I have no choice but to end matters, and embrace my spinster state.'

There was a lot of satisfaction to be had from detective work.

Chapter Fifty-Five

I got a note from Benjamin to say he had returned, so I shot over as soon as I could. The time had come to tell him the truth about Mr Knight, because a crisis was beckoning and Mr Knight was starting to scare me. I was a little shy, because it was the first time I had seen Benjamin since our night at the museum, but, like all weaknesses, shyness must be overcome.

I asked him to sit down and offered to make the coffee, but he insisted on making it, which was probably wise. Then I outlined everything that Mr Knight had said and done.

He listened as always: beautifully, without judgement. 'You should have told me sooner,' he said, predictably, once I had finished. I didn't remind him that I had tried to tell him when we first met. But now I had a great deal more evidence that Mr Knight was not a proper detective with principles, like him.

'I'm a big believer in instinct,' Benjamin said. 'You have a sensible head on your shoulders, I would trust yourself. I'll look into Knight for you. He's an odd fish. He's only been here a few months and he hasn't taken on any cases but yours, judging by the number of people pestering me.

I've been meaning to look into it for a while. And if you are feeling threatened, don't go near him again until I find out what is going on.

'I went to London mainly to look at furniture,' he continued. 'But while I was there I asked in some of the big theatres about Evelina Joyce. I found out a bit more about her, not enough. She was quite a popular actress until a few years ago, not quite a big name, but popular with the crowds. Her touring schedule was ferocious, the length and breadth of Britain and back again. She hasn't performed in a few years, though, as far as I can tell, and the trail has gone quiet. I managed to find a photograph of her, here.' He handed it to me.

It was a photograph of a woman in a fur-trimmed satin gown, laughing from behind a fan, her chin hidden. She had a mass of black hair piled on top of her head, sparkling eyes, a ribbon collarette around her neck. I was briefly reminded of my mother because she, too, had been beautiful and had laughed at the camera with unfettered joy, but this woman was a complete stranger.

'I do not know her,' I said. 'But it is something, isn't it? You are getting somewhere. Thank you.' I felt strangely emotional, because he had investigated matters in London for me. And as I didn't know how to express my gratitude, I picked up one of his big hands and kissed his knuckles again.

'Well,' he said. 'Well.' He kept hold of my hand, turned it over and looked at it for a second, ran his thumb across my palm and then placed it gently back in my lap. 'I'll go and get some more coffee,' he said, and he shot off to the back room. I had not known such a big man could move so fast.

⋆ ⋆ ⋆

I had not meant the kiss in a flirtatious manner. It had been purely a professional kiss. I couldn't of course practise the art of flirting with Benjamin, because he was essentially a business associate and a married man.

Things had not really been the same since our night at the museum. I had a new consciousness of him that I couldn't avoid. I was aware of the way he moved, the shift of his muscles under his shirt, his smile, even the place where his hair curled into the nape of his neck. Sometimes he rolled up his shirtsleeves and then my eyes got caught on his forearms. It was intensely irritating, and although I tried to squash it down (with the other uncomfortable feelings, under my ribs on the left-hand side), it kept popping up again when I least expected it.

There were many reasons why this awareness had to stop. We were working together for a start, and then there were the multiple children and his affectionate wife. And if the awareness was linked to a physical attraction – which was plausible, I admitted reluctantly – if attraction meant wanting our physical bodies to get closer, then that of course wasn't possible, not only because of his marital state but because of the sheer horror to follow. At some stage of the process, presumably, my body would start to feel repelled rather than attracted, and I would have to run out of the room screaming.

He had been kind to me, I told myself, and given me a new idea of what life could be, and I was grateful. That had to be mostly what it was. Perhaps my body just wanted to hug his, out of gratitude, although the flush that went through me when I thought of those hugs did not feel entirely straightforward.

I longed for advice. I longed for someone wise, who knew

about these things and would not laugh at me or offer to show me, to tell me everything. Who would explain to me honestly, straightforwardly, and without any drama, what happened in the bedroom and how to survive it. I thought of Mrs Monk, and wished the world was modern enough that I could go and ask her. But she would laugh at me, of course. I thought of Hildebrand, but she had looked so tired and unhappy in that bed, I did not think I would like what she would tell me.

Meanwhile, I would just have to do my level best to redirect these inappropriate feelings.

'It is very slovenly of you, Benjamin,' I said the next day, 'to be always wearing your shirtsleeves rolled up when I am around. Please remember I am a lady.'

He looked at me with mild amazement and rolled them down. 'Got out of bed the wrong side this morning, did we?'

'Proprieties are important, and we must not forget them even though we are spending a great deal of time together,' I said.

'Point taken, Lady Violet,' he said. 'Should I bow when I come into the room? And while we are at it, what about you and your ankles? I can see them, when you sit on the sideboard. Is it right, that you are constantly flashing your shapely ankles at me?'

'Levity is not necessary at this juncture,' I said, sliding off sharply. 'I have finished your invoices. What should I do now?'

'Well,' he said, 'we've been asked to follow someone's wife. Her husband thinks she is being unfaithful. I could get one of Agnes's brood on it, but—'

'It is intensely irritating that you keep calling them Agnes's children,' I said. There, that was out in the open.

'But they are her children,' he said.

'Yes, but they are yours too, and both parents should take equal responsibility for them,' I said. 'They didn't just pop out of Agnes, without some cooperation from you.'

'Some cooperation from my father, actually,' he said, lazily, watching me. 'Agnes was my father's second wife. It seems easier to call them her brood, than half-sisters and half-brothers, but perhaps I should just drop the half and accept they are here for good.'

'But they called you Father.'

'Yes, because they know it makes me soft, as Agnes says. It's not so long ago he died, and they are good at playing the fatherless card on me. We were all pretty cut up about it. He hasn't left them badly off, financially, but they do miss him. The youngest is only five. God knows, I miss him too.'

'So who,' I said. 'So who is your wife?'

'No one,' he said. 'I am not married, yet.'

I turned back to my desk and piled the sheets of invoices together while I thought about that.

'Have I shocked your sensibilities? Are you upset that you have spent the last few weeks in the company of an unmarried man?'

'I am a little discombobulated, that's all,' I said.

'I thought you knew. But I have not overstepped any lines, have I? Beyond the wickedness of shirtsleeves and shaving off my beard when you owned it. I rescued you from a blanket box, remember.' He was laughing at me, only perhaps for the hundredth time.

This was a disaster of horrific proportions. Because if he was unmarried, that meant he was Available, and there was nothing, no solid reason, to stop my imagination from meandering along salacious alleyways, however misguided.

His marriage had been a reassurance, a defence against possibility. Without it, I would have to face the full shame of my ignorance.

'I have to go,' I said. 'I have an appointment. At… I have an appointment.'

I could not get the door open, and when I finally wrenched it wide the bell rang so wildly, I thought it might fall off.

'Violet,' I heard him say behind me, and perhaps there was affection in his voice. But I didn't stay to find out.

Chapter Fifty-Six

My worst nightmare came true a week later, when Benjamin called on me. I had not been back to his shop, and I was not ready to see him. It had been a great, long, exhausting week of self-recrimination, where I did little beyond castigating myself for behaving like a woman instead of a practical, pragmatic man.

I was knitting, because Mrs Cherry had given me some wool and needles as a thank-you present. I kept accidentally casting on extra stitches, so the rows were getting longer and longer. It would be a triangular scarf.

Edith showed him into the parlour. I had never seen her so smiling and pleasant. Her eyes were all lit up, and I suspected it was to do with Benjamin's handsomeness.

'She's not always so happy,' I said, in front of her. 'She must have been on the brandy again,' which was just plain nasty. She glared at me and slammed the door. It was her last day, anyway.

'Hello,' he said. He was hardly limping at all. He wended his way to a chair and sat down.

If I lifted my knitting to a certain height, there was no way I could look anywhere inappropriate. That was the answer.

'Nice flag,' he said. 'Did Mrs Cherry give you the wool?'

'Yes,' I said.

'Good work on that case, by the way.' He stretched out his legs in front and put his hands in his pockets, staring at the ceiling.

'Thank you.'

'Come on, Violet,' he said. 'Why did you run away? I've said I'm sorry. I really didn't know that you thought I was married. Are you truly that worried about your reputation, with all the dangerous things you've done?'

'Thank you for reminding me,' I said.

'If it's marriage you want, we can think about that,' he said, and my world crumbled. 'I miss you. I miss you coming to the shop, typing away on that great monster, arguing with me, trying to sell me footstools. I didn't mean to upset you. If propriety matters to you and marriage would make things better, let's think about it.'

'I have never in my life wanted to get married,' I said. 'I have always done my level best to avoid it. So, you are quite mistaken there. I was not upset. Your marital condition is entirely your business. And I had to leave anyway, because I had an appointment.'

'So, what can I do? What can I do to set things right between us?' he said.

I thought about asking him to make me a proper Lady Detective, but of course my father would never allow it, because no respectable lady worked as a detective in real life. And there was also the fact that I didn't want to spend my time mooning around a shop after a gentleman who would consider marriage if I wanted it.

'I think it is time I stopped gadding about town, being foolish,' I said. 'I think it would be best if I went back to my charitable work, Mr Blackthorn.'

'There's something else going on here,' he said, frowning. 'I'm going to find out what it is. We were getting along fine, and this has all blown up out of nothing. I'm damned if this is over. We haven't sorted Knight out yet. I've sent off a few telegrams, but I haven't heard back yet.'

The parlour door opened, and my father came in.

It was mildly awkward, but because Benjamin could manage most social situations, we all got through it. He introduced himself as the owner of a furniture shop, and they talked about wood for a while. Rosewood was proving difficult to import, apparently. Benjamin didn't mention that he was a detective. And then because I was numbly unable to say anything at all, he politely took his leave.

My father poured out two sherries and gave me one.

'I know I have been urging you to get married,' he said. 'But there seem to be rather a lot of gentlemen calling on you these days. Is there any one of them you prefer above the others?'

'Absolutely not,' I said.

I wondered how far Benjamin's apathy would go. Perhaps we would be standing naked opposite each other, right next to a bed, without any clothes on, and he would say, 'Well, yes, we can copulate, let's think about it, if that's what you want.'

I may have cried a bit in bed that night. Nigel the stuffed

cat was becoming irritating, his glass eyes shiny in the dark. I wonder how many people had stroked him, to get so worn and ratty. I opened the window and threw him out, and he landed on the lawn with a thump.

Chapter Fifty-Seven

I knew I was a fool, would always be a fool, until I found out what intimacy entailed. I would forever be terrified, unless I understood it better. It was no good, gadding about town as a fully grown female, knowing so little about an act that so much of the population must have participated in, and survived. I was beginning to understand, from the way I dreamt and woke startled in the night, that it was possible my mother's explanations were more than unsatisfactory.

I had to do something to end it. I went and hired an hour in a bathing carriage, donned my scratchy mohair blouse, knickerbockers and skirt and flung myself into the sea.

It was the ladies' section of the beach. It was early morning, and the sea had not yet been warmed by the sun. There was no one else around. The sun was still low in the sky and it spun red and blue shadows across the water. The cold shock was enough to make me gasp and splutter. I swam along the shore and back again, just the humble breaststroke, watching the birds wheeling and diving and feeling my bones start to warm up again.

Then I made a plan to sort out all my problems, one by

one. I was not going to run away from life any more. Or at least, if I ran, I would choose the direction, and I would run purposefully and with determination. There were three people I needed to speak to, to sort out the swirling chaos that surrounded me. I had already said goodbye to Edith, hired Hildebrand. I had solved cases for Maria Monk and Miss Turton. Surely, I could manage my own life.

Mackenzie looked pleased to see me at the door and showed me in immediately.

'I have just come to check that the case is resolved to your satisfaction,' I said to Mrs Monk.

'Of course,' she said. 'We discussed this at the time, and I have settled my bill. I am quite content.'

'Excellent,' I said.

'So you can feel quite free of conscience in the matter,' she said.

'Well, that's most satisfactory,' I said, but I was finding it hard to leave.

'Violet,' she said, 'is there something else you need to tell me? Or ask me? You seem a little... upset.'

'I am quite well,' I said. I ignored the tear that was making its way down my face without permission. The rest could wait.

'Tell me what's upsetting you,' she said. 'In fact, come to my back parlour. It's cosier there.'

It was much cosier. It was full of the things she loved and, as we sat down, she told me about them. There was a beautiful lamp made of green stained-glass and another in gold, in the form of a woman dancing, inspired by the Folies

Bergère in Paris. In a glass case in the corner lay lumps of shining, colourful rocks: red-orange agates, purple amethyst, citrine and jasper, as well as the fossils she had been searching for on the day we met. I burst into tears. She took one of my hands and awkwardly patted it until I stopped.

'There's not much in life worth crying over,' she said. 'But I appreciate it might ease your burden. So do get it all out. But not for too long. It makes me uncomfortable.'

Sometime later, when she had given me a handkerchief and I had blown my nose, she asked Rose to fetch tea and cake.

'Right then, out with it,' she said. She was wearing a blue satin dress with jewels on the bodice and looked far too regal to be confided in.

Where to start?

'Are you the Maria Monk,' I said. 'The one who wrote a book about being in a nunnery, and naughty goings-on with priests and suchlike?'

'I am not,' she said. 'But I do know of my namesake, and I have read the book. It is fairly disappointing, all lurid hints and insinuations. It's likely written by someone who knew as little as you do. But no, I never spent any time in a convent, for my sins.'

'Ah, yes,' I said. 'Now you've mentioned it, I wondered whether you might tell me about it.'

'About what? Convents?'

'No, about –' I took a deep breath, 'marital relations.'

'Sweet flower, I didn't have any,' she said. 'I've never been married. I had plenty of extra-marital relations, I suppose, if we are talking about other women's husbands. But no, the blessed intimacy of marital intercourse, I've never known it. It might be sprinkled with some holy brush of extra special joy.'

It was going to take all my courage to ask what I wanted to know.

'How did you survive the wrenching pain, over and over? And the horror? And the blood? How did you manage to breathe? Did it make you want to peel your skin off? Does it really look like part of a turkey? Where can I find the right mushroom?'

The tea arrived along with cake, a delicate affair, decorated with sprigs of lavender made of icing.

'Christ alive,' Mrs Monk said. 'Let's all take a deep breath. I think there are a few facts needed here. Who told you what you know?' she asked.

'Just my mother.'

'And what did she tell you?'

I told her the story, in all its colourful detail, and her eyes widened.

'Send her over here,' she said. 'I'd like to have a word with her.'

'She disappeared,' I said, and then I had to tell her that story too and so we went around the houses a bit before we got back to what I wanted to know.

'Right,' she said eventually, and she plunged into an in-depth explanation of intercourse while I blushed red from the top of my head to my toes. She used words like 'erection', 'arousal', 'ejaculation', and so many terms for male and female parts I had to ask her to stop and explain them all. I stowed it all away in my mind, a shell-shocked squirrel storing nuts. I wished I had my notebook with me.

I was not a saint. There was a tiny Mrs Withers waving her arm in the corner of my brain, shouting: 'This woman is a common slut! Do not let her sully your innocence!' but I had never liked Mrs Withers anyway. I squashed her with the heel of my boot.

'Stop,' I said to Mrs Monk. 'You mentioned pleasure.'

'I was lucky enough to find a few good men,' she said. 'Not all of them, but I didn't spend all my life on my back like the ones at Tibbs' place, poor souls. I had one man at a time, mostly, and some of them were ugly gibfaces. But,' she said, 'most of them, I could teach. They were always better prepared for other women, once they had been with me.'

'But you mentioned pleasure? For a woman?'

She laughed. 'There were a few I had a good time with – James, for one. If he was still alive, who knows, he might have married me one day, or at least lived as man and wife. We were very close.'

'But—'

'Yes, Violet. If you are with the right one, intercourse can be an uproarious, joyful, rip-roaring, ecstatic, whale of a time, for a woman just as much as a man. There is no reason at all it shouldn't be.'

I chewed over that fact. It was very new and shiny. 'How do you know it's the right one?'

'Ha. Well, there's the rub. I happen to think there can be a few right ones, but you might not know until you are holding their John Thomas in your hand. That's the trouble with matrimony, as I see it. You spend all that time getting to know the superior workings of one person's mind and then you fall into bed and they're a flapdoodle. And Holy Mary, you're stuck with them for life.'

'So, the pain?'

'It was your mother's first time, and she reacted badly,' Mrs Monk said. 'If she'd kept at it for a while, who knows, it might have improved. It might have been your father's fault, it might have been hers, it's likely it was both. Some men can be cruel or selfish, and that's another reason for not marrying them first. There are some women who don't like it much, often because a man has bollocksed things up in the past… and there are others who don't like men. This world is made up of more than one kind of person, and, hopefully, there's room for us all.'

'What's the difference between not liking it and not liking men?'

'Ah, we'll leave that one for another day,' she said. 'Your eyes are as round as dinner plates. I hope you are not too shocked, and that you feel more cheerful.'

'It has been remarkably instructive, thank you,' I said. I gave her a hug and after a pause she returned it, stiffly.

'There's only one thing,' I said. 'I might be a lot less worried if I could actually see it. See a man. Before I actually have to do anything. Descriptions are all very well, but my imagination is inclined to run away in the wrong direction. In any of the statues and paintings I have seen the area is covered in fig leaves, or floating bits of cloth.'

'Goodness, just look at a horse,' she said. 'That's close enough, and they have no embarrassment about waving it around. Most men's are smaller.'

'All right,' I said, but I was a little fed up of being referred to third-party objects. She must have spotted it in my face, because she sighed.

'Friday morning, six o'clock. Meet me by the bottom of the path up East Hill, by Tackleway. Yes, Tackleway. Don't be late. Wear dark colours.'

Chapter Fifty-Eight

The morning I met Maria Monk was sunny and clear. The birds were up early, chirping and singing, darting around the bushes and trees, full of life and purpose. She was already waiting for me by the small white cottages on Tackleway and she nodded at me, looked all around us and then began speedily clambering up a narrow path.

'Where are we going?' I asked.

'Shh,' she said. 'Keep quiet, in case anyone's around.'

It was a fair climb, but I had gained some elemental fitness in running after Mr Prout. There was no one else around, apart from the birds and a small fox that stared at us and then shot across our path into the bushes, sly and sleek.

After fifteen minutes we reached a gate, and she looked over it and around at the field beyond.

'No bull today,' she whispered, and we climbed over the gate and ran across the field. Beyond it there was a rough area of brush and bushes, and suddenly the coast was before us, dropping sharply to the sea. The vista across Hastings and St Leonards was stunning – the new houses, white cliffs, the empty promenade and the blue, blue sea.

Maria wound her way among the bushes until we reached a small patch of grass already warmed by the sun, protected by bushes on either side but with a clear view of the majesty below.

'What an admirable view,' I said, once we were seated, but she shot me a frown and shook her head, so I shut my mouth again. She had been carrying a small wicker basket, covered with a cloth, and now she uncovered it to reveal ham sandwiches, cake, lemonade and apples.

We sat in the sunshine, looking at the view and eating. A chiffchaff was chiffchaffing away on a branch not so far away from us, and the seagulls were whirling and swooping across the sea below. I felt absurdly content and at peace.

'There,' she said in a low voice, and following her pointing finger I saw that there was movement on the beach below us. She reached into the basket next to her and took out two pairs of binoculars, handing one to me.

'Look there,' she said. 'Fill your boots.'

It took a while for me to get the focus right, but suddenly I saw what she had been pointing at. Seven men, no eight, stripping off their clothes, and striding into the sea. I could hear them talking now, their laughter travelling faintly to where we sat.

'They are naked as the day they were born,' I whispered, horrified, fascinated.

'I don't blame them. I would ditch my clothing myself to swim, if I were a man,' Maria said.

I held my breath and looked again. There were so many bodies on display, completely without clothing. There was a great variety of shapes and sizes. Some bodies were fat, some thin. Some men were aged, some younger. Some had hair on their backs, their legs, others were smoother. My fear faded. They looked… ordinary. But…

'They are all walking into the sea,' I said. 'I can't see…'

She laughed at me. I deserved it.

'Patience,' she said. 'They have to come out again.'

A magpie flew off sharply from a bush not far away from us, and I heard the unmistakeable sound of a giggle. I started to get up, but Maria put a staying hand on my arm.

'We are not the only ones here,' she said. 'Let them be.' The men were splashing around in the sea, some swimming, others just floating. One started singing, and a few of the others joined in. It was a distinctly naughty song, about a woman who kept losing her clothing accidentally. As if any woman would be so careless. Did they know how long it took to get undressed?

It was lovely, sitting on the hillside in the sunshine, drinking lemonade and waiting for men to come out of the water. There were bees buzzing, and the smell of heather and flowers hung in the air. It was a little like being at an open-air theatre, but free. I smiled at Mrs Monk.

'Thank you,' I said.

She gave the female equivalent of a harrumph. 'Well, better this way than being tupped by a stranger at fourteen,' she said, bitterly, but I knew she was not really angry with me any longer.

The men were leaving the sea, and I lifted my binoculars again.

It was like Salome and her veils, a slow reveal. There were some I wanted to see more than others – I avoided the aged, out of respect – but there was a particularly fine specimen, who had swum strongly up and down the bay, who was taller than the others, and wider in the chest – oh God.

I lowered my binoculars abruptly and put my head in my hands.

'What's the matter?' Maria said.

'Nothing,' I said weakly. 'Nothing at all.' I picked the binoculars up again, and there he was, striding out of the sea. He looked like Neptune, but beardless. I almost expected the waves to part before him. Was it right, for one man to be so much better made than the others?

As the sea reached his waist-level, I put the binoculars down again and took a deep breath. It was not ethical, surely, to ogle a man I knew. God would smite me for it. It was not a thing that a polite, respectable lady should do.

But I wanted to know. I snatched them up again and took Benjamin in, in all his glory. I watched him walk until the waves were at his ankles, I watched him as he strode onto the sand and reached his pile of clothing and began to dress, and then I lowered the binoculars. It seemed worse to watch a man dressing.

Maria dropped her binoculars abruptly. 'Dammit,' she said. 'Old Killjoy Crabbins is out in his boat.'

There was indeed a man in a small boat, rowing furiously to shore.

'Who?' I said.

'Mr Crabbins,' she said, rising swiftly and packing everything in the basket. 'It's his job to make sure we don't do this. The indecency patrol. He hasn't found this spot yet, but he might have seen the glint from someone's binoculars.'

'Time to go, ladies!' She raised her voice marginally and

there was a flurry of quiet squeals and activity from the bushes around us. 'Crabbins is coming. He's still berthing his boat so it'll take a while for him to reach us, but best scram.'

We started back the way we had come, and I could see flashes of dresses and hear rustlings as other women scattered across the hillside. How many of us had there been?

'Don't run,' Maria said. 'Let us take our time, like the ladies we are.'

Halfway down the hillside, we ran into Mr Crabbins. He was bright red and sweat was dripping down his face. He had obviously been belting up the hill.

'And where have you ladies been at this hour?' he asked, panting, without introduction. There was triumph in his voice.

'Birdwatching,' Maria said. The frost was back in her voice, and I was glad it wasn't aimed at me.

'You expect me to believe that, madam? I know what you ladies do. I saw your binoculars. They'll be in your basket. You'll have to come with me, to the police station. It's dirty business, what you're up to, and there'll be a fine in it, at the very least.'

'For birdwatching?'

'You haven't been watching birds, and you know it,' he said. Some of his puffed-up importance was deflating.

'We saw a green woodpecker,' she said. 'Three jays, four blue tits, a chiffchaff and a reed warbler. With our binoculars. We also had a picnic. Are you really going to fine us for that?'

'Yes, but what else did you see?' he said, leering, and stepping too close to Mrs Monk. 'What else were you looking at? It's my job to stop indecency, and it's my belief you were committing it.'

'You might do best to step back,' she said, firmly moving the basket between them, 'or I will be suing you for assault. I am a lady, as is my companion, and I am acquainted with the Sussex constabulary. I would recommend that you desist this distressing behaviour and let us pass.'

I wondered why she was bothering to give him so much of her time, and then I saw a flash of beige from behind a bush, that likely belonged to a lady moving at speed. The Misses Spencer often wore beige. Could it be... surely it could not be? They were far too prim to be doing any such thing.

'I know,' he said. 'I know that you...' But then he abruptly ran out of steam and stood aside.

'If you are interested in birds,' Maria said as we passed him, 'they are always most active at this hour, and I am sure I saw a great tit not long since.'

It was only eight o'clock, and I had already expanded my world quite considerably. It had been most illuminating, and I would need to write Maria Monk a letter of thanks. My courage in asking her had proved very fruitful.

Now, emboldened, I had to go and see my father. He was the second person on my list, and I had a confession to make.

Chapter Fifty-Nine

I had not given my father a chance to understand me, I realised. I had not talked to him properly, to show him I was a different person now, wiser, more grown-up than the girl I had been when my mother had left. If I confessed to him about recent events, Septimus Patmore would have less hold on me, and maybe my father might even be able to stop Mr Knight. Perhaps he could threaten to close their banking accounts or tell all the merchants in town that they did not pay their debts. Men often had mysterious powers to moderate each other's behaviour.

My father was still at breakfast, eating toast one-handed while reading the paper, so I sat down opposite him and began. My delivery left something to be desired. I felt it was best to get the most dangerous points out at the same time, which meant it lacked an element of order. I wasn't going to tell him everything, but perhaps I was still too truthful.

'You have hired a floozy as our servant?'

'Ssshh,' I said. 'She is not a floozy. She is just someone who has fallen on hard times. She is actually a very fine knitter. I thought I should tell you in case anyone comes around from her lodging house and tries to get her back. She has large fists. Not Hildebrand, the owner of the lodging house, Mrs Tibbs.'

'That is not—'

'Hush, please,' I said, 'I have more to say. I wanted to find my mother. I have always wanted to find my mother. I know you have not felt the same. A couple of months ago, I hired Frank Knight, the detective by the seaside.'

'You—'

'I changed my mind quite quickly, but he wouldn't stop. He uncovered all kinds of things about her that you and I didn't know, and I've been trying to stop him ever since.'

'Things?' My father had never listened to me so much in my life. I think it was the shock.

'She posed for some pictures, indecorous pictures. Scantily clad, in her... undergarments. On a bicycle. On a bed. The photographer sold them in Brighton and made money out of them. Did you ever know? Do you want to see them?'

'No,' he said.

'The photographer sold them to a few men in town, here. I'm not sure what to do about it. Mr Knight has also given copies of them to Dr Patmore, who is not at all a good candidate for marriage by the way. He is trying to blackmail me over them.'

'Violet,' my father said. 'What is this mess you have got yourself into?'

'I am not sure it was entirely my fault. I know you do not care about my mother any more. I know things were not as they should be, that you were not happy. But I needed to find out. I had to hire him, but things have got a little... difficult.'

He dropped his toast, flung his napkin on the table, stood up and began to pace the room.

'Do you know what it was like for me, living with her?' he said. 'She was unnatural. She expected me to worship her, without ever – I don't expect you to understand.'

'I do understand,' I said. 'I have learnt all the things married ladies should know from a friend. It must have been hard for you. But at least you have met Mrs Beeton, who looks as if she would be very jolly between the sheets. I am sorry. I think I have over-loosened my tongue, and it is running away with me.'

He didn't say another word for at least another half-minute. He just stood by the window and stared out into the garden.

'Your breakfast will be getting cold. Mr Knight thinks that you might have hurt my mother,' I said at last. 'I told him that you would never have hurt her. But he won't stop investigating, even though I have asked him. I wondered if you might have the power to stop him.'

'Stop him?' he said. He had still not turned around.

'I don't think he is a very good detective,' I said. 'He seems angry, and he's not investigating any other cases but this one, and he has been quite threatening to me and about… my mother.'

'So, she has done it again,' he said, still looking out the window. 'Your mother has managed to overturn our lives again, even though she is entirely absent.'

'It is not wholly her fault,' I said. 'The photographer should not have sold them on so… freely. And Dr Patmore is less than savoury as a person. It is not fair to blame her for this.'

'Fair?' he said, spinning around. 'Fair? Do not talk to me about fairness. I want to marry Mrs Beeton. I finally have the chance of warmth, the chance to catch up on all the things I've missed out on. What will your meddling get me? A conviction for murder? When all I ever was with your mother was patient?'

'I can't forget her,' I said. 'I want to remember her, and I need to know what happened. She might be… might be dead, but at least we would know.'

'And all I have ever wanted, from the day she disappeared, was to forget and move on. But I am not to be allowed, am I? She is not dead. She sent you a letter, a year after she left.'

The world slowed down. I noticed the quiet steady ticking of the clock on the mantlepiece, although I had not noticed it for years. Who wound it?

'She sent me a letter?'

He may have looked uncomfortable, but I could not be sure. It was not an expression I saw often.

'It was some nonsense about fungi. It made no sense. She signed it with a false name, and she disguised her handwriting, but I could tell. She always curled her capitals. When have you ever been interested in mushrooms? It was a coded message for you, because she did not want me to know.'

'Why did you not show it to me? Please fetch it,' I said, and he frowned as if to argue, but then he saw the expression on my face, a new one for me too, and he went to his study and fetched it without another word.

'*Dear Miss Hamilton*,' it read. '*Thank you for your enquiry. I hope this letter finds you well. I would like to clarify that the mushroom you asked about is a Stinkhorn, not a Matterhorn. The Matterhorn is of course a mountain in the Alps. I am also well, although mycology is often a difficult path to follow, without my favourite flower to brighten my way. I am sorry for any troubles my confusion may have caused you.*

With kindest regards,
Professor L. Valley, FRSA'

'She wrote to me,' I said, wonderingly. 'She wrote to me, and you did not show it to me? You opened my letter?'

'She was no mother to you,' he said, colour high on his cheekbones. 'She left you. She abandoned us, her marriage, any claim to respectability. It was in your best interests for us to let her go, let her stew wherever she had gone.'

'She has been alive,' I said, 'all these years, and you did not let me know? You *lied* to me? You lied to my face about it, only a few weeks ago?' I had thought he held himself to high standards, but apparently those standards were only for other people.

'She was not good for you,' he said. 'Sending you secret messages as if you were a little coven of two. What does her letter *mean*? Where did *I* come into it? Why could she not have let me know?' His voice was high on the last word, and I briefly saw the depth of his betrayal and confusion. It did not excuse him.

'I loved her,' I said. 'She was my mother, and she has been *alive* all these years? While I worried and wondered and grieved? How could you do that to me?'

'She was better off dead to us. Your own behaviour has not been sterling,' he said, and I realised it was the closest I might ever get to an admission he might have been wrong. 'I cannot believe you have risked our lives, our reputations, by hiring a detective. Where is your decorum, your decency as a young woman? You keep our home with the barest of care, I know you have ignored me regarding chaperones. And now you employ a harlot in my house?' His face was a picture of indignant outrage, whipped up in order to right his wrong, and I saw how he must look at the bank, issuing orders to hapless clerks.

'I blame your mother for this ridiculous sense of independence,' he said. 'You are not free to do as you wish, Violet. You are not free to gad about town, careless of your reputation and mine. Your mother must have given you these wild ideas. She was a terrible influence. You have indeed been better off without her.'

'Well, considering how so-called wild my behaviour has been in her absence, that is doubtful,' I said. 'Does this mean you know where she is?'

He sat down at the table abruptly and finished his half-eaten toast in two bites. Then he drank a cup of tea, picking up his paper and throwing it down again without reading it, while I waited.

'No, I do not know, and I do not care,' he said eventually. 'But we are talking about you. I am not here to catch your runaway horses. If you are going to behave like a hoyden, do not expect me to pick up the pieces. I will think about Mr Knight and Dr Patmore, but it may be that you have got yourself in so deep that matters cannot be mended. If that is the case, we will need to think about whether you continue to live in this house, or whether I need to find you a place to retire in the country, where you cannot get up to mischief. Yes, I may need to have a serious think about where you live.'

I watched him, giving this speech, and he sounded so firm, so in control, but he still had his office face on and, for the first time, I wondered. Perhaps, underneath, he was not really so certain of his world and how to handle it. It was an odd feeling, to look at someone who had always presented himself as so sure of life and wonder if he was merely bumbling his way through it. He had certainly bumbled spectacularly, taking a letter that was meant for me, which would have changed my whole world, and lying to my face about it. My failings were irrelevant by comparison.

'I do not think I want to live here any longer, myself,' I said. It was a bold, perhaps stupid thing to say, but it was true.

'Is that so,' he said, after a pause. There was a look of something that was almost hurt on his face, but he shuttered it fast. 'So you wish to become a tramp like your mother? Well, then, you must make your own bed, young lady, and lie in it.' He picked up the newspaper again, threw it pointlessly across the room, and then stomped out of the room and the house.

She was alive. She was alive. It was like being showered with gold coins, pain and joy at the same time. I sat still for several minutes, staring out of the parlour window, allowing my thoughts to settle, the feelings to churn through me, and then I picked up the letter again.

I understood that she had talked about mushrooms because it was a message that only I would understand, because she had not wanted my father to know. But it was such a short, sparse letter. Why had she been so cloak-and-dagger about it? What was the danger, in just telling me the truth, without revealing her whereabouts?

I turned the letter over. It was the kind that folded up to make its own envelope and it bore a postmark.

The postmark was for the same place as the postcard of orchestral frogs I had found in the crack between her bedroom floorboards. Buxton. She had written from Buxton.

Benjamin was already the third person on my list, but now it was even more urgent I see him.

Chapter Sixty

I had made up my mind, I must bury any feelings I had for Benjamin. This was the part of life I was still running away from, but at least I was deciding the trajectory. I had seen him entirely without clothes, and he had proposed to me in a manner that was decidedly lukewarm, but these matters must be set aside, because I needed him. I needed him to help me find my mother, help me with Mr Knight, and train me to become a Lady Detective, all practical goals that would only be hindered by emotion. I would behave exactly like many men did and bury any feelings so deep that they could never be found again. I could do it, because I was Violet Hamilton, newly frozen inside.

There was a man in the shop when I arrived. He was looking for a bookcase. He had a very specific idea of what he wanted, and in fact had brought several books of different heights with him to try on the shelves. Benjamin shot me a look and nodded grimly. 'Two minutes,' he said to me.

'I think that might suit,' the man said. 'Oh, no, there's too much of a gap above that book. I don't like gaps.'

This went on for several minutes, before Benjamin took

them all off him and jammed them all together on their side on one shelf. 'Just put them like that and they'll fit everywhere,' he said.

'Well, that's rude,' the man said, and left without buying anything.

'Hello,' Benjamin said.

My primary goal was to act calmly, rationally.

'I think I have found my mother,' I said. 'At least, where she might be. I think she might be in Buxton. She is alive, or she was nine years ago… look.' I handed him the postcard and the letter and pointed at the postmark on both of them. 'She might still be living there. Do you think she might be still living there?'

'A postcard of frogs and a letter about mushrooms?' he asked, and I had to explain about them both because context was important, although I didn't explain exactly what stinkhorn mushrooms meant. I simply said we had shared a fondness for collecting fungi.

'She wrote you this letter, and he didn't share it with you?' he said, and his frown was ferocious.

'I know,' I said. 'I think that was very wrong of him. What does Bubbins mean?' It had bothered me ever since I saw it.

'I've never heard of it,' he said. 'But if I was to make a guess, it's an affectionate word for – a bosom.' He may or may not have looked at mine, very briefly, as he said it, but my frozen self did not notice.

'So someone living in Buxton liked my mother's bosom?'

'Apparently. I'll send a telegram to a contact I have near Buxton to see if anyone's heard of your mother or Evelina Joyce.'

'Yes,' I said. 'Thank you.'

While he wrote out what he wanted the telegram to say, I sat on my typing chair and looked at my feet.

'I'm sorry I've been a bit off recently,' I said. 'I've been having a difficult time. I still am, actually, but I've decided to try to rise above it.'

'I don't want us to fall out,' Benjamin said. 'I can be a bit pan-handled with words sometimes, so I'm sorry if I've said the wrong things. I've missed you.'

'You too,' I said.

'About what I said about marriage,' he said.

'There's no need to bother about that. My essential point is that I want to keep on working for you, and I think that a marriage between us would be a distraction. It will be best if we keep it purely businesslike from now on and work side by side, like brother and sister.'

'Brother and sister?' he said.

'Yes,' I said. I clung to the icicle inside me. It was not without a pang, as attraction was not so easily dismissed as all that. But I would fight it with every cold bone in my body, because I had a bigger, purer goal. 'I want you to train me to be a Lady Detective.'

'I don't think it will be possible, to work side by side, a single lady and a bachelor,' he said. 'You were right to worry about your reputation, and I was wrong to treat it so lightly. I think we should consider our options. I have been feeling—'

'I am distracting you from the telegram,' I said. Feelings were off the cards forever more. And as far as my reputation went, I would handle it by wearing a disguise all the time. I could dye my hair blonde, adopt a limp, so that people could not recognise my walk; I could dress as a man or travel everywhere in a closed barouche. I would find solutions.

'And about working together...' he said.

'It's worked well so far, as it is,' I said. 'Let's just carry on as we are. Will you convey the urgency of the matter? Perhaps I can come back in a few hours to see if you have had a response.' And I shot out of the door like a rabbit, before I melted.

Because I did not want to go home, I passed the afternoon wandering along the promenade. It ran for miles in the direction of Bexhill and Eastbourne, a great, flat, white expanse of wide-open road stretching towards the horizon. I thought a lot of thoughts, about my father's betrayal, my mother's letter, about what she might have been doing all these years, and I let the vast panorama of empty sea calm me down, gentle waves washing away my confusion. Eventually, I thought about my feet again, as they were starting to get sore, and as the harsh afternoon light began to turn to the gentler rays of evening, I retraced my steps to see Benjamin.

He was pacing the floor with excitement. 'I've heard back,' he said. 'There is an Evelina Joyce living in Buxton. I have her address. We can go together tomorrow.'

'No, I'll go,' I said.

'We can go together,' he said. 'I can book the train—'

'No, I'd like to go alone,' I said. He looked a bit hurt, so I biffed him on the shoulder, in a manly fashion, and he jumped.

'Thank you, Benjamin. Thank you for investigating this for me.'

'It's the least I can do,' he said, and he gave me the address.

'Wait,' he said as I was running out of the door. 'Wait. Something else I've discovered. Mr Knight is not Mr Knight.

The lease on his office says Herbert Winkler. I'm trying to find out what it's about, but don't go near the man for now. He's not who he says he is, so stay away from him until I find out what's going on.'

'Herbert Winkler?' I said. The name meant nothing to me, but I was wholeheartedly glad to know my suspicions were founded and that I had Benjamin, finally, fully, on my side. 'I have never heard of him, but I shall be delighted never to see that man again.'

I went home, because it was still my home for the moment, and ate my dinner in my room. I was not ready for any more confrontations with my father. Then I went to bed too early and spent the night tossing and turning, waiting on tenterhooks for dawn to break and for it to be an acceptable hour for me to get up and catch a train to Buxton. It was the longest night I had ever spent, apart from the nights when she first disappeared.

I caught the first train the next morning, at seven o'clock, more than ready for the day to begin. I hoped that such an early train would mean I would not run into anyone I knew. My heart was in my mouth, and the butterflies in my chest were as big as seagulls.

Half a minute before the train pulled out, the door to my compartment opened, and Mr Knight climbed in.

Chapter Sixty-One

'Going somewhere nice?' he said and he sat down opposite me as the train pulled away. He looked surprisingly dishevelled for a man who prided himself on his blazers. His moustache was trimmed slightly shorter on one side than the other, and his eyes were bloodshot. His holiday panache had definitely faded.

'I am going to visit my elderly aunt in Edinburgh,' I said.

'Is that so? You will be changing trains to catch one from King's Cross, then?' he said. 'I am going that way myself. I will be glad to see you safely onto your train. It would be a shame for you to cross London on your own. But now you have me.'

We went into a tunnel and the carriage went black, and I put my hands up before me, blindly, because I was terrified as to what he might do.

But he stayed silent, and when we reached the other side and the daylight came into the carriage again, he was merely sitting there, watching me. I lowered them to my lap again.

'Why have you come?' I said. 'How did you know—'

'Credit me with some sense,' he said. 'You've likely been

telling Blackthorn things you wouldn't tell me, if he's got between your legs. I've been following you, and it seems you've found out something good. Where is she?'

'Who?' I said, but of course it was hopeless pretending he didn't know. 'Why do you need to know, so badly? Why is it such an obsession for you? Why are you lying about your name? I know you are Herbert Winkler.'

'My name is my own business,' he said, and it was almost a snarl. 'I don't like to be played by anyone, especially a woman. And you've played me, haven't you? Running that article, getting Blackthorn onto me, lying, always lying. Women are always lying, and I'm sick of it. Where is she?'

'Why do you want to know?' I repeated. He pursed his lips and turned his head towards the window.

'It's a long journey to Edinburgh,' he said. 'I'm sure you'll decide to tell me at some point.'

I looked at him closely for the first time, searching for answers. He turned his head to glare at me briefly, the fury and hate in his eyes so extreme, so over the top, that I pressed back against the seat involuntarily. It reminded me of someone. It reminded me of someone who had had the same irrational anger in his eyes, a long, long time ago.

'Was it you?' I said, after a while. 'Was it you, in the silk muffler, who gave me the parcel for my mother?'

He was silent for so long I thought he would never answer. The train stopped at a station, and carried on, before he spoke.

'I loved her,' he said. 'I would have given her everything. I worshipped that woman, every step she took. I had money, I would have kept her in luxury, I would have kissed her feet every day, if she had asked me to. She knew that, but she left me anyway. Yes, I gave you a gift for her, a gold watch, one of many gifts, and she sent it back, and then she disappeared.'

'Were you together?' I said, bewildered, horrified, because I could not see my mother going near him at any time in history.

'She smiled at me,' he said. 'We met at an afternoon gathering in the spring, at Crystal Palace. I remember the day clearly, even now. We were standing by the Egyptian statues in the entrance hall and she smiled at me, several times. I knew what it meant. She touched my elbow with hers in passing. It was a promise.'

'She smiled at everybody,' I said. He frowned, and I remembered that I had called the man in a muffler a nobody.

'I should be a wealthy man,' he said, sitting back against the seat. 'My father is a viscount. I am a second son, but I have prospects. My brother is poorly, his wife a weakling. I could have any woman I chose, and I chose Lily.'

'But it is so long ago,' I said. 'Why would you still care about someone who left you so long ago?'

'Because I know she cared for me.' He spat it out. 'She was always polite, modest, retiring, pretending to reject me, but I knew. It was in her eyes. She sent me messages with her eyes. Even when she returned my gifts, my flowers, I knew she did not mean it. Your father must have made her leave London.'

'But that was eighteen years ago. Why would you hold onto her memory for so long?'

'I need to know what happened,' he said. 'I need to know where she is. Real devotion doesn't end when a person is absent. And now on top of it all, I'm angry. Because she played me for a fool, didn't she, all these years? She was a trollop and she could have given me a piece, but she pretended to be modest, and I fell for it. I think she needs to know she can't play games. I think there needs to be a chat. And she must be alive, mustn't she, if you've jumped on a train on your own, without any luggage? Where is she?'

'But –' my brain was slow as if it was swimming through a bowlful of porridge, 'but you are a detective. How did you know I would hire you?'

'I didn't,' he said. 'I found out she had lived in Hastings last year, and I came to find out what had happened to her. I decided to be a detective, because it was a good way to ask questions. I've had a few professions. I ran a gentlemen's club for a while, a good one, until the gentlemen said I was overcharging them for whisky, and I got bored of it. I was a gamekeeper in Africa too, until I shot the wrong beast and they sent me home. I like variety. I might as well be a detective as anything.'

'But how did you know I would hire you?' I repeated, because things were still not making sense.

'I couldn't be sure,' he said. 'I put a leaflet through your door, thought your father might want it sorted. It was a surprise when you turned up. I'd been working on a very lucrative case too, for a real lady. Paranoid her husband was having an affair. I could have strung her along for weeks. But when you came along, I gave it up to look for your mother. You should be grateful to me.'

And then the ticket inspector came past and after he had stamped my ticket, Frank Knight-Winkler took it straight off him, smiling his tiny smile.

'Buxton?' he said. 'Well, there we go. Not Edinburgh, after all. I'll have a ticket to Buxton too, please, inspector.'

We sat in silence for the rest of the journey to London Bridge, because I did not know what else to say.

I spent the time thinking furiously, desperately. I had to get rid of Mr Knight at London Bridge station, and delay him, somehow, so that I could get to Buxton before him, find my mother, and warn her. It was a long shot, but I knew where she lived, so my only hope was that I could get there first.

It was too unbelievable. I knew that men admired my mother, but for eighteen years, with no encouragement? I also knew that she had been pleasant to everyone, but that it meant nothing. She charmed as effortlessly and as thoughtlessly as she served tea, as part of her social armour. I knew now why the hairs on the back of my neck had stood up as soon as I met him. Some part of me had recognised him.

I was only a woman, but I could not let him find my mother. I felt hopeless, angry, confused and a dozen other emotions all at once, and I spent the journey packing them all tightly together into one, manageable parcel that coalesced into a resolve to escape.

Could I call over a stationmaster or find a constable and accuse Mr Knight of harassment? Scream for help? I had well over an hour to think about it but, when we arrived, they seemed as practical as the ideas in a penny dreadful.

'Best behave,' he said into my ear as we disembarked, taking a firm grip of my upper arm. 'Don't try to run, or you'll suffer for it.'

I had two small advantages. The first was that he still thought I was a weak female. I had never shown him otherwise. He did not know that I had followed someone, broken into a museum, visited a brothel, stopped a theft. He didn't know my mother was alive, and when he threatened her, he unleashed a lioness. If an opportunity came to stop him, I would take it.

The second was that I had been through London Bridge station before, as trains came there from Crystal Palace, and I knew it was the most confusing station in the world. It appeared Mr Knight-Winkler had forgotten.

Today it was incredibly busy, travellers running around in all directions, porters pushing barrows full of luggage. Mr Knight stopped dead in the middle of them all, which caused some chaos as people bumped into us. But his grip on my arm was too tight for me to wriggle free.

'Where is the platform for the Buxton train?' he said, but I was not inclined to help. There was a board listing all the trains going south, but not north.

'I need to use the necessary,' I said, but 'No, you don't,' he said. 'You can go on the train if you have to.' He pulled me sharply onwards.

Mr Knight walked me around the station twice and found no answers. I hadn't yet found mine. Salvation came in the form of a cart piled with barrels of beer.

Mr Knight was looking about him, fiercely, as if his determination alone would give him answers. The cart stopped behind us, briefly, as the man pushing it tried to navigate through the crowd, and I noticed there were taps on the barrels. Mr Knight had a hold of my left arm, so I twisted towards him and pointed across the station to where there was a stationmaster, surrounded by a crowd asking directions.

'Over there,' I said, helpfully, and he turned to look, and I reached over his head and turned the tap on the very highest barrel, immediately above him, and the beer thankfully came out in a great gush. I think, for a second, he had thought I was going to kiss him.

'What the...' he said and let go of my arm for a single second to look up and work out what was going on, and I vanished into the maelstrom.

I knew I had to cross a bridge to the other half of the station because I had worked it out, so I ran weaving through the crowd as fast as my legs would take me, ducking down low so that hopefully he would not see me. I was short anyway. I flung myself across the bridge and into the side of the station where trains went north, and I found my platform in seconds.

Luck was on my side. The train was about to leave. I threw myself into a compartment, shut the door, and shook a little beer off my sleeve and my hat.

I had won this latest battle. Now it was a race to find my mother, if she was actually in Buxton. I would probably find that Evelina Joyce had never heard of her.

Chapter Sixty-Two

When the train pulled in at Buxton it was raining hard, and water ran ankle-deep like a river down the road outside. I ran to ask the stationmaster where to go, and he pointed to the left, making a curving motion with his arm.

'Follow the road as it bends to the right, go straight ahead,' he said, 'when the street runs out of straight, turn left up the hill, go straight past the fountain, through the park, take your first right, cross the bridge and it's on your right. You can't miss it.'

'Thank you,' I said, silently screaming inside at the complexity of his instructions, and set off running again. My heart felt like a bird jumping about in my chest. How foolish I had been, not to come with Benjamin. He could have picked up Mr Knight with one hand and popped him out of the train window near Tunbridge Wells, if not before. How had I thought to manage this, on my own? How could I be sure that Mr Knight had not somehow made the train and was even now on my heels? I looked behind me, but I could not see him.

It was too far. It was too far uphill, and by the time I got to the small house I was exhausted. It was very pretty, with camellia bushes and roses by the door, and I didn't care.

The woman who answered was the lady in the photograph with the black hair, and I wanted to lean against the pillar and weep with relief.

'I need to speak to Lily Hamilton,' I said, because there was no time for anything else. She looked me up and down, a beer-spattered woman with her hat falling off, and started to close the door, but I put my foot in it and pushed back against her.

'She is in danger,' I said. 'I am her daughter, and she is in danger, and you have to listen to me. Are you Evelina?'

She opened the door abruptly and I fell across the doorstep onto my hands and knees.

'Violet?' she said. 'You must be Violet? Come, come,' and she encouraged me to crawl in far enough that she could close the door behind me.

'Come and have some tea,' she said, and I clambered to my feet and followed her into a small parlour, but—

'We don't have time,' I said. 'We don't have time. He's coming after her, and I have to warn her.'

'Who? Your father?' she said, and she tried to push me bodily into an armchair. 'Sit for two seconds or you'll be no good to anyone.' But I couldn't sit so I just stood there, swaying.

'No, Frank… Herbert Winkler,' I said, and she looked at me blankly for a second and then shook her head.

'Never heard of him,' she said. 'Never mind. I know where your mother is, so we can go and find her. But I think you need a second to get your breath back.'

'I can't go as I am,' I said. 'He is on his way, and if he sees me, he'll follow me. I can't go as I am.' Logical thought had been replaced by a kind of panicked exhaustion.

'You can borrow some of mine,' she said, looking me up and down. 'You're a bit shorter and bigger in the bosom than your mother, I think. Give me two ticks. I am Evelina, by the way. Nice to meet you.'

I had never met a calmer, more competent woman. She shot out of the room and was indeed back in two ticks, with a dry dress that fitted and a short red wig.

'No time for modesty,' she said, and she helped me out of the wet dress and into the new one, buttoning me up the back; she pinned my hair neatly under the wig, and gave me a blue coat that was hanging in the hall. I let her do it, gathering my breath and my energy again, as it was mostly the run up the hill that had knocked the stuffing out of me.

'Right then,' Evelina said, and she took my shoulders and gave me a gentle shake. 'Fit for purpose?' When I nodded, she opened the door, and I would have shot out, but she held me back.

'Don't run,' she said. 'We'll walk fast, but don't run, or you'll attract attention and we'll be no good to anyone when we get there. Walk with me.' And she set off, at a fast clip, down the hill, and I followed.

The rain had stopped. The sun came out and there was a faint rainbow in the sky.

Evelina walked down a narrow road that took us up past a sweeping crescent, with a colonnade of elegant shops, up around a curve to reach the Buxton Theatre, and into a park. There was a lake, a stream and several colourful flower borders. She reached a point between a bandstand and the entrance to a huge glass conservatory and waited.

'We must,' I said, desperate, but, 'No,' she said, 'Wait.'

Two women came out of the conservatory, an older lady, a stranger, in a red woollen coat, and a golden-haired woman in blue velvet. Then the golden-haired woman turned her head towards us and shock ran through me. My brain, slow to catch up, rearranged her features into familiarity, but something deeper in me had already recognised my mother.

She saw Evelina, and pleasure spread across her face. Then she saw me, and there was shock and joy in her face, and then, quite clearly, a plea. She shook her head, and I froze.

My mother walked towards us. 'Lady Bourne,' she said to the older lady in the red coat, 'you know my friend Evelina. This is my cousin Viol— Viola Smythe, who is visiting us from Edinburgh.' She gestured towards me, still with an appeal in her eyes.

'Scotland, how nice. You have chosen a good weekend to visit,' Lady Bourne said. 'Now that the rain has stopped.'

'Virra pleased tae meet ye,' I said, and then I mostly stayed quiet, because I had accidentally channelled Mackenzie's deep voice and I wasn't sure I could maintain it. We were forced to walk the whole of the park together, while my mother talked about the weather, a cake shop we should visit, the theatre and any number of things that mattered not a whit, while I looked frantically from side to side, searching for Mr Knight and clutching Evelina's arm so hard it must have hurt her.

Eventually, after the sun had passed around the earth a thousand-and-one times, Lady Bourne said her polite farewells and left, and the three of us stood and looked at one another.

'Violet,' my mother said. 'My Violet,' and she took my hands in hers and held them.

'We don't have time,' I said. 'We don't have time. He is coming after you. Frank Knight is coming, and he's angry, and I think he's a lunatic, and we have to escape, somehow.'

'Frank Knight?' she said. 'Who is he?' And I wanted to scream in frustration, because no one was getting it, and my brain couldn't adjust to a Winkler when he had tormented me for so long as a Knight.

'Herbert Winkler. The man in the muffler,' I said. 'The angry man, who gave me a parcel for you when we lived in Crystal Palace, before we moved to Hastings. I think he is obsessed with you, and he's angry that you left him, and angry with me because I poured beer over him, and—'

'Herbert?' she said. 'Herbert Winkler? I thought I had left him behind long ago. That evil little runt has found me here?' She looked older, but she was still breathtakingly, regally beautiful and I couldn't believe she was standing there, in front of me, and we were having to talk about someone else.

'Yes, he's been searching for you, for months,' I said. 'He pretended he was a detective, and I hired him and he followed me. He will have taken a train not long after mine, as soon as he changed his clothes, I expect, and I have really never met anyone so absolutely, furiously angry. It can't just be at us, that anger, can it? It seems too much.'

'He has always been angry,' she said. 'Mostly at women, for not giving him the attention he thinks he deserves. And he has been threatening you, my Violet?' She took a deep breath and straightened her shoulders. 'Well then, I must sort this out.'

'Lily,' Evelina said, a warning note to her voice.

'No, Evelina,' my mother said. 'It's time to end this nonsense. Threatening my daughter, all because I wouldn't pay him the time of day eighteen years ago? That's ridiculous. Does he know where we live, Violet?'

'No,' I said. 'Only that you might live in Buxton.'

'I don't want him to come to our home,' my mother said. 'Very well, let's meet him at the caves. That's gloomy enough to suit his temperament. But how do we get word to him?' She thought for a second, then spun around in a circle and called over to a small boy who was loitering by a row of carriages just outside the park.

'I need your help, Billy,' she said. 'I need you to go to the station and meet a man off a train called Herb— no, Mr Knight. I need you to find Mr Knight and tell him that the person he seeks is at Poole's Cavern. That's all. No need to mention names. Here.' She gave him a coin.

'What does he look like?' Billy said, and a small hiatus ensued, because my mother had not seen Mr Knight for eighteen years and, when it came to it, he was fairly nondescript.

'Small teeth,' I said. 'Brown hair, a moustache like flat ivy. Not tall.' And the boy stared at me askance and I felt an utter failure as a detective. 'He might be wearing a beige and white blazer, or he might not, because it was covered in beer. His moustache is trimmed slightly smaller on one side than the other.' Eventually the boy shot off, still visibly unimpressed, and I turned to my mother.

'Go with Evelina,' she said. 'I'll meet him alone.'

'I'm not leaving you,' I said, and she looked at me with tears in her eyes.

'This is for me to sort out, Violet. This should not have

touched you. We left London because he had come near you, and now he has been threatening you? That is enough. Go with Evelina. I will sort this.'

'What are you planning, Lily?' Evelina asked, but my mother just shook her head. I would not go, so eventually Evelina left, on her own, and my mother and I went together to the caves.

Chapter Sixty-Three

As I found out from my mother later, Poole's Cavern was not one but a series of caves, set beneath Grin Low Hill, formed over centuries by limestone dripping on the rock, slowly dissolving it. Once visitors had had an uncomfortable crawl into the cave's first chamber, but fifty years or so ago it had been enlarged by removing tons of sediment and blasting away the low roof space.

'It is closed to the public this week,' my mother explained, 'because they are repairing the path. But it is easy enough to get in, for those that know. Wait here for a moment, and I will light the lamps, so we are ready.'

I was not sure what she had planned, but I let her go in through the narrow door, while I sat on a moss-covered rock outside and waited. It was a warm day now, and it was pretty here on the hillside, with the hill stretching far above us. There were birds singing and everything seemed unreal. What was she planning? Surely not murder?

She came out again and sat beside me on the rock.

'What do you intend to do?' I asked her, and she smiled and took my hand.

'So many private battles are fought between men and women,' she said. 'And so often we do not know what happened, because the women are silenced. I do not know what I will do. But I will not let this man, who is so unimportant to you and me, who is so angry that he is unimportant to us, to invade our lives any more. I am sorry I left you. Did you get my letter? Did you understand it? That I was sorry?'

'Father kept it from me,' I said. 'Until yesterday. So I didn't know you were still alive.'

I could see the shock in her face, and I felt anew the tragedy of it myself. I could not believe how perfect she looked, how untouched. She was older, certainly, with fine lines beside her eyes and a softer chin, her hair turning to grey, but otherwise she did not look as if hard times had touched her. I felt selfish for wishing she would be riven with some outward sign of all that she had put me through.

'I... will never forgive him for that,' she said. 'I am sorry.'

I didn't know what to say, so I didn't respond. Instead, I sat for a while looking across the hillside. It was so peaceful here, so contrasting to the tumult of emotion running through me. I wanted a Hastings storm, wild seas, grey skies, pummelling waves and driving rain.

'Shouldn't we go to the police?' I said. 'And tell them about Mr Knight – Mr Winkler – and then they will arrest him, and we can talk properly?'

'Arrest him for what?' she said. 'Devotion? The police are not good at arresting people for devotion. I have a life here, Violet. A secret life, a difficult life, but there are moments when it is a good one. I do not want to risk upending it for him. I do not want to risk your wellbeing any longer.'

'But what will you do?' I asked again, and she shrugged a little.

'If I am harmed,' she said, 'I want you to know that I loved you, and that I'm sorry I left without telling you, and you did not get my letter. I asked the Reverend to look after you.'

'He knows?' I said. 'He knows you are alive and well?' Somehow that hurt more badly than anything, that he had held that secret for ten years, when he had known I was suffering. It seemed as if everyone knew then, that she was still alive, and it was just me, flailing about, imagining death.

'I asked him to keep an eye on you,' she said. 'I am sorry I did not let you know, Violet. I am sorry.' She put her hands over her eyes, tight, and I knew she did care, that she had not left me easily, but the wound was still there, and I did not know how long it would take for me to forgive her.

'You must go,' she said suddenly. 'You must go and leave me to speak to him. I never told him to his face he meant nothing to me, because I did not want to create a scene in the street, at someone's house. For the sake of politeness. I think we are beyond that now. Leave me, and allow me to speak with him, and I will make him understand it is hopeless. All will be well. But I cannot risk you. Leave me here.'

I looked at her and saw she planned some great self-sacrifice, a penance perhaps, and I could not allow it. 'As if I would leave you alone with him,' I said. 'After ten years? I don't think so.'

She looked at me afresh, and I realised she had still thought I was eighteen and biddable. She did not know I had changed.

'Your father would not be persuaded to speak to Mr Winkler,' she said. 'He would rather move to Hastings than create a scene. And he did not entirely believe I had not done something to make Mr Winkler think there was hope. As if there was hope, for such a pompous, ridiculous popinjay.'

'Why didn't you let the Reverend tell me you were well?' I said. Because that was all that mattered, mostly. Mr Winkler was merely an inconvenience to be dealt with, madman or no. What mattered was why she had chosen to move to a distance of half a day away on a train, and not make sure I knew she was alive. The hurt of it was swallowing me whole, shrivelling my insides and shrinking my heart.

'He wanted to, but I couldn't risk it. I knew you would not rest until he told you where I was, and then you might tell your father, and I was not ready. The life I have built is so fragile, so delicate, Violet. No one knows my real name here. The letter was the most I could risk at first, and then later... I thought you might not forgive me.'

'Why did you go?' I said. Her lack of trust was not something I wanted to explore.

'It was a whim, Violet,' she said. 'A running away together in the moment, which we couldn't undo. Because I was miserable, and the chance came for happiness and I took it, without enough thought. When it was too late to come back, I realised what I had done. How terrible it was. But I was miserable with your father. And the life we have built together – we could not have built it, without a fresh start.'

'You are fond of fresh starts,' I said. 'I am sorry to have been your baggage.'

'No, no, Violet,' she said, and she reached out a hand to touch my arm but withdrew it again, hesitant. 'I did not mean that. I do not mean... I loved you. Love you. You were all that was good in my life. I just... please, will you let me deal with this... man, this weevil, and then we can talk? Properly, without anger, without interruption. Will you go now, so I can get rid of him from our lives?' She was crying again, elegantly, but something inside had hardened and I did not feel moved by it.

'Of course I will not go,' I said in a small, stubborn voice, and there was some argument and more tears on her part, but after a while she gave up and we sat together on the hillside, waiting for doom.

Mr Winkler's arrival was not sudden or dramatic. We saw him from some way away, toiling up the slope, a tiny figure at first, getting bigger, and it seemed ridiculous, that such a man could threaten our peace of mind. He had found an outfit somewhere, a linen safari suit and a pith helmet, and he looked like he should be exploring the African savannah, not climbing up a small hill in Buxton. He looked tired and sweaty.

I picked up a rock and my mother smiled at me. 'No, not that,' she said. 'More subtlety, I think,' and she seemed more like the mother I had known, who had met life with courage.

He reached us eventually and stood gasping in front of us for a second, his hands on his hips.

'Lily Hamilton,' he said. 'There you are. I've been looking for you.' And it was so banal I wanted to laugh.

'Mrs Dixon, now,' she said, but light-heartedly, so it was a reprimand and a joke at the same time. She stayed sitting on her rock, as if she did not care to rise. 'It's been a long, long time, Mr Winkler. What are you doing here?'

'You know why I have come,' he said, and I could see that she was disarming him already with her charm. He was striving to ruffle his own feathers and hold onto his rage, so that he had a battle to fight.

'To see the caves,' she said. 'You have come to see the caves. They are a sight to behold, so it will be worth it. Or are you too tired, after your climb?' It was a challenge he could not ignore.

'No, I am not tired,' he said. 'Very well, although you know quite clearly, I have not come for the caves. I think you have some explaining to do.'

'She doesn't have to explain anything to you,' I said. 'You are a nobody. A tin-pot fake detective with a pathetic obsession. I think you should go home.'

'Violet,' my mother said, warningly, and Mr Knight-Winkler started towards me in fury, but then he stopped and put his hands in his trouser pockets, relaxed, and I realised a part of him still cared what my mother thought. I stored the thought away. It might, perhaps, be an advantage.

'Your daughter lacks charm,' he said. 'Is that why you came here to Buxton? I am curious to know why you left. Is it possible you have been leading a double life, Mrs Hamilton?'

'Let's go into the caves,' she said, rising, 'and I'll tell you all about it.'

I rose too, but my mother put out a staying hand. 'Violet will stay here, I think, because it appears you are not friends. Violet, stay,' she said, and although I was not a dog I sat down again automatically because she was my mother and I had always done as she wished.

She started to make her way towards the narrow door that led to the caverns, and I rose again, because Mr Winkler was following her, grimly, and I could not let her face whatever tragedy lay ahead on her own. I put the rock in my pocket.

None of us expected a small, overexcited woman in a flowery hat to pop out of the bushes.

'Mrs Dixon,' she crowed in delight. 'Mrs Dixon! I am so glad I am in time.' She was covered in flowery clothing from the giant sprigs on her hat to her coat and her dress, and she had a giant parasol covered in roses over her arm.

'I went to your house and they said you were here, and I thought, well, I haven't been to the caverns in ages! An adventure, I thought. Thank you for inviting me. And look, I am just in time. Is it about to begin?'

I stared at her in wonder. It was Evelina Joyce, looking like a completely different woman, ten years older, a hundred times more foolish and exuberant. What was she planning? We all stood, frozen in time, while we worked out what to do.

'I wasn't expecting to give a tour,' my mother said, slowly.

'But you must! It will be a secret tour, if it is only the four of us. I cannot miss that! As soon as they said in the post office that's what you planned to do, I thought, well, I must be a part of it. I have never wanted to be part of the crowds. What a delight! Lead the way. Do I need to be careful of anything? Is it very dangerous? Are these the right shoes?' She held out her foot, almost a slipper, covered in embroidered pansies, and wiggled it.

'It is fairly dangerous,' my mother said. 'You might slip. Perhaps you might want to change your mind.'

'Oh, no, I couldn't possibly,' Evelina said. 'I've lived here all my life, and I may never get the chance for a private tour again. I remember, when I went to Chatsworth House…' And she was off, wittering about nothing, while we all stared at her in shock.

Eventually, my mother gathered herself.

'Well, let's go,' she said, and she opened the wooden door and led the way, as stiffly as a puppet jointed at the hinges. And Mr Knight-Winkler, the one of us most likely to protest, followed her without a word.

It was a remarkable change, from the sun outside to the dark and cold of the cavern within. There were gas lamps on the walls, that flickered and cast shadows, but the light could not reach everywhere and the caves were immense, stalagmites and stalactites reaching from every angle.

'We cannot just walk silently,' Evelina chirped. She had not been silent for a second. 'I am Mrs Legg, by the way, Mrs Legg with two "g"s as well as two legs, as my husband always says,' and she insisted on giving her hand to Mr Knight, although he dropped it quite quickly, and on us introducing ourselves, although it was not easy on the narrow walkway. Mr Winkler introduced himself as Mr Knight, and I saw my mother raise her eyebrows.

'Be careful, it is slippery in here,' my mother said.

'But you must give us a tour!' Mrs Legg said. 'It is so exciting! These caves are so frightening! It must be haunted! I am sure there is a face over there, staring at me, over there. Do you think it is haunted?'

'There is a stalactite that looks just like you,' my mother said. 'In the next cave, Mr Knight. Let us go and see it.'

She led the way, and we all followed, Evelina twittering on as Mrs Legg, the situation so bizarre I did not know what to make of it.

'There is a narrow set of steps here,' my mother said. 'Please take it slowly and be careful. There is a steep drop on the left, as you can see.'

We all took her advice and took them steadily, one at a time, but when we got halfway up, Evelina stopped.

'I could do with an arm,' she said. 'Mr Knight, I could do with an arm,' but he wasn't stopping, he was following my mother up the uneven steps, so Evelina reached out her parasol and hooked it over his arm abruptly, and pulled him backwards, almost sideways. 'Mr Knight,' she said.

He lost his balance abruptly, grabbing at the left-hand rope, but it wasn't made for a heavy fall from above and the loop of it swung him out further over the deep drop below.

'What the,' he said, his arms windmilling wildly. 'What the—' And then Evelina, who was holding firmly to the right-hand rope attached to the wall, let go of her parasol and, because it was the only thing holding him, he went over the rope. He fell down into the depths of the cavern with a long cry, taking the rope barrier and its flimsy wooden supports with him. There was a thud as his upper half hit the wall opposite, bouncing him off it further into the darkness, and then another as he hit the bottom.

There was a pause, and then a long silence, that stretched out until my mother turned and looked at Evelina, with tears in her eyes.

'Evie,' she said. 'Oh Evie.'

'What were you planning, you fool?' Evelina asked. 'To take tea with him? I'm not in favour of self-sacrifice. Let's get out of here quickly. It's too cold.'

She sounded bullish but the ebullience of Mrs Legg had gone, and the woman who remained seemed smaller, hunched in her clothing as if it was too large. Even the flowers on her jacket seemed to fade and shrink into themselves. She had leapt to my mother's defence like a warrior queen, but she already seemed crushed by it.

'Is he – gone?' I asked. No one could have survived a fall like that, but the word 'dead' was impossible to say. The cold in the cave hit my bones, and I realised I was shivering.

'Yes, he's gone, thanks to Evie,' my mother said. She put her arm around Evelina and I felt it sharply, even though I was not the one who had just committed murder and in need of comforting.

'Are you well, my Evie?' my mother said, and Evelina nodded her head, barely.

'I always knew you were a bundle of trouble, Lily,' she said, and they shared a glance of survival. For a second, I might not have been there, and then my mother reached out her hand and took mine.

'Let's get out of here,' she said, pulling us both towards the entrance. 'I'm so sorry for all this, Violet. Let's get back out into the light, so we can think about what to do.'

As we emerged into the sunlight, blinking, I remembered that Benjamin had said something similar to me about bringing him a great deal of trouble when we had first met. And at that second it was as if I had conjured him up, because there he was, racing up the slope at great speed, determination in his stride.

'Oh heavens, who is that now?' Evelina said.

'It's my detective,' I said, shielding the sun from my eyes.

Chapter Sixty-Four

Benjamin was, as in all things except marriage proposals, magnificent.

He had gone to Evelina's house and the maid had told him where we were.

'He was a bad one,' he said to us. 'I was coming to find you, V— Miss Hamilton, because as soon as I clocked he was Herbert Winkler, the answers came in fast and I uncovered a lot of stuff I didn't like. He was convicted a year after you moved to Hastings, ma'am, for walking down pavements and randomly pushing women off them – like skittles. Any that walked past. One girl broke quite a few bones.'

He listened to us, about how Mr Winkler had tragically tripped on the stairs, and he took it at face value, although I knew he knew that more had gone on.

He went into the cave, carefully clambered down, and checked that there were no signs of life in Mr Winkler. There were none. But he brought back the umbrella and gave it to us.

He seemed to understand that the truth would help nobody, and he helped us shape our story, that Mr Winkler was a stranger passing through Buxton, no one any of us knew, who had come to visit the cavern, and we had tried to stop him from entering the second room, because the steps were narrow and being repaired, but Mr Winkler had ignored us.

Benjamin went to the police first, and although we were interviewed, it was from a position of respect, because they knew of Benjamin's father, and because he carried a natural authority. Everyone trusted his word, and no one questioned if Mrs Dixon was Mrs Dixon or not, or indeed if I was Viola Smythe. It had been a tragic accident for a man who, despite his change of jacket, smelt strongly of beer.

Billy was a small loophole in our plans, but we hoped he would not connect Mr Knight with Mr Winkler.

I was glad that Mr Blackthorn's firm principles could be flexed a little, when circumstances required.

I was in shock, of course. I had never seen anyone die. I had been told I was taken to see my father's mother in the drawing room where my mother had laid her out before her burial, but I had been so little at the time, only three or so, that I did not remember it. I had vague memories of her smell, camphor and lavender, and the stiffness and shininess of her black bombazine dress, but I did not remember the knowledge of death at all. She had been a fierce martinet, by all accounts, who had not approved of my mother's frivolity.

In contrast, Mr Winkler's death left me shaking and horrified, and I fought the desire to lean on Benjamin as if he was a wall to hold me up.

However, underneath my disturbance lay other emotions, which I did not care to analyse too deeply. They lay hand in hand with the knowledge that death, no matter how horrible, was as much a part of learning about life as nudity and marital intimacy. The scene in the caves was life's horror in all its reality, without any of the cotton wool or obfuscation normally ladled out to a lady. I wanted more of it. Not death, of course, but to see and experience all of life's challenges as clearly and honestly as men did, and to have the freedom to deal with them the way I saw fit. Evelina had been brilliant and decisive, and I could not help but admire her for it. To add to my confusion, the shameful thought occurred to me that Mr Winkler's death was an important step in my preparation to becoming a Lady Detective. If I could handle death without falling into a fit of the vapours, I could cope with anything.

Benjamin went to stay in lodgings around the corner that evening, but I stayed the night with my mother and Evelina. Any courage had fled, leaving behind three exhausted and stupefied females huddled together around a parlour fire in summer, drinking cocoa.

'Do you think he felt pain?' Evelina asked, and my mother rushed to say no.

'It was so quick,' my mother said. 'I doubt he had time to feel anything at all. Plus, Evelina, he was utterly awful. You have done not only us but the whole world a favour. She is a great actress, don't you think, Violet? A brilliant actress.'

Evelina looked embarrassed and said my mother was overly sentimental. I was beginning to see they held a firm friendship, a relationship forged over years, interweavings of give and take, affection and familiarity, but it did not hold answers to why my mother had left.

Our reasons for leaving Crystal Palace as a family were clearer. My mother told us that Mr Winkler had stalked after her for months before she left London, on no encouragement at all. She had passed him at the Crystal Palace and smiled at him without thought, as she smiled at everybody, and, before she knew it, he was giving her lavish gifts, calling on her and pledging his affection, the wedding ring on her finger no deterrent. She had never been 'at home' when he called, had avoided him at gatherings, had looked past him in the street, but still he had persisted, his devotion turning angry, his letters threatening, his handwriting as spiky and disturbing as it had been for me.

'Your father did not believe me,' she said. 'Because he never saw Herbert. I have always had some charm, but this was different. The man was everywhere I went, and he frightened me. His pursuit did not seem rational. When he spoke to you in the street, Violet, I knew we had to leave. We needed a fresh start anyway, away from London. I thought Hastings might be a chance to repair things with your father, start again.' She stared into the distance, and then shook herself. 'Anyway, I thought we had got rid of weevil Winkler after that. Why on earth would he still come after me, after so long?'

'He found the photographs,' I said. 'Of you… of you in your scant underthings. They seemed to make him angry. And I had hired him to find you, after all. Why did you pose for those photographs?'

My mother shot a startled look at Evelina, another small smile of something shared, and then she rubbed her brow, and somehow Evelina read it as a message and got up from her chair.

'I'm going to retire to bed,' she said. 'I'm exhausted. Violet, it is lovely to meet you after so long. You are just as your mother told me, though very much a grown woman now. I'm sorry today was… what it was. Lily… talk as long as you like. Sleep well, both.' She left the room, and my mother frowned after her in concern.

'She will not forgive herself easily,' she said. 'Even though she has saved my life, both our lives, possibly, from a very horrible man, I will still need to convince her.' She sighed and then looked back at me and sighed again, in a way that ran through her whole body, and I knew seeing me again meant something to her.

'I posed for those photographs for Evelina,' she said. 'We met at the Pier Pavilion, around four months before I… left. She was performing there, and I went to the after-party, and she bowled me over. She was dressed in a pink silk wrap, laughing at the world, at me, and right away I knew, although it took a while for me to admit it to myself. She was… everything. We had only a few days together, and there was sunlight again, after so many years of cloud. It was when you had the flu and were bedridden, do you remember? I still came home to mop your brow but, in between, we had the days together, because she was performing in the evening.'

'You posed for photos in your underthings… for another woman?' I said, because I did not understand.

'You are shocked,' she said. 'You disapprove, I can see it in your face. You always were so very prim, my Violet. A little deer frightened at trees. I am sorry I have not been there to guide you through life.' Her eyes were full of tears.

'Are you saying that Evelina wanted to see you in your underclothes?' I asked. It appeared there were still some bewildering gaps in my education.

'Yes,' she said. 'Violet, Violet, I was wrong about intimacy. I was wrong about it because it was with the wrong person. I am sorry, for my cod advice. I hope you have worked it out since.'

I nodded. I didn't tell her I had only worked it out a matter of days before.

'She carried on touring the country, but she asked for a photograph of me, to remember me by, and I decided it would be a lark to pose for... more private ones. Ones that only she and I would understand. I put her name on them, so she knew they were meant only for her. I was drunk on happiness, I think. I did not mind if men liked the photos too, if they made me money. I am sorry if they upset you,' she said.

'I was mostly confused,' I said. 'But they did damage my reputation. So, to be clear... you and Evelina are... together? Like a man and a woman? Did she send you the postcard about... Bubbins?'

'Yes. Please do not hate me,' she said. 'Please do not judge us. It may seem... unusual... but what we feel is more real than anything I have ever felt. Have you heard of the Ladies of Llangollen? We are like them, I think. Two ladies, living happily together. Oh, I can see it in your face, you hate me now.'

'Of course I do not hate you,' I said. I did not know what to think, but my first instinct was to go and ask Maria Monk. Life still held more surprises than I had dreamt of. 'This is just new to me, and I am trying to understand. So, you left with Evelina, that night?'

'I was not happy with your father, as you know,' she said. 'And then... Evelina came back. She was coming to the end of her tour, and she spent a week in town, and I saw a glimpse of what life could be. She offered me a holiday with her, only a holiday. It was a whim, and I took it without thinking.

'Your father and I had argued the night before, because he had seen my happiness. He accused me of having an affair. It was all the more insulting to him, I suppose, the idea that I would look at another man, because he knew I did not welcome their intimate attentions. I could not tell him the truth. After I left… I only intended to stay for the holiday. I planned to come back. To have my little bit of joy, and then go back, and repent, and take up my life in Hastings again. But the longer I stayed away, the harder it was to imagine I could go back. Or to think that anyone would forgive me or understand. I am sorry.'

I had not known they had argued. My father had not seen fit to tell me, although maybe if he had I would have been more inclined to believe Mr Knight's wild theories of murder.

'Tell me how you have been, my Violet,' she said then. 'The Reverend has written to me regularly, but I want to hear it from you. I thought you would have married by now, settled down. Have you not found a young man you like?'

I stared into my empty cup of cocoa because there was ten years' worth of answering in that question, and because she had left me with a barrel of baggage and no answers. It hurt afresh, that the Reverend had been corresponding with her. As a kind man, he likely sent her nothing more than platitudes. He knew very little of my inner struggles and if he had, would likely be too thoughtful of her feelings to share them.

'I don't think I am your Violet any more,' I said at last. 'I have not had an easy time of it, on my own. But I am getting there.'

'And that young man, Mr Blackthorn? He was very quick to race to your defence,' she said.

'He is a good detective,' I said. I had wanted her to ask about me, but now that she was, I did not want her to know. She could not make up for ten years of distance in five minutes. And she only knew me as that eighteen year old, innocent, foolish. Did she think I had just been fluttering through life like any other young lady? I could not tell her of my grand plans for my life. It was best to change the subject, because she looked like she was going to cry again.

'Father is not so very dour these days, by the way. He has a fancy woman, a nice lady he wants to marry.'

'Does he indeed? Well, I wish him all the best,' she said. 'Although, heavens above, we are still married. Goodness, Violet, will you tell him? What will you tell him? Would you keep it a secret, if I asked?'

'I am not sure,' I said. 'I will need to think about what's best. He is threatening to send me to rusticate in the country, because I hired Mr Knight.'

'Ever a giving man,' she said. 'You can come and live here, if you like, with Evie and me. We are accepted in society here, as two friends. Although that might change, if your father finds out.'

'Thank you,' I said. We talked a little more but shortly afterwards I expressed my wish to retire to bed. I was feeling a little woebegone. I had too much to think about and, oddly, I wished Benjamin was here. My feelings were not proving easy to freeze. I hoped I was not coming to rely upon him.

Chapter Sixty-Five

I slept heavily, which was a surprise, considering I had raced across the country and a murder had been done the day before. At breakfast, I told my mother and Evelina that I was going home.

'But you must stay,' my mother said. 'You must stay for longer, and we can catch up on… on all that we have missed.'

'My father does not know where I am,' I said. 'He may begin to think me a strumpet, if I do not go home soon. There will be other opportunities, I am sure.' I could hear how cold I sounded, but I could not find more warmth. 'I do not know yet,' I added, as she looked ready to speak. 'I do not know what I will say to him yet. I have the train journey to think about it. I need time to consider everything. I will not tell him, without letting you know first. Will there be more opportunities for us to talk, or will you disappear again?'

My mother started to speak but Evelina got in first. 'Of course we will not disappear, Violet,' she said. 'We will be here, and we will face whatever happens. Please know how wonderful it is for me to meet you. Your mother has spoken of you so often, and I know how sorely she has missed you.' I did not know yet what I thought of this woman, who had taken my mother away from me, who had apparently made her happy, while I had been left alone to be miserable. Did they realise how many years I had spent imagining the worst?

'Well, that's good,' I said. 'I am glad you discussed me. Well, I must be heading off.'

Benjamin came to meet me, and my mother insisted on giving me a fierce hug goodbye.

'We will talk again,' she said in my ear. 'We will talk properly, and I will try to explain. You must forgive me, Violet, in time. You must. I am so glad you came. I am glad you have changed and are strong.' She gave me a little shake as if I was a doll, and then set me loose.

'Shall we go, B— Mr Blackthorn?' I said. 'It is a long journey. It was delightful to meet you both.' Which was stupid, of course, because I had met my mother before.

We headed for the train station, and home.

It was a very different journey from the one I had taken yesterday, because I was with the right detective.

We talked about the day before for a while.

'How did she leave?' Benjamin asked.

'They dressed as travelling clowns,' I said. 'Evelina knew some of the trapeze artists in the circus that was travelling through, so they bought a couple of costumes from them. Evelina's contract with her theatre company had ended, so they planned to spend a week together in Buxton, where Evelina had lodgings, and they dressed on the pier in the public convenience, caught the steam tug to Rye, and then travelled most of the way to Buxton dressed as clowns. No one questioned them. Apparently, it was easy.'

'She only planned a week away?' Benjamin said. 'That was a long week.' He frowned, and I could see it was a second frown on my behalf, and whatever ice remained in my chest turned into warm water and puddled somewhere around my heart. This was no good. I had to get hold of myself.

'I am concerned about what I should tell my father,' I said. 'He will not be able to marry Mrs Beeton, now that I have found her. He is already displeased with me and set on sending me to the country.' I did not tell him about my father's perfidy, because I had had enough drama for the day.

Benjamin stroked his jaw. 'As I see it,' he said, 'it's best to be truthful, unless you think he might decide to ruin your mother's life. You know him best. He himself has a couple of options. He can push for a death certificate, if we all conspire not to reveal your mother is alive, or he can simply pretend he has married Mrs Beeton elsewhere, and they can live as common-law husband and wife. There are many more common-law marriages out there than you realise.'

I thought about my father, his deceit, his pretence of uprightness, his dourness. I thought about the light in his eyes when he looked at his buxom lady love, and I wondered. Could I persuade him to abandon some of his self-professed morals to live the life he wanted? He had apparently already been planning to declare her dead, when she was not. Could I try to make him see me not as his wayward daughter but as a person with some wisdom and agency, who could occasionally dispense advice worthy of being listened to? I did not know. But it seemed worth a try, as it was well past time that he moved forward in life too. And my anger might give me the courage and the gravitas to say what I needed.

'I shall raise it with him,' I said. It might end badly. My father might decide to lock me up in an asylum for my impertinence. But he had to be faced, and life had to be faced. Perhaps we could salvage a relationship. Perhaps Mrs Beeton could help to show him that life, in all its colours, was better embraced than stifled.

I was in a reflective mood and we fell into silence. I was able to watch the countryside and to think, relatively peacefully, about life, about secrets, about myself. I knew that I wanted to be a Lady Detective, above all. I wanted to discover what made people tick; solve their problems, unwind their complications, soothe their troubles. A door had been firmly opened, and I would never let it shut again. I was ready to deal with everything, head on.

'So now that we are alone and you cannot run very far,' Benjamin said. 'Shall we talk about us?'

Chapter Sixty-Six

My heart stopped in my chest and I half rose to flee to another compartment. But what kind of detective ran from a conversation? If I could not even face a feeling, squash it back to where it belonged, deal with it practically, logically, how could I solve cases? I had to face it, beard him in his beardless den, exactly as I would face being a Lady Detective, with a cool, calm head. I sat back down.

It was strange how easy it was, to hide gale-force gusts of emotion.

'Of course,' I said, primly. 'On what topics in particular concerning us would you like us to converse?'

His mouth quirked.

'You are the most frustrating firework I have ever had the misfortune to come across. No, listen,' he said, as I rose from my seat to flee again, and he took both of my hands in his and pulled me down to sit next to him on the seat, 'I'm fond of you. More than fond. You made me laugh when I was prepared to wallow in misery, you've got me interested in detective work and perhaps even the whole of life again, and you've somehow wedged your way into here' – he placed one of his hands and mine to a place on his chest that might have been his heart – 'and if you remove yourself, it will hurt. I'd miss your funny ways. So—'

'I am not sure I want to be your own personal clown,' I said, instantly annoyed with myself because I was being irrational, pushing him away again, when I already knew I needed him too, for his manly, forthright detective ability at the very least.

He only laughed.

'Violet. You want to work for me. You want me to teach you all I know. That cannot happen – no, it will not happen – unless you and I are on a path to be wed. I will not play with your reputation any more. If you want to be a detective, if you want this, us, then it's marriage or nothing.'

I turned our hands over so that mine were on top, and I thought about what he had said for a while, for at least the length of seven fields rolling past the window.

'I have always been quite determined not to marry,' I said. 'And I do not know exactly how I feel about you yet. I admire your skills as a detective, immensely, and I know there is a lot you can teach me, but I do not know how I feel about you as a *man*. As a husband.' It was not really true, as there were feelings swirling inside me that fully acknowledged that he was a man. I had seen him in his glorious nakedness, as only wives were meant to. But I was not entirely ready to commit to marriage, even yet.

'I'm hopeful you might come to admire me in those areas too,' he said. 'I'm fairly practised at being a man. Being a husband would be new, but the novelty might help.' He was laughing at me again. 'Seriously, though, I'm prepared for us to take our time and get to know each other while we are engaged. I'm clear how I feel about you, but I'm happy to wait until you feel the same too.'

It was not a passionate declaration of love, but it felt more *real* a proposal than any of the others I had had. More honest, more caring, definitely aimed at me and me alone, less about lust for my bodily parts. It was the perfect protection from Patmore. An engagement could also be ended, if I changed my mind. I clutched our hands as several thoughts occurred to me at once.

'If we were to become engaged,' I said, 'it should be a long engagement. And I want my own desk and a sign with my name on it. And I might change my name to Loveday. She is a very good detective, even though she is not real. And also, I should warn you, I would wish to practise before we get married.'

'Practise?'

'My mother was not… fond of marital intimacy,' I said. My cheeks burnt. 'I do not know yet whether I might be the same. So, I think it would be expedient for me… for us… to experiment before marriage, so we are not disappointed and regret it. I am very knowledgeable about bedroom activities in a theoretical, abstract sense, but I haven't practically attempted them in person at all.'

He rolled his shoulders as if his coat was too tight. 'You want to experiment on me?'

Why could I not get the words right? 'Perhaps more in the nature of an investigation,' I said. 'Is it improper of me to suggest it? It is only… I should not like to shriek and run away on our wedding night. Is there anything we could try a little, some respectable intimacies… which would not lead to… offshoots?'

He did not answer. He had dropped my hands on my lap, crossed his arms and was looking over my shoulder at the landscape outside, his jaw working. Things did not look hopeful. It could be the first time I had scared away a suitor without meaning to. Perhaps he considered me a brazen hussy and would stride off alone down the platform when we arrived, never to be seen again.

'If you would prefer not to,' I said with dignity, 'I will understand.' My eyes felt prickly. It must be the stale air in the carriage.

'You should not change your first name,' he said, after a while. 'It is your decision, of course, but Violet Blackthorn will suit you well. The desk, the sign, yes, you can have them. As for the other, I expect I could suffer it. Purely for your sake, I'd be happy to dally in some respectable intimacies. So that's agreed, then. We'll get married.'

'Yes,' I said, but then I couldn't say anything else, because, 'Shall we start now then?' he said, and he took my head in his hands and kissed me expertly and with great determination, until I was so fully flustered and hot that when he let me go I dropped back against the seat limply and stared at him, dazed. One of my gloved hands had somehow become entangled in his hair. I removed it carefully and placed it back in my lap.

'If you want to take notes, that's fine,' he said. 'I appreciate you might want to keep track as you learn.' And he smiled at me, his wicked pirate smile, and I wondered whether I had got myself into a great deal of trouble.

I could handle it. I would handle it. In future, the second I recovered from my befuddlement, in fact, I was going to handle absolutely everything that came my way, with élan and aplomb. After all, I was going to be a Lady Detective.

Acknowledgements

Thank you.

I am so grateful to everyone who has made me laugh in life, intentionally or otherwise. It has made this book what it is today.

I would especially like to thank my family, who have been hugely supportive over the years and greatly encouraged my sense of humour by cracking better jokes.

Thanks all my brilliant friends, especially Karen van de Graaf, who was with me at the Horniman Museum as I shrieked to discover I was longlisted for the Comedy Women in Print Awards; and Karen Payton, who has promised to fill a shopping trolley with copies of my novel. Fellow writer Lindsay Ford has been a font of wisdom and writerly encouragement. Emma Thompson, one of life's brightest stars, left this planet too soon, but not before gifting me a notebook to write in. I hope she would be proud. Many other dear friends, some I have known since childhood, others who came into my life later, have encouraged, supported and laughed with me along the way. I hope they know who they are and how much they mean to me.

Huge thanks to my wonderful agent Diana Beaumont at Marjacq for championing my book so brilliantly, and to Claire McGowan for believing in my writing enough to introduce her to me. Especial thanks to my Editor Rachel Faulkner-Willcocks and all at Head of Zeus for making it look so beautiful, sharing it with the world and polishing every word to make it shine. I am very happy to know that kippers are made from herrings, not mackerel.

I am of course incredibly grateful to the amazing Helen Lederer and all at the Comedy Women in Print Awards for nominating my novel in November 2021 – this competition is truly life-changing for women writers and transformed my grey lockdown year into a frenzy of excitement and hope.

I loved researching this book, spending long weekends wandering the streets of Hastings, haunting the premises of The Old Hastings Preservation Society and diving into books on Victorian Hastings such as *Strange Exits from Hastings* by Helena Wojtczak and *Secret Hastings and St Leonards* by Tina Brown.

Finally, thanks to my lovely readers for reading it, without which it would just be a story written during lockdown, to cheer myself up. I hope it has brought you joy.

About the Author

Hannah Dolby's first job was in the circus and she has aimed to keep life as interesting since. She trained as a journalist in Hastings and has worked in PR for many years, promoting museums, galleries, palaces, gardens and even Dolly the sheep. She completed the Curtis Brown selective three-month novel writing course, and she won runner-up in the Comedy Women in Print Awards for this novel with the prize of a place on an MA in Comedy Writing at the University of Falmouth. She currently lives in London.

You can follow Hannah on Twitter @LadyDolby.